THE
PERFECT
SHOE

THE PERFECT SHOE

KIMBERLY T. MATTHEWS

URBAN BOOKS
www.urbanbooks.net

URBAN SOUL is published by

Urban Books
10 Brennan Pl.
Deer Park, NY 11729

ISBN-13: 978-1-59983-018-6
ISBN-10: 1-59983-018-3

First Printing: March 2007
10 9 8 7 6 5 4 3 2 1

Printed in the United States of America

Intro

The Shoe Dictionary: A Guide to Understanding the Men in My Life.

—*By December Elliott*

The Workday Pump
This shoe describes a woman's best platonic male friendships. Just as a pump is a very standard, practical shoe that one might wear to a general nine-to-five, the Workday Pump is a basic type of brother who maybe works with you every day, listens to you complain about how much you hate your boss, and offers good male advice. The Workday Pump will loan you a dollar for a soda and will change your car tire for you if you don't have AAA. The thing to remember about the Workday Pump, however, is that although your relationship with him is purely platonic, he appreciates your finer qualities, finds you attractive, and is not above taking some if you offer. He may, from time to time, express that he doesn't know why your boyfriend is trippin', because he would date you in a heartbeat if given the chance.

The Flip-flop
Flip-flops make a lot of noise but offer no true protection for the foot. If you drop a can of sliced peaches on your foot while wearing a simple flip-flop, no matter how sweet the peaches may be,

you can kiss your pretty little toes good-bye. The Flip-flop man is much like this shoe. He constantly confesses that he loves you, and you're the woman of his dreams and he can't live without you, and one day the two of you will do this and have that. He's just full of empty promises and future commitment dates, but when it all boils down to it, talk is cheap. Just like that can of peaches falling on your toes would have you screaming out in pain, messing with a Flip-flop will ultimately lead to painful heartbreak if you're not careful.

The Winter Boot

Every girl has had at least one pair: the boot that, once on, takes the help of another individual (usually a sister or best girlfriend—and sometimes a brother) to get off. Many sisters have taken a hard push in the behind because of this type of shoe. The Winter Boot is the man you just can't seem to get rid of, no matter how hard you try. Simply saying "I'm not interested" is not enough for this man. Nor is cussing him out, talking about him behind his back or to his face, telling everybody that he's gay, purposely letting his dog run away, or accidentally wrecking his car. He's crazy about you and will stop at almost nothing to have you. The only thing that will stop this man is your (or his) being committed to someone else. However, as soon as you become free again, he will be right there to let you know that he is still awaiting his turn to show you how wonderful life with him could be.

The House Shoe

In the same sense that your house shoes (those slippers spattered with fried chicken grease, which make that shick-shick sound when you walk across the kitchen) are only good for things like taking out the trash and checking the mail, you can see the House Shoe only in the comfort and privacy of your own home because as much as you enjoy his company, he will embarrass the crap out of you if you take him out in public. He does stuff like show up at your company's formal dinner party, with his jeans hanging off his behind, with a T-shirt four sizes too big underneath a plaid sports coat, and greet your boss with a fist pound and a "Wha's up dog? I won't waisin' no money on no boo-gee tux man, 'cause I cain't be nobody but me." Or he will take you out on a date, then, after eating like a fat king, will announce, "Oh snap! I left my wallet at home!" Don't even go to the grocery store with him; House Shoes are for the house only!

The Bedroom Shoe

The Bedroom Shoe is soft, warm, inviting, and luxuriously comfortable. You must be extremely careful not to confuse the Bedroom Shoe with the House Shoe. They are indeed different. Although your bedroom shoes should not be worn outside of the house, they are not, I repeat, are not for taking out the trash or other around-the-house activities and chores. Bedroom shoes are strictly for pampering, thus bringing relaxation to your entire body. A really good bedroom shoe (both the actual and the man version) will bring the wiggle out of your toes and a moan from your lips. The same way that the bedroom shoe feels good to your very sole, the Bedroom Shoe man feels good to your very soul!

—Special note: While the House Shoe could be a great Bedroom Shoe, the best Bedroom Shoe is a Stiletto (Stiletto description provided below). It is most important to take extreme caution to ensure that Bedroom Shoes do not become House Shoes. Carelessness and overuse for general purposes can cause this to happen very, very quickly.

The Stiletto

The Stiletto is a very sexy shoe . . . tall, makes your calves more appealing, and is very versatile. You can wear it with a formal gown or with a pair of cuffed jeans and a blouse. It draws the attention of other envious shoe wearers. "Ooh, girl, those are nice! Where did you get those!" Now the Stiletto man doesn't necessarily have to be tall, but he must have the same versatility and sex appeal as his shoe counterpart. He has to look good on your arm no matter what the occasion. He can casually hang out at the mall, escort you to a business mixer, and wear a tux like nobody's business. Although you already look good, he makes you look even better . . . with his sexy, fine self! (If he is not sexy and fine, no matter how versatile he is, he simply is not a Stiletto.)

There are many other shoe styles that appropriately describe other men in my life, but I find my man closet mostly filled with the first four in my dictionary. My actual closet today holds exactly 365 pairs of shoes, a pair for every day of the year, a pair for every occasion you could possibly think of. Shoes for working all day; shoes for dancing all night; shoes for grocery shopping, errand running, picking my granny up from the doctor's office, looking cute at my best friend's baby shower; shoes for running through Atlanta's Hartsfield Airport to catch the last flight home; shoes for just in case it's raining by the time I get to work; and shoes for finding a man. That's right. I have several pairs of man-finding shoes. I just can't seem to find the right pair for attracting *the* man. You know, the One.

One

I sorted through the stack of envelopes I'd just pulled from the mailbox. Maybe today would be the day that God would show me crazy favor and let an unexpected check show up. Slipping out of my Louis Vuitton kitten heel mules, my soles were instantly massaged by my warm suede floor covering (it was way too classy to be referred to as a simple rug). While my toes curled around bits of fringe, I was reminded of what an incredible deal the rug had been. There was nothing else that comple-mented my living room so perfectly. What else would go with a butter-soft off-white leather couch, accented with warm shades of caramel, other than a gorgeous mocha-colored, crinkled suede rug . . . I mean floor covering? I was lucky enough to find it on sale for about thirteen hundred. A little expensive, I know, but I ordered it, mak-ing the decision then and there always to have a room with shades of brown somewhere in my home, making this a justifiable lifetime investment.

I tossed my purse and keys on the couch, then sank into my favorite chair, a plush chaise lounge sized for two, which strategically sat opposite my fireplace. The chaise was comforting enough for me to enjoy alone, but I looked forward to the day that my Stiletto man would lounge beside me, holding me in his arms after lighting a mood-setting fire, and would whisper something like, *"December, you are the most incredible, sexy, intriguing woman I have ever met. Your very essence just speaks to my soul and calls me from a place of vagueness right to a place of decision."* (Yes, my Stiletto man would be deep like that.) *"And I have decided that you, baby, are my everything. I never want to leave your embrace. . . ."*

When I bought this chaise, I must have sat in it with my eyes closed for a solid twenty minutes, just imagining the possibilities.

"Girl, I've only dreamed about a woman like you, but never did I think in a million years that I'd be holding that woman in my arms . . . tonight." Stiletto was closing in for a kiss. Not a regular kiss, but the kind where the man creates a tiny bit of a vacuum and sucks my lips into his ever so slightly. Mmm! *"December, I just have one question for you. Will you . . ."*

"Ma'am, we can't allow you to sleep on the showroom floor!"

My eyes popped open to see a saleswoman, whose facial expression conveyed total disdain for my presence. Actually, she wasn't a saleswoman; she was a salesman who wanted to be a woman, dress and all. As a matter of fact, she looked just like Tom Hanks on *Bosom Buddies* back in the day. I smoothed my skirt, swung my legs to the side of the chaise, and rose gracefully, then glanced back inconspicuously to make sure that I hadn't slobbed on the pillows. Thank goodness there were no dark, wet circles left behind. When I turned back to face "Sabrina," her nose was turned high in the air, as if to say, "You sssstink!" That was until I whipped out the small piece of plastic from my purse.

"In that case, I'll take it," I said. She wasted no time snatching the card from my fingers and transferring the embossed numbers onto a sales order form to take care of the down payment. Within twelve seconds, she was chatting with me like we were best friends, telling me about her dog and her hometown.

"Thank you so much for coming to see us at Tosalina Furniture," she said, escorting me to the door after setting up my delivery date and trying to up-sell me with ten other items.

Tosalina was the first envelope in my mail stack; I flipped past it. Next were VISA, Target, Lord & Taylor, Hecht's . . . Yeah, yeah yeah, nothing but bills. Just before I dismissed the stack in my hand, my eyes lit upon a light blue envelope exposing my name through a clear window, right beside my favorite mail words: Pay to the Order Of. In an instant I tore through the seal and pulled out my "check" for $100,000 if I refinanced my house.

I owned a luxury two-bedroom, two-and-a-half bathroom condo, which was perfect for my lifestyle. No grass to cut. I fell in love with it as soon as I walked through. It was incredibly spacious and had a second-level loft overlooking the living room and a beautiful deck outside the master bedroom. For some reason unknown to me, the seller had been desperate to get rid of it and gladly sold it to me for well under market value. Since I'd been there, I'd made several upgrades: put in cherry hardwood floors, installed custom lighting, tore out the ceiling in the master bedroom and had it restructured cathedral style, with skylights, added a garden tub. I absolutely loved my house!

I rose from the chaise and made my way to the kitchen, dropping the mail onto my dining-room table/desk on the way. I'd study each piece over dinner . . . for real this time. To solidify my intentions, I pulled my Franklin Planner from my workbag and added it to the pile of things on the desk side of the dining-room table. I'd open the bills, look at my calendar, then pencil in pay dates to remind myself to take care of them. The only reason why I decided to use a pencil rather than a pen was because sometimes I had so many things to do at work, I would need to shift items around on my planner pages, so I needed the flexibility of being able to erase and rewrite.

As long as I remembered to rewrite. Last month, I didn't do that important step and ended up being charged twenty-nine dollars and thirty-nine dollars in late fees on all of my accounts. I couldn't afford to let that happen again.

Fresh salad greens, warm grilled chicken, candied walnuts, cherry tomatoes, sliced cucumbers, California raisins, and a sprinkle of parmesan cheese—paired with a glass of wine—made for the perfect "enjoy your food but watch your figure" meal. With a quick click of my stereo remote, KEM's mellow voice crept around the walls via surround-sound speakers. I took a seat, forked down a few mouthfuls, then started on my task. First, prioritize. I transferred the easily identifiable bills to the back of the stack, placed the unmarked envelopes (disguised bills) to the middle, and the "interesting but probably junk mail" pieces to the front. I needed to be eased into the part of the mail that would require some thinking and possibly bring on depression.

An offer to have satellite TV installed in four rooms, with a free DVD player . . . trash. A brochure from the local business school, informing me that there was no better time for me to start my new career in the medical field . . . trash. And an envelope stuffed with coupons. It wasn't long before the wine/jazz combination shifted me right into relaxation mode as I sorted through a variety of money-saving fliers. Most of the products were things that I didn't normally purchase, but I could be inclined with a coupon to buy sugar-free cookies, plug-in room fresheners, and veggie burgers. I separated the coupons into two piles; one pile went in the wastebasket, while the other pile would go on the kitchen counter, readily accessible for me to review when I made my grocery list. On to the next group: unmarked envelopes.

Good Fitness Entertainment, DVD Club
Third and Final Notification
Ms. Elliott,
   Your account is seriously delinquent! Please call us immediately to prevent your account from moving further in the collection process. Representatives are available at 1-888-PASTDUE to assist you from 8:00 a.m. to 10:00 p.m. central standard time.
   Time is of the essence!

At the time that I opened this DVD club account, I really could see how receiving a new set of kickboxing DVDs every month was a necessity. It would keep me from doing the same routine over and over again every day. Well, maybe not every day but every other day. Okay, whenever I got a chance to work out . . . which was hardly ever nowadays. My eyes floated to the ceiling as I tried to recall what I did with last month's shipment . . . and the shipment from the month before that. Hmmm. I'd look for them sometime over the weekend and get started back on my workouts. In the meantime, I jotted the DVD club's number down in my planner (writing just the number and not the company name), under the nine o'clock slot, and made up a contact person's name to list beside it. That would make it look like a real appointment to anyone who'd pass by my desk and see my open planner. My lips twisted as I viewed the rest of the page; it was totally blank. I'd have to fill it up with something prior to leaving it out on my desk.

Anyway, back to the bills. At nine tomorrow, I'd call and make a payment over the phone with my VISA. Easy. Done. On to the next letter.

Life Financial Bank and Trust, VISA Department
Ms. Elliott,
Why haven't you called us?

We've noticed that no payment has been made on your account within the last sixty days. Thus your account has been suspended, but we want to help.

Everyone experiences hard times due to lost wages or unexpected expenses. That is why we are happy to tell you that we have programs especially designed to assist you in your time of need.

If you have already made a payment, please accept our apology and disregard this letter. We will process and post your payment as soon as possible. If you haven't made your payment yet, please call today to speak to me personally so that we can discuss options for bringing your account current.
Sincerely,
Margaret Campbell
Accounts Manager

Although there was no one in my presence, I was embarrassed. I listed the bank's number under the eight thirty slot, gave it a few seconds of thought, then decided to log on to my computer and send them a quick e-mail.

I took a seat at my computer, went to their Website,

pecked in my user name and password, then clicked on the *Contact Us* link.

> Dear Life Bank and Trust,
> I have all intentions of paying on my account and apologize that I have, in the past, been late. I've been in the process of realigning . . .

No, no, no. That was all wrong. Delete, delete, delete.

> Dear Life Bank and Trust,
> Please accept this e-mail as an explanation for the delinquency of my account.

I stopped for a minute and thought about what I could type next. There was a reason I hadn't paid on time; there had to be. I mean, other than I just didn't. Oh yeah. I had intended to pay it, but I had been distracted by that huge sale at Bare Feet Shoes. That was when I picked up those awesome black Aldo boots with the buckles up the back. I'd been eyeing them for weeks. And I got those brown macramé sling backs to match the crocheted halter top that I'd been dying to wear but never had the shoes to match. And then I had to get those wraparound, crystal heel slides because they were just too hot to be left in the store. I definitely couldn't put that in my e-mail; I needed something to motivate my thinking.

I ran to my front closet, where all three pairs of shoes were still in the bag, and pulled them out. Before slipping my feet into the slides, I stripped out of my work clothes, down to my lime green lace boy-cut panties and matching camisole. I picked up my remote, switched CDs to Faith Evans, and skipped tracks to get to "Mesmerized."

"One, two, three, four, hit it . . ." My hips rotated, and my arms flew upwards. I took it down to the floor, brought it back up again, then strutted across the living room, cutting my eyes over my right shoulder, as if Stiletto man were there dancing with me.

"Work that thang girl," he said. My lips puckered forward while I ran a hand slowly through my hair. Quick drop to the floor one more time.

"You like that, baby?" I teased.

Before I could show him what I was really working with, the phone rang. Dancing my way across the room to the bar, which separated the kitchen from the dining area, and lowering the music's volume on the way, I picked up without giving a thought to the caller ID. I hadn't even said hello before the voice came across the line.

"Hi. We have an important call for you. Please hold for the next available representative."

Just like that, Stiletto was gone again. I held the receiver for a few seconds, knowing that I should be accountable, but then hung up. If whoever it was didn't have sense enough to call me live, I didn't have patience enough to wait for them. My eyes floated back over to my half-written e-mail and the other envelopes I had not even opened yet. With a heavy sigh, I kicked out of the slides, slunk in the chair, and started on a new e-mail, to Andre, my Workday Pump.

Andre,
Will you be free for lunch tomorrow? Well, today, by the time you get this.

It took me six tries to type the next line.

Just wanted to spend some time . . . Nah. Too date-ish.

Long time no lunch! Uh-uh. Too cute.
I need to talk to . . . No. That sounded like I was in a crisis.
Can you help me with something? Backspace.
I need some help with my bills. Sounded like I was asking for money. Nope.

Finally, I keyed,

I'd like you to look at something for me . . . my checkbook!
Deece

I could count on Andre to help me without being judgmental. I clicked on *Send* before I could give it another thought.

Two

Although traffic was the typical nightmare, I was feeling pretty good when I pulled into the parking lot at work. It wasn't the crisp French cuff, side-zip blouse or the fitted black pencil skirt with the kick pleats that met the back of my knees. It wasn't even my new tangerine water bra (which added a full cup size to my bustline) or the matching thong panties, which had me walking on sunshine. It was my Enzo Angiolinis that had me high stepping. I sported a pair of gorgeous black supple suede pumps with ribbon stitching and a flower ornament at the toes. I could almost swear that I heard somebody singing, "Ba-ba-ba-bad (dun-dun-dun-dunt), bad to the bone," when I stepped my foot out of my 2002 Sports Trac.

Tucking my clutch under my arm, I strutted across the lot, trying my best not to look down and worship my own two feet. My coworkers made up for my self-deprivation no sooner than I crossed the threshold into the office.

"December, girl, them some bad shoes!" Portia began. I barely glanced down, as if I didn't care.

"Where'd you get those?" Leslie asked, circling me to see my shoes from all sides.

"Oh. Thanks. I don't even remember," I lied, knowing full well I'd picked them up at Nordstrom Rack a few weeks ago. Waving a dismissive hand, I smiled smugly inside. I took two steps toward my office, then turned back toward the receptionist desk, purposely leaving one foot cocked out to the side so the ladies could get another freeze-frame look.

"Did, uh . . ." I really didn't have anything to say, so I paused pensively, with a crinkled brow, and rested a finger on my pursed lips. "Oh, never mind. It's at nine o'clock. That's right," I said, referencing a pretend appointment. I spun on my heels and walked off confidently, with Leslie and Portia still eyeing my feet.

I was currently working as a senior account manager at Wright-Way Staffing, which assisted individuals with finding temporary to permanent employment. I had started there as a temp myself but was hired onto the internal staff in less than three months and had worked my way up the ladder.

Before I could get my computer on and pull up my task list in Staff Suites, Andre popped in, toting a Chick-Fil-A bag and a drink carrier with two large sweet teas.

"Extra lemon?" I asked.

"You know I got you," he chimed as he took a seat in front of my desk.

"You are too good to me. Did you get my e-mail?" Digging right in, I lifted a biscuit from the bag, then tapped my straw against my desk to remove its paper wrapping.

"What e-mail? The one about throwing Shelley a book shower?" He popped a potato round into his mouth after dipping it into a pool of ketchup.

My girlfriend and coworker Shelley had just gotten a

book deal and would soon be a published author. I'd be giving her a party to celebrate her success.

"What's a book shower, anyway?" Andre said. "What do we do? Throw books at the guest of honor?"

"No, stupid, you give gifts that a writer needs. Just like at a baby shower, you give gifts that a mother would need for a new baby?" I said, with a "do you get it?" tone.

"What kind of stuff would a writer need, though? Pencils? Ink pens?" He unwrapped his sandwich, peeled the top half of the biscuit away, and squirted mayonnaise on the biscuit.

"We can talk about Shelley's party later; it won't be any time soon. I'm talking about the e-mail I sent you inviting you to lunch today . . . on me. Of course, you would bring breakfast on a day that I'm trying to take you to lunch."

Andre had a strict rule about eating no more than one not-from-home meal per week, even if he wasn't paying for it. "It costs too much, and it's not good for you in the first place," was his reasoning. Everyone in the office knew he was right, but generally speaking, we lacked the discipline that he seemed to have an abundance of, and shucks, we just didn't care. That was his rule, not ours.

"Why are you offering me lunch? What's going on?" He eyed me suspiciously.

"What? I can't show my appreciation for a great friend by buying him lunch?" I took a long swig of tea while I batted my lashes at him.

"I'm listening." He chuckled.

"I just need your help with something, that's all." Andre nodded his head, signaling me to go on. "I need you to help me . . . um . . ." I was starting to stall, and he could tell.

"Listen, call me at my desk when you get yourself together. I don't know why you are acting like you can't talk to me." He got up and started collecting the remainder of his breakfast, threatening to walk out.

"Okay, okay!" I whined, sucking my teeth. "I need you to help me catch up on my bills. I don't mean pay them for me, but help me come up with a strategy to keep up with them."

"Didn't I tell you to at least freeze those credit cards in a cup of water so you could think about what you were buying first? As long as you can whip 'em out of your wallet whenever you get ready, you'll continue to be in this dilemma that you're in." He looked me straight in the eyes, giving me a father's reprimand.

Actually, I had tried that. My cards were in the freezer for two whole days, but once I received notification of Victoria's Secret's semiannual sale, all it took to loosen those cards from their icy prison was four minutes and a pot of boiling water on the stove. In no time flat, they were fully recuperated and snuggling in their designated crevices of my wallet. Besides that, I had the card numbers (expiration dates and security codes included) memorized in my head from frequently shopping online, so, really, keeping them frozen wouldn't have done me any good. Well, it probably would have curbed my mall spending a little . . . and my eating out.

"I know, but see what had happened was . . ." Andre burst into laughter. "I had put them in the freezer, right? But then I got an e-mail from Victoria's Secret saying that their semiannual sale was going to start like that next week, and you know I'd been wanting to get that new sexy, smoothing, lifting, and so on bra they have. It was going to be on sale for like 50 percent off. And getting three new bras was way cheaper than getting breast implants, 'cause you know I've been thinking about that, too."

Andre picked at his fingernails the whole time, pretending not to listen to a word, although I saw him glance at my breasts, with his eyebrows slightly raised, when I mentioned the boob job.

"So really, I saved like three grand by not leaving my cards in the freezer," I added.

I intentionally left out the part about me ignoring the care labels, which clearly told me to hand wash the bras and lay them flat to dry. After wearing each bra one time only, I threw them in the washer with my regular department store bras. When I pulled them out of the dryer, they had to be added to the underwear that is only to be worn at night during my period. Andre and I talked about a lot of things, but he didn't need to know all that . . . not today.

"So . . . will you help me?" I asked. He didn't respond. "Pleeeease?" He sighed before finally speaking.

"Yeah, I'll help you. And I'll tell you where we're going to start."

"Okay," I readily agreed.

"You will not be buying me lunch today. That is money saved right there. Why don't you meet me at the gym instead so we can pump some iron? You're already paying for a membership. No sense in wasting it another day, and I know you still have the gym bag thrown in the back of your truck like you work out all the time," he teased.

"Whatever!" I smiled. "I am overdue for a gym visit, not to mention a little overdue on some—" Portia's voice via phone intercom broke through our conversation.

"Deece, you have a call on line four. Renee from CPS?" she said, with a question in her tone.

"I'll meet you there at six," Andre said as he stood, brushing invisible crumbs from his plain blue oxford and starched khakis. A pair of sensible worn leather Dockers were on his feet. Very white boyish.

"Thanks." I winked before picking up the phone. "This is December speaking. How can I help you?"

"Ms. Elliott, this is Renee calling from the Center for Plastic Surgery. How are you?"

"Pretty good, thank you, and you?"

"Great, great!" Her voice was overly chipper as she continued. "I just wanted to confirm your appointment for Wednesday morning at eleven. Is that time still good for you?"

"It sure is."

"Great," she replied, extending the "a" sound. "Bring any questions that you have, any questions at all. We'll make sure that they are all answered before you leave the office."

"Now how long will this take again? Because I will be coming during my lunchtime."

"Generally, it takes between fifteen to thirty minutes. It all depends on how many questions you have. And then the wrap-up takes about ten minutes, so all in all, I would say forty-five minutes, give or take." I could hear her fingers tapping on a keyboard in the background. "I'm going to go ahead and mark your appointment as a lunch visit so we can get you in and out as quickly as possible. . . ." Her voice trailed off as she struck more keys.

"That would be perfect. I appreciate you doing that for me."

"No problem. We'll see you on Wednesday at eleven."

Portia had to be watching the switchboard like a hawk. No sooner had I hung up than she came sticking her nose where it didn't belong. "Is everything okay?" Her eyebrows were nearly touching her hairline.

"Is everything okay with what?" I asked. I barely looked up at her as I flipped through my client reports, determining who I would call today to try to get my hours up.

"I mean CPS? Child Protective Services?" I kept thumbing through my report. "You don't have any kids, so . . . What did you do? Turn somebody in or something?" She took a seat in front of my desk as her eyes scanned its surface for any potential clues.

"That's not your business," I sang.

"Mmmh! You let me find out you 'round here abusing kids." She stood, disappointed that she couldn't pick me for information. "Anyway, you have an interview waiting."

I had seven back-to-back interviews, all for clerical work. The next few hours were spent rotating the applicants between different seats and computers for the small battery of assessments we had all clerical applicants complete. When I made it back to my desk and glanced at my planner, I realized that I'd missed my reminder time frames to make payments on my VISA and DVD club accounts. I picked up the phone and started to dial one of the numbers, but then dismissed the thought based on the fact that later on Andre would be helping me to come up with a winning strategy to get my accounts paid off completely. I'd call tomorrow.

Instead, I dialed Andre's extension.

"What do you want?" he said. He obviously read my extension number, displayed on his phone, before answering.

"I have my appointment at CPS this week." He sighed before he responded.

"Deece, you know I'm here to support whatever decision you make, but you really need to think about it and make sure that you're doing the right thing."

"What makes you think I haven't thought about it? I have thought about it. I've thought about it a lot as a matter of fact. Plus, it's just a consultation. Nothing is set in stone yet. The consultation is part of the decision-making process."

"Well, let me know how it goes . . . that is, if you want to talk about it. I'm here for you, but I think you look great just the way you are."

"Thanks, Dre. I'll keep you posted."

I must have had this conversation with Andre at least three other times, but he was the easiest to talk to. He was the most neutral. Both Kisha and Shelley gave me grief whenever I would bring the subject up, making me regret that I'd tried to discuss my wanting implants with them at all.

That's why I loved Andre so much; our friendship was just as wonderful as the pumps I had on. Comfortable, perfect for work. Okay, maybe he wasn't as stylish, but he was definitely great for my "friends" collection.

Three

Andre had already finished his stretching routine by the time I arrived at the gym. He gave me a few minutes to get my muscles warmed up; then we walked together to the free weights.

"Are you serious this time?" Andre asked. He slid two five-pound weights on the bar and spotted me while I struggled through a few bench press reps.

"Hold on." I winced, doing my best to force my arms upwards. He practically did the last rep for me, grasping and lifting the center of the bar, then bringing it to a rest on the stand. "Yeah, I'm for real this time. I gotta do something."

"December, we've been through this before." He added a hundred pounds to both sides of the bar, then positioned himself on the bench.

"You know if you can't lift that, I can't help you, right?" I barely made it with ten pounds and the weight of the bar.

"I'm good." I was quiet as he did his reps, straining a bit during his last set. He stood up, wiped away his sweat on a face towel, then swatted the seat. "So how much debt are you in?"

"I don't know." I quickly shrugged. "Not that much, I guess."

"What do you mean, you don't know? Is it a couple of hundred dollars, a couple of thousand, ten thousand?" He added weights onto an arm curl machine and gestured for me to sit.

"I think I could catch up on stuff if I had maybe five hundred dollars or something." I caught his look of disapproval at my answer from the corner of my eye. "How are my hands supposed to be on here again?" He placed my hands and gave me quick instructions before I started curling. "Why are you looking at me like that?" I puffed.

"Because I have told you I don't know how many times that if you don't know what you owe, there is no way you can successfully catch up. And just forget about getting ahead." He paused while we switched places. "Suppose I drugged you up, knocked you out, blindfolded you, took you ten miles from home, kicked you out of my car, and pulled off. How would you get home?" He easily guided the apparatus back and forth, lifting four times the weight he had set for me.

"Do I have any money?"

"Yep. You got all the money in the world."

"What kind of shoes do I have on? My tennis shoes or some work shoes?"

"Whatever shoes you want to have on."

"Well, if I have on my tennis shoes, and I'm only ten miles away, I can walk to the bus stop probably, catch a cab, or worst-case scenario, walk. If I have on work shoes, then I'd call a cab or get somebody to come get me."

"Come get you from where?"

"From wherever you dumped me half-nekkid and left me for dead!"

"Which would be where?"

"I don't know."

"You get my point, though. The very first thing you would do, no matter how much money you had or didn't have, regardless of your shoes, and whether you have your phone or not, is to determine where you are so you can figure out how you are going to get home. It is the same thing with your finances, Deece. You need to know exactly just how much money you owe, monthly and altogether, how much you make, and what you can afford to pay. You need to know where you are."

We moved to the fly machine next. "All right, all right! Let me think."

I started calculating numbers in my head, thinking of the stack of bills I'd looked at yesterday, plus a few more that I knew were coming or I'd already received. Trying to count reps and count debt dollars was a bit challenging. We changed places, with me still doing some math. When I arrived at an estimated figure, I was too embarrassed to share the number with Andre.

"Well?" he asked, grunting through his sets.

"You want me to actually tell you the number?"

"I thought you wanted some help."

"I do, but I can't tell you *everything*."

He led the way to the pectoral deck machine, shaking his head. I took a seat, pressed my back against the rest, then brought my arms together in front of me, contracting my chest.

"Well, let me just give you some quick tips then," he said, a hint of exasperation in his voice. Andre helped me squeeze out the last few presses, then took a seat.

"Number one"—he groaned—"cut those credit cards

up." His face contorted through a full set. "Number two, make a list of everything you owe, and prioritize the accounts by amount or by interest rate." He completed another set. "Which one of your cards has the lowest interest rate?"

"My, uh. . . ." I honestly had no clue. "My Capital Finance VISA," I answered, picking one out of the air. I followed him to the cable pull machine.

"Well, at least you know that much. Do you have any available credit on it?"

"Yeah, a little." By "a little," I meant forty-two dollars.

"Okay, transfer as much debt as you can onto that card to pay as little interest as possible. The less interest you pay, the better off you are." I nodded in understanding, knowing full well that I wouldn't be able to transfer anything to a card that had less than fifty dollars in available credit.

"Next, pay off the smallest bills first," he continued. "As you pay off the small bills, add that payment amount to the next bill's payment."

"Huh?" I crinkled my brows in confusion.

"As you pay off a bill, instead of spending the money on shoes"—he paused from his set and gave me a scolding eye—"Add that amount that you were paying to the payment amount of the next bill you are going to pay off."

By this time, I had started to tune Andre out, not seeing the feasibility of the solution he was attempting to explain to me. My mind drifted to those three bras that were now ruined. For all the money they cost, why couldn't they be machine washable? Who came up with the theory that the more money something cost, the more fragile it was? I should write the lingerie companies a letter telling them that they should use more durable lace and stuff. And could they please secure their underwires a little better? Some of my formerly favorite bras now had one underwire missing from them. Once, I was at work, in the middle of an interview, when I looked down to write the candidate's response and felt something poke me in my chin. It was the underwire! It had crept up and out of the casing and was protruding from the opening of my blouse. Luckily, the interviewee was so nervous, she wasn't giving any kind of eye contact. I kindly excused myself, went to the ladies' room, and slid the wire out completely. Instantly, the lift was gone from my right side. There I was, stuck in the office all day, looking like Lopsided Louise.

"Does that help you?" Andre asked. He was pouring sweat. I bobbed my head excitedly.

"It sure does! Thanks, Andre!"

On my way home, I stopped by the mall and picked up three new bras.

Four

Janice caught me on my way out the door.

"It's a little early for lunch, isn't it?" she asked. She flashed a bright smile, but it wasn't sincere.

"I just need to take care of some personal business." I shrugged. "And, by the way, I need to swing by Drake, Lynch, and Lewis around two to meet with the office manager. We may be able to squeeze another admin in there." Janice didn't respond right away but looked at me probingly.

"We weren't talking about you or anything, but Portia mentioned to me that you got a call from social services," she whispered, then waited for me to confirm. But I kept silent. "I don't know what's going on, and I'm not asking you to tell me your personal business," she added, quickly throwing her hand up. "Just let me know if you need to take some personal time off, December."

"Thanks, Janice. I am so glad to be working for you," I lied, touching her hand lightly, feeding into her ego. I knew I shouldn't have, but she was holding me up. I needed to get to my appointment.

"Bring some hours back with you!" She smiled again, then winked. My eyes rolled into the back of my head as soon as my back was to her. And as for Portia, lucky for her, I'd never learned how to fight, because she was forever doing something to make me want to kick her behind. I just didn't know how to do it.

"Who is your appointment with today, ma'am?" The receptionist at the Center for Plastic Surgery looked to be in her early thirties. She had incredibly white teeth and burgundy hair, which was razor cut into a wispy style that made her look young-spirited. She had on a sheer black blouse, which covered a black camisole that dipped in the front, exposing her cleavage. Did she have them done? Just because she worked at CPS didn't mean she'd been a patient, right?

"Umm . . . I didn't have a preference." It didn't matter to me who I saw, as I was not familiar with any of the doctors in the office.

"Okay, that's fine. Go ahead and fill out the paperwork on this clipboard, and we'll be right with you just as soon as you're done."

As I took my seat and filled in blanks with my personal information, I made a quick sweep over the other individuals in the waiting area, wondering what they were there for. *Middle-aged white woman, face-lift. Younger white woman, implants. Thirty-something black woman, reduction. Twenty-something white dude, hmmmm . . . chin lift maybe? Who knows.* I was being stereotypical in my assumptions, but they were probably making assumptions about me, too.

"Ms. Elliott," a thin, blond woman called from a

cracked door leading to the examination rooms. "Hi, I'm Barbie." It took everything I had not to burst into laughter. A woman named Barbie who worked at a plastic surgery center? She had to be making that up. "I'll do the initial part of your consultation. Then Dr. Patrick will come in to do an initial exam and chat with you a little bit."

I tried to stroll confidently along with her, but how confident could I be when asking somebody to look at my tits and make them bigger? She led me to room number ten, pointed out a book that displayed before and after photos of various breast procedures, and instructed me to replace my blouse and bra with a gown, opening to the front. At least it wasn't made of paper and accompanied by a stupid paper "sheet" like at my ob-gyn's office.

I was quick to undress, grab the photo book, and start looking at the before and after shots, starting with lifts only, then implants only, then a combination of the two, and ending with tummy tucks. The photos were actually impressive, giving me confidence about what I was trying to decide to do. But then again, if any of these doctors botched anybody up, that would never be found in a photo album for potential surgery candidates.

Although there weren't many to focus on, I concentrated on the photos of black women because . . . well, because I was most like them. There was one woman whose breasts hung waaaay low and flat, looking like those socks with an orange in them that I'd only heard about, but her after picture had her boobies looking the bomb! She had had both the lift and implant procedures, or as properly stated in the book, a mastopexy and augmentation. I had brought the book practically to my nose, examining the photo for scarring, when Barbie walked back in.

"So what'd you think of the photos?" she asked, taking a seat on a rolling stool in the corner.

"I'm impressed," I said, nodding. "Impressed and convinced."

"Did you have an opportunity to look through the procedure brochure?"

"Actually, I didn't, but I will take it with me." I had been so anxious to see the photos, I never even saw the informative pamphlet on the counter, by a small sink.

"Well, let's take a look. . . ." She stood and practically snatched my gown open. "So you are looking for size increase, or volume, or . . ." She left the sentence open for me to clarify why I was there. The thing was, I didn't really know. They were the professionals!

"I guess I just want to be a little fuller," I said, looking down at my nipples, trying to avoid eye contact with Barbie." I lost about twenty pounds last year, and I think some of that weight came off my breasts. They used to be rounder and fuller, but ever since I lost weight, they have just seemed not as full to me."

"How did you lose weight?" she asked, jotting down a few notes.

"Drinking meal replacement shakes mostly. I thought I was getting married, but . . ." I shook my head, thinking about how Terrance, my flip-flop of an ex-boyfriend, had strung me along all that time, knowing full well he had no intentions of marrying me. "It didn't work out."

"Awww." Okay, she could have saved the pity voice. "What cup size would you like to be?" she asked next.

"I actually like the cup size I am now, which is a C, but I just don't have the firmness or roundness I used to have. I just want them to be like this," I replied, cupping my breasts and lifting them up to try to demonstrate the look I wanted to achieve.

"I see. Well, let me go get Dr. Patrick, and he can talk

with you about some options that I'm sure will give you the results you're looking for. Go ahead and keep the robe on, and he'll be right in."

"Okay, thanks. Would you mind handing me one of those?" I asked.

"Sure." She passed me one of the trifold brochures and disappeared.

My jaw dropped to my chest as I read a paragraph that explained that it was sometimes necessary that a woman's nipples be removed as part of the procedure. I suddenly became not so sure of the whole thing as I read not only about the nipple removal, but also that the nipples could become overly sensitive or dramatically lose sensitivity.

I already had a look of shock on my face when the door slowly opened, but I became even more horrified when Dr. Patrick stepped in.

"Good morning. I'm Dr. William Patrick," he said cordially, eyeing me through his rimless specs.

This doctor was six feet three, solidly built, with a trim waistline, jet-black hair, and a gorgeous mocha complexion, which looked to be carefully pampered with somebody's facial rejuvenation cream. That's right, a mocha complexion. The doctor was a brother. A handsome brother at that . . . no, not just handsome, he was beautiful . . . with no ring! I wanted to sink right through the floor! How was I going to let this fine man look at my low-volume boobies! Why didn't I research the doctors before I came? I could have gone on the Web site, looked at the photos, and picked Doctor Vladamir, who would probably be Indian or something.

"Hi," I responded, suddenly embarrassed. I forgot all about the nipple removal, sensitivity gain or loss, scar lines, and all of that, and could only think about how this fine man was about to see my shame.

"So you've lost some volume due to weight loss?"

I could barely concentrate. Trying not to stutter, I answered; "Uh, yes. I think, um, when I lost weight, I uh, they um, got a little smaller. Well, not smaller, but less firm."

With perfect bedside manner, he approached and opened my gown, then used his right hand to gently lift each breast, while tilting his head slightly. Then he pinched a few times on the top and at the sides. I could feel the blood rush to my face. When had I ever, ever, in my life been seen by a black doctor? My current ob-gyn was an old white man; before him, it was an Asian lady. When I got on the pill at seventeen, it was some young white guy. In reality, I'm sure somewhere along the way, I'd been seen by a black physician, but *why* did the breast man have to be black! I didn't even know there was such a thing as a black plastic surgeon. Well, really, I did, but I never expected to meet him like this!

"You do have a little loose skin, but your nipples are not below the breast crease line," he began, using a silver pen as a pointer. He pinched underneath my left breast and continued. "You could go with an augmentation. That would fill you in nicely and give you more shape and volume."

He paused, then continued. "And we could also do just a little bit of a lift, if you'd like. You really don't need that, because your nipples are in proper placement to the crease line. If your nipples were below the crease line, you'd be a perfect candidate for a lift. During the lift, the nipple is removed, and we'd cut away the extra skin right along here"—he did more pen pointing—"then replace the nipple."

He tilted his head again to get a look from a different angle. "If it's placed too high, it won't look natural." He closed the gown and made a few notes. "Did you have any questions?" he asked, without looking up. I actually had a whole bunch about that nipple removal thing, but I was too mortified to remember any of them.

"Uh, not right now."

"Well, you can call into the office if you think of any later, or set up a second consultation if you'd like. Good luck, now." With that, he was gone, leaving me with Bambi . . . I mean Barbie. I let out a puff of air.

"You okay, sweetie?" she asked. That snapped me back to reality; I hated when people called me sweetie as if I were five years old. I was twenty-eight and was nobody's sweetie. Not to some bimbo Bambi girl, anyway.

"I'm fine, thank you."

"Are you sure you don't have any questions?"

Yes! Why didn't you tell me the doctor was a fine, single black man! "I'm positive, thanks," I said calmly.

"Okay, well, once you're dressed, come down to the office at the end of the hall, and Carrie will do your financial consultation, and if you think of anything at all, just give us a call." She shut the door behind her.

While I re-dressed, I searched my mind for any thoughts of dignity. *He does this all day every day; this was no big deal to him. He probably has forgotten all about me just that quickly.* I neatened up my make-up before leaving the examination room, just in case I bumped into him in the hallway. Maybe if my lipstick was fresh enough, he would forget all about my flattened breasts and would be like, "Who was *that!*" I wasn't really convinced, but it would have to do.

Luckily, I didn't see him on the way to the finance office. I sat in yet another waiting room for about two minutes before another woman with very round tatas came and got me.

"I'm Carrie," she said as she extended her hand for a shake. "Come on over. I'll be going over the pricing and financing options with you." She gleamed. I found a reciprocal smile from somewhere and followed her across the hall. She tapped on her computer, then pulled a few sheets of paper from her printer and placed them upside down on her desk. "Are you okay? You look a little razzled."

"Oh, I'm fine." *Okay, December, snap out of it.*

"And you're considering the mastopexy and/or augmentation, right?"

"Exactly," I confirmed.

"Let's start with the augmentation, which is the least expensive of the two." She flipped the first sheet of paper and pointed to a figure a little over four thousand dollars. I wasn't expecting the procedure to be cheap, but I had a little bit of sticker shock. "This amount is all inclusive, and we do all of our procedures on-site. We have a state-of-the-art facility, with an on-site anesthesiologist, so you would not get a separate bill for that. Your follow-up visits are also included, for your stitch removal and to make sure that you're draining properly."

She must have noticed the overwhelmed look on my face. "I know it sounds like a lot, but really, it's a pretty easy and low-risk procedure," she continued. "The doctors here are the best. I'll tell you, I got both the lift and implants about six months ago, and I *love* them. I decided to have them done after I had my son, and I had some droop going on. I was like, 'Oh, no way. I am way too young to look like my nana, you know?'"

"Right." I laughed with her, not because I found her to be humorous, but only to make her feel good.

"Let me show you the mastopexy pricing." She flipped the next sheet, and I nearly fell out of my seat. It was in excess of six thousand dollars. "Now if you get both procedures together, it's discounted by fifteen hundred dollars, so you save quite a bit by doing them at the same time."

I didn't have $8,500. I didn't even have $850. As a matter of fact, I think there was $242 in my savings account, and $120 of that needed to be transferred to my checking before the check I sent for my power bill bounced.

"Wow, that's pretty reasonable," I fronted. She reached back and handed me a financing brochure.

"We do require 100 percent of your procedure paid for up front and two weeks prior to you coming in for your surgery. Now we do have a couple of financing options for you to consider. We accept cash, MasterCard, VISA, and Discover, and this company"—she pointed to a brochure—"does offer financing for cosmetic procedures, and can approve you in just a few minutes if you apply online."

I nodded as if I was ready to sign up right then. "So what would be the next steps after paying?"

"We'd have you come in for a fitting so you can determine what size you'd like to be. You'd try on a few padded bras; that will give us an idea of your desired cup size. When you come in that day, I would recommend that you bring a few different shirts with you, to see how you'd look in each of them, because different shirts will lie differently on your breasts."

"Right." While she continued, I scanned the financing brochure, wondering if I could get approved for a few grand. The matrix of estimated payments just about had my full attention.

"We'd then have you come in for some lab work, and then your actual surgery, which, again, would be done right in this facility." She paused, waiting for my next question.

Maybe I could split the cost between my four VISAs and then work really hard toward my bonuses and pay them all off. Let's see. I had the $42 VISA, another which had about $600, card three had about $175, and my fourth card, which was reserved for emergencies, had $1,400. I had only used it once, and that was when those cream-colored, open-toe, leather wedged-heel Prada sandals were released. They were almost six hundred dollars, but a worthy investment, as they matched several of my spring and summer outfits. Not that I would wear them frequently . . . They cost too much for that.

Anyway, I had about twenty-two hundred dollars in credit, and I could easily come up with the rest just from going to work every day, or I could apply with this finance company and just have it all on one bill. I placed the brochure in my purse for later review.

Concluding that I had no other questions, Carrie began again. "Did you want to go ahead and schedule your surgery today?" She flipped the page of her desk calendar forward to the next month and pointed out the third week. "Dr. Patrick does his surgeries on Wednesdays, so we could have you come in on the twenty-sixth to do your lab work then have you back in the following week, on the third,"—she flipped to the next month—"to have your procedure done."

"I actually need some time to review this brochure and think about some things Dr. Patrick shared with me in the consultation before I decide to move forward."

"Okay, that's fine. These are your copies." She folded three sheets—one with the mastopexy price, one with the augmentation price, and one with both procedures combined—and stuffed them into an envelope. "I just need you to sign our copies, indicating that I did review these with you." I scribbled my signature on each sheet.

"Call me if you have any questions," she ended, sliding me her card.

I looked for Kisha's screen name on instant messenger and was glad to find that she was signed on.

Deece79: There?
KQN0602: Yep. Whassup?
Deece79: You would not believe what happened to me today.
KQN0602: What?
Deece79: I told you I was going to get implants, right?
KQN0602: You better not do that mess!

I sighed, then continued typing.

Deece79: Can you just listen (read) please?
KQN0602: Yeah, but don't get that mess!
Deece79: Anyway . . . why did I go to the dr today for a consultation, and I'm in there half nekkid, with my tits looking all sleepy, like they saying, "Mama, we tired!"
KQN0602: LOLOLOLOL!! ☺
Deece79: LOL! Girl the dr walks in, and he is this FINE black man!!!
KQN0602: What????
Deece79: I was so embarrassed!!
KQN0602: That is what you get for going in there in the first place! I told you you don't need that mess.
Deece79: Kisha, he was FINNNNNNNNNNNNN-NNNNNNNE!!!! Suppose I see him at McDonald's

or something? He gone be like, "There go that girl with them flat titties!"

KQN0602: December, your breasts are not flat!

Deece79: Yes, they are!!!

KQN0602: NO, they not!

Deece79: Okay, they not flat, but they need some help! They not round and pretty!

KQN0602: Stop trippin'. All you need is a good bra.

Deece79: A good bra ain't gone help me when I take it off! I want them to stay up when I take my bra off!

KQN0602: Ima send you a Vic Sec gift card.

Deece79: No! Send me 'bout $5000 so I can get my jonks fixed!

KQN0602: You crazy.

Deece79: You think I'm playing!!!

KQN0602: You better be!

Deece79: I ain't! Why that man had to be black??? He could have at least been ugly!

KQN0602: Was he married?

Deece79: No!!!!! Sigh!!! I bed' not ever see that man again!

KQN0602: Girl, please, he probably ain't thinking 'bout you. He looks at breasts all day and has seen a lot worse, I'm sure.

Deece79: Potatoes.

I immediately closed the dialogue box. Whenever a *Potatoes* alert went out, all typing immediately ceased. *Potatoes* was our code word to indicate that the IM had the potential of being read by an onlooker. We had decided on *potatoes* because potatoes have eyes, thus, the perfect signal that someone was looking. There would be no more messages sent until whoever sent the alert gave clearance for the conversation to continue.

"I didn't realize you were back," Janice said as she came in and took a seat in front of me.

"My lunch hour is just that, an hour. Why wouldn't I be back?" She was here to play the nosey game.

"Oh, I know if you were going to be late, you would have called to let me know." She paused, waiting for me to confide in her. "You're still eating this junk, huh?" she asked, looking in disdain at the bag of cheese curls, which served as my midday meal. "You're not going to learn your lesson about eating junk until you are carrying around an extra fifteen pounds on that caboose of yours, and when you get there, I'll share my Slim-Fast with you." She winked. "I've lost two pounds so far."

"Did you need me to do anything?" *In other words, what the heck do you want?*

"No, no." She stood and turned toward the door. "If you need to talk or anything, you know where my office is." She was trying her best to be sincere, but I knew better. "I always have my people's back."

"Thanks, Janice." *Yeah, right.*

She wasn't cognizant of the fact that I had come out of my office just a few steps behind her and thus was clearly able to hear her when she rounded the bend to Portia's desk and said, "I know she doesn't have kids. I'm going to find out what's going on with her. If you find out anything before I do, let me know."

Five

"December, line two," Portia announced. "It's Eddie Thomas."

"December Elliott speaking." Eddie was one of my best clients, but he was also my Winter Boot. He owned a small but popular little hole-in-the-wall restaurant that had the absolute best barbecue and ribs. His business had taken off over the past year, making him good for a couple hundred billable hours each week. I primarily had him to thank for the huge bonuses I'd received over the past seven months and my receiving the Top Account Manager Award for two quarters in a row.

"Ms. Elliott, how are you today?"

"Great, thanks, and you?" I'd learned my lesson about saying, "I'm fine," which always caused him to say, "I know you fine, but I asked how you doin'." After two or three times, I got sick of it.

"I'm pretty good, but I'd be better if—" I cut him off at the pass.

"If I sent you how many workers?"

"Actually, I was gon' ask you to check your schedule

for tomorrow night at seven to see if you free for dinner. I got a slew of weddings coming up in a coupla weeks, and I'ma need a super-sized crew. I thought we could sit down and review some numbahs and rates. Now you gotta eat. Last time I saw you, you look like you could use a little bit more rump on your rump roast. And you know I can whip you up somp'n that'll make you slap yo' momma girl."

"Eddie, unless I want to die an early death, I won't be slapping my momma anytime soon." I laughed, although I didn't appreciate his rump roast comment. I flipped through my planner, hoping that he would hear me turning pages. "I can absolutely assist you with your staffing needs, but I'm afraid that tomorrow night is no good for me. I have something scheduled every night this week."

My evenings were actually clearer than the summer sky in June, but in my book, business and pleasure only mixed well if I planned on sleeping my way to the top, which just wasn't part of the plan.

"Why do you give me such a hard way to go, December?"

"How do you mean? I take great care of you," I replied. Not wanting him to respond, I redirected him back to the business at hand. "I can have some quality workers lined up for you by morning. Just tell me what you need." He sighed in defeat, which he'd only temporarily accept.

"I'll need about twenty-thirty people, preferably with server and/or short order cook experience."

"How soon will you need them, and for how long?" My fingers danced randomly on the keys of my calculator. I was already thinking about bonus dollars.

"Monday at seven thirty. Just send them on to the restaurant. I'll need them for about three weeks." *Oh yeah!* Thirty temps at hopefully forty hours a week for three weeks could mean a shopping spree for me!

"No problem, Eddie. I'll go ahead and set you up for forty-five heads to make sure you get the thirty you need." Overbooking was the name of the game in keeping clients happy and billable hours up. I always used the "add half" rule: whatever the client asked for, book that many heads, plus half. Doing so ensured my client's needs were well covered when folks decided just out of the clear blue sky that they didn't want to report to work, or their baby got sick, or they suddenly remembered ten minutes after the start of the shift that they had to report to court. Leslie, the lowest-performing account manager, didn't seem to understand that concept, which explained why she was always under her hours goal.

"What you gon' charge me an hour," Eddie asked. I quoted him rates for both servers and cooks, and after he agreed to both, I ended the call.

Typing a few key words into the database produced a list of sixty-seven candidates I could contact for Eddie's job order. I printed the list and blocked out the afternoon to make calls, then clicked on the Internet icon to check cruise prices on Priceline.com. I had yet to experience the often talked about "all you can eat twenty-four hours a day" cruise and decided that that was how I'd reward myself for all my hard work when I received my next bonus check.

Royal Caribbean had inside cabins as low as $219 in late November. A cruise would be the perfect way to spend some time with my girls, Kisha and Shelley. We hadn't had a girl trip in over a year, although we promised to make girl trips a yearly ritual as long as we were single. Not one of us had a ring yet; we could hardly find a worthy suitor, let alone a ring! I dialed Shelley's extension to run the idea by her. She picked up on the third ring.

"What are you doing?" I began.

"Working." Like I didn't know that.

"It's girl trip time. Let's go on a cruise."

"No, it's I got cramps time," she moaned. "Let's go to Starbucks and get some tea." I glanced down at my planner. There was nothing listed except my afternoon calls.

"Okay," I agreed. "How soon will you be ready?"

"Give me two minutes to file these I-9s. I'll swing by your office."

"Cool." I looked at the small pile of applications and I-9s on my own desk, then jotted "filing" in my planner, at 4:30. It was then that I noticed a small area in the lower left-hand corner of the page, designated for tracking daily spending. Actually, I knew that box was there all along but would always forget to use it. "Track daily spending" was now listed in the 5:00 P.M. slot. I'd make a habit of listing any money I'd spent during the day before I left work.

"Let's go." Shelley leaned against the door frame as she dug through her BCBGirls shoulder bag. "Who's driving?" Shelley drove a black BMW truck. I had to get me one of those.

"It doesn't matter. I'll drive since your 'aunt' is visiting."

Out of respect, we swung by Janice's office to let her know we were leaving. I couldn't stand Janice but had learned to play the office politics game, smile, and feed her ego. She asked for a venti something or other and handed me a five-dollar bill.

"Did you get that?" I asked Shelley as we rounded the corner in the hallway. I slid on my Coach wraparound shades and applied a little gloss to my lips before step-ping outside. Never knew who I might run into. Once seated in my truck, I popped in John Legend and skipped to my favorite riding track.

"Yea, yea, yea, yea, yea!" I sang.

"Girl, turn that down for a minute so I can tell you what happened last night." Shelley reached for the volume knob while she spoke. "You got some Midol in here?" She began digging through the storage of my armrest.

"You know I don't get cramps," I said. She continued searching, anyway.

"How about Advil, Tylenol, something!"

"We can stop at the drugstore on the way back. What's going on?"

"I heard a posting is going up for a new regional manager," she began. "The person is supposed to be in place by the end of the month."

"How do you know? Is Janice going to post for it?"

"Yep!" That was enough to make my day. I was sick of working under Janice's stuck-up, high and mighty behind. The fact that she was a sistah didn't help any. Really, she wasn't a true sistah; she was mixed but seemed to be ashamed of her black side when she got around the big-wigs. "I was standing at the printer when her internal application and resume' came rolling off. You should have seen the way she came bucking around that corner, trying to make sure nobody saw it."

"Did she say anything to you?"

"Girl, no. Her eyes about popped out of her head when she saw me standing there, leafing through papers. She asked what was I still doing in the office and snatched those papers out of my hands so quick, talking about, 'Sorry for snatching. I didn't know you were still here. I just printed some confidential documents.'"

"Who is she gonna sleep with and step on to get that

promotion?" I asked. Janice had a terribly promiscuous reputation.

"I don't think there is anybody left." Shelley chuckled. "You can just go through the drive-thru. I don't feel like getting out."

"Look at the line. We'll be there all day. Come on here," I coaxed after pointing out that the Starbucks drive-thru line was backed up to the street. Once we got inside, I regretted having gotten out of the truck. Standing at the counter, about six people in front of me, was Terrance. I started to turn right back around and get in the truck, but then I remembered how fly I looked. I'd look even better on my new Motorola Razr (which I had to sign a whole new two-year contract for. Cell phone companies got you coming and going). I quickly pulled it out of my clutch and dialed *86 to listen to my saved messages.

"When'd you get that!" Shelley tried to take the phone from my hand.

"Shh!" I jerked away and nodded my head in Terrance's direction, although Shelley had never met him.

She instantly lowered her tone, while her eyes shifted suspiciously around the shop. "What?" she whispered.

"That's Terrance," I mouthed, turning my back to him just in case he turned around.

"Who?"

"I'll tell you later." He looked over his shoulder just as I turned around, but I didn't make eye contact. I crinkled my eyebrows and studied the menu board instead, holding a pretend conversation with a voice mail message Kisha had left me last week that was never deleted.

"Girl, turn on Sex and the City*!! This is the one I was telling you about, when Carrie got slapped by that*

Russian man, and her and Mr. Big end up getting back together! Hurry up and turn it on! You better watch it tonight!"

"Right . . . right . . . Well, when I last heard from her, she said the reservations had been made, and he was scheduled to show up at two . . . No . . . exactly . . . Well, let me give his admin a call to find out the status, because I've already received payment, and the transaction can't be reversed."

To save this message, press nine. To delete, press seven. To skip this message and go to the next, press . . .

"Great! Just shoot me a quick e-mail once the compensation portion is finalized . . . Okay . . . okay, bye." I snapped the phone shut and slid it back in my bag, then turned to Shelley.

"They are so inefficient. And Diane needs some development on her e-mail etiquette," I said.

"Deece, 'sup, girl?" Terrance said from a distance.

"Oh! Hi, Terrance," I replied, acting as if I hadn't seen him already. His eyes looked me over from head to toe at least three times.

"Deece, he is fine," Shelley whispered, barely moving her lips. Terrance grabbed his coffee cup, then excused himself as he moved backwards through the line, past the customers that stood between the two of us.

"I see you're still doing your career woman thing," he said.

I nodded, with a smile. I was actually smiling because he looked so good, even dressed down in a pair of baggy jeans and what I called a Blue's Clues shirt, a dark and light green-striped, long-sleeved, white-collared rugby. A green ball cap sat tilted on his head, and his feet were covered in a pair of Nike Air Force Ones. He had just the front hem of his shirt tucked inside his pants to show off a light green belt.

"And I see you're still trying to live your teen years," I responded snidely. "Not quite ready to be a man yet, huh?" He chuckled.

"Oh, you got jokes. Okay, okay," he said. He searched my eyes for just a second or two before glancing at Shelley, then randomly at the others in line. "Can I speak to you over here for a minute?" He touched my elbow, coaxing me from the line.

"That was a venti White Chocolate Mocha Latte," I said as I handed Janice's money to Shelley and winked my eye. Terrance and I stepped over to a small, high-top round table at the window.

"Is that all I gotta do to get back in your life? Change my clothes? 'Cause as fine as you look, I'll do whatever it takes!" said Terrance.

"I think it's going to take a little more than that, Terrance." He licked his bottom lip and folded it into his mouth while he tried to read past my nonchalant expression.

He traced his finger back and forth across his mustache, then tapped his lips twice. "What happened to us, Deece?" I shrugged my shoulders, knowing that anything I said had the strong potential of sending me into a relapse. "You know I still love you, right?"

I nodded my head like a bashful little schoolgirl but said nothing. Silence lingered between us while I pretended to be distracted by a group of teenagers shooting down the sidewalk on in-line skates.

"What do I need to do, Deece? Girl, I could kiss you right here and now," he murmured through clenched teeth, edging closer to me. As hard as I was trying to avoid it, I blushed. His eyes darted over to the counter.

"Here comes your friend, so I guess I gotta let you go. Can I at least get a hug?"

He didn't wait for my response but moved forward, wrapping his arms around my back, then gliding them downward until his hands rested on my hips. I fought hard to keep from pressing my pelvic bone ever so slightly into him. Oh, he had me!

"Can I call you, Deece?" he whispered in my ear. I pulled back gently and looked up at him.

"Terrance, I . . ."

"Not at home, not on your cell. Just at work . . . sometimes." He was enticing.

"Okay." *Okay! Okay? December, what are you doing!* I reached in my clutch and retrieved a small leather card holder, then handed him my business card.

"Thanks. Take care of yourself." He walked off just as Shelley approached, never turning back.

"All right girl, spill the beans!" she began, blowing into the small hole in the lid of her tea.

I smiled knowingly at her while I sashayed to the truck. "Can't tell you everything," I teased.

"You're gonna tell me something! Who was that, December?"

"My ex."

Her mouth dropped open as she twisted her neck nearly full circle, trying to catch a glimpse of Terrance pulling out of the lot in his tiny Mazda Miata. "And you let that go? Are you two going to get back together?"

"Girl, please. Don't nobody want him." I refrained from watching him drive off, but she read right through my façade and could tell that in my mind, I was already having him. Only for old times' sake, or better yet, "it had been a long time" sake.

"Mmmm-hmmm," she said disbelievingly. "I see that look in your eye."

"Whatever. I wasted five years of my life on that man. I'm done with that."

"Well, give me his number," she tested. "'Cause I could put something on that bald head of his that he won't wanna let go of!" She rotated her hips in the seat, suddenly turning John Legend back up.

"Good lawd, you got body for days. . . . ," she sang. I snapped the stereo off immediately.

"I thought your cycle was on, nasty!" I said, with my nose turned up.

"Oh yeah, I forgot." She laughed.

"How did you forget when you've been crying all day about cramps? Get out before you make a mess on my seats with all that scootching around!" I joked. We both hopped out of the truck, headed for the drugstore, but I made a U-turn. "I'm going to run in Barnes & Noble real quick," I stated. I had to have a sugar cookie.

On my way to the café, I stopped by the African American Interests table. I picked up Mary Monroe's *In Sheep's Clothing*, read the back cover synopsis, and tucked it under my arm. Next, I picked up Glinda Bridgforth's *Girl, Get Your Money Straight!* Flipping through its pages, I took note of the chapter headings and read a few paragraphs.

"That's a pretty good book," said Shelley. She had come in behind me and was now browsing through titles. "I'll be back." She wandered off to the business section while I moseyed over to the café, my nose still in the same book. By the time I ordered and received my cookie, along with a cup of ice water, I had chosen to put both books back, remembering that I rarely had the time to read. But then I thought, I could squeeze in a few chapters a night, at least one chapter. Did I want to read for pleasure or to learn something? I contemplated both titles momentarily.

"Come on. We have this coffee for Janice," Shelley said as she took both books from my hand and laid them on the nearest table. "And she knows exactly what time we left the office. She's probably counting minutes."

I'd come back and get the books another time.

Six

Right away, Terrance began to call. I had two voice mail messages from him by the time I got back to my desk.

"Deece, it was so good running into you today. I know you don't believe this, but I have thought about you every day since the day we broke up. I was trippin' girl. I don't know why I let you get away from me." There were a few seconds of silence. *"Well, I'm not going to talk you to death on your voice mail, but I hope we can see each other a little later. No pressure, just maybe hang out or something, see a movie, you know, something like that. Hit me back on my cell at 555-2507. You're still beautiful, girl. Peace."*

There were two other messages sandwiched between Terrance's first and second message.

"I'm sorry for calling right back like this, but you just got me spinnin'. I can hardly concentrate on my work

anymore 'cause I'm thinkin' 'bout you. Look, why 'on't you call me when you get off work, and we can just meet up at Applebee's or something and get something to eat. You gotta eat, right? I just wanna see you. Ah-ight. Call me."

I knew that Terrance was no good for me, so I'm not sure why I gave a moment's thought to his invite. I guess it was because I was lacking male attention, and it wasn't like I didn't know Terrance. We went way back.

Terrance owned a mobile car wash company and had become increasingly popular and successful over the last few years. Actually, it was through his business that we'd met. He had been coming out to the parking lot of the office where I worked as a receptionist (prior to being employed at Wright-Way) quite regularly, but I never paid attention to him or his crew. I was on my way into the building one morning when he called out.

"Excuse me, Miss. You want your car washed?"

At the time I was driving a bright yellow, sporty little Honda Prelude that my dad had picked up for me at a car auction. I stopped to talk to him for a while, asking about his prices and that sort of thing, and at the same time absorbing his features. Six feet two, straight white teeth, chiseled chest. (He got points deducted for being out in the street in just a wife beater, but then again, he was out in the hot sun, scrubbing cars, and the wife beater showed off his well-defined biceps, triceps, and all the other ceps in between. Instead, of taking off three points, I took off one only and a half. He still could have had a shirt on.) And, he was a business owner (major points earned). I agreed to let him wash and detail the yellow bee.

"Ima take care of you," he promised. "By the time you

walk outside to leave work, she gone look brand new. Matta fact, you don't even have to pay for this one. This one on me."

When I did get off work, I found that he hadn't lied! That car was so spotless and shiny, I had to check the license plates on it twice to make sure it was really mine. He had left a single rose on the driver's seat, with a small card that read, *I'd be most honored if you would have dinner with me tonight.—Terrance Reeves, 555-5211*

I didn't take him up on his dinner offer right away; I mean, I did believe in the whole thrill of the chase theory. And every woman's guide to successful dating book that I'd ever read constantly advised that a woman should never give a man the idea that her schedule was open and available to him. Even if she had absolutely nothing to do, she should act like she did to make herself challenging, and thus more desirable.

I didn't even bother to call him, although I had picked up the phone no less than eight times and dialed 555. By making him chase me a little bit, I got two more free car washes out of the deal. In retrospect, calling him without delay is exactly what I should have done to make him lose interest in me from the get-go and move on, rather than allowing myself to get so tangled up in a relationship that did nothing but run laps around the track of nowhere for five years.

I thought Terrance and I had really good chemistry. We were both business-minded, although his business was a lot more labor intensive than mine. We, for the most part, shared the same values and beliefs and seemed to connect right away. Before I knew it, we had been dating for two enjoyable years. He'd met my friends, and I'd met his. I'd cook dinner for him; he'd take me out. We were taking three-day weekend trips every other month, regularly spending the night at each other's homes. He'd make my toes curl, and I had him tearing the sheets slam off the bed!

It was around the two-year mark that I began to think more futuristically about our relationship and posed some not too pressing questions about where we were headed.

"Terrance, where do you see us in, say, another year?" We were all tangled up in his sheets, tracing our fingers on each other's bodies in a euphoric aftermath. He pulled me close to his chest and kissed my forehead.

"I see myself right here with you, baby," he whispered. "Right here . . . right here . . . right here . . . and right here," he said lowering himself beneath the covers at each statement and planting kisses. His fourth "right here" landed him three inches below my navel, and from there I couldn't even remember what I had asked him. That one night carried me right into year three, but the next time I asked him about our future, I made sure that I was fully clothed.

"Terrance, where is this relationship headed?"

"What do you mean, where is it headed? I think we've got a great thing going, and I am enjoying every minute of it. I'd say it's headed in the right direction."

"Which is where?" I was in the kitchen, sautéing some boneless chicken breasts and onions in my special, secret-ingredient tzatziki sauce to make chicken gyros for dinner. He came up behind me and wrapped his arms around my waist.

"Wherever you want it to go, baby. I'll take you to the moon if you just say the word." He leaned down and nuzzled my neck. I bit into my lower lip, contemplating my next words. Now, all of the woman's guide to successful dating books strongly advised against saying what I was getting ready to say, but I took a chance. I mean, how right could ten different books be?

"I want it to go to the altar." I held my breath. He kept nuzzling. I stirred the chicken. His nuzzling turned to kisses. I turned the heat down. He turned me around and kissed me fully on the mouth.

"Well, let's go then," he whispered.

Oh, snap! See! The books were wrong! I guess I couldn't believe everything I read. I immediately started the initial phases of planning my wedding in my head: buying wedding magazines, researching catering companies and menus online, drinking Slim-Fast every day. I was happier than a . . . than a . . . shucks, I was just happy.

It took him another nine months to take me to Maryland to meet his mom. And when I did meet her, he introduced me as Deece.

"Ma, this is Deece. Deece, this is my mom," he said. We were at her house for a hot ten minutes before he had a flash of nostalgia and wanted to go to some chicken shack. Over a plate of fried chicken smothered in a rich onion gravy over rice; a large, rounded scoop of macaroni and cheese; collard greens sprinkled with hot sauce (complete with running juice); and a thick square of buttery corn bread, he looked at me and said "You satisfied now?" I couldn't even find it in myself to give a response.

Once our meal was over, we hopped back in his Cherokee, and I assumed that we were headed back to his mom's house. Much to my surprise, he pulled onto I-95 South and headed back home.

I rode six hours round trip in one day and didn't even get to stop at Potomac Mills for that?

* * *

What finally made me open up my eyes about Terrance was when Kisha, after hearing me bellyache for two consecutive years about how unfulfilled I was in my relationship, sent me a new book, *He's Just Not That Into You*. It arrived in the mail out of the blue, with a card attached to the front that read:

> *Don't get mad at me for sending this to you, but I love you and only want the best for you and want you to be happy.*
> *XOXOXOXO,*
> *Kisha*
> *PS: The author was on Oprah today. Call me after you finish reading so we can talk about it.*

I must have read the book five times over and had several girlfriend counseling sessions before I mustered up the gumption to let Terrance go . . . or better yet, let myself go.

I changed my phone numbers, packed away all of our photos (I didn't have the heart to throw them away), hid my car down the street, snuck in the back door at work, whatever I had to do to get him out of my system.

Of course, he showed up at my house one night, acting a natural black fool. I had just started my job at Wright-Way and had attended my first business mixer. By the time I got home, I was totally exhausted from being in training all day and rubbing elbows all night, not to mention my feet were killing me, having been stuffed in a pair of Carlos Santana calf skin sling-back pumps all day. I knew that they were a smidgen too small when I'd put them on that morning, but I didn't have anything that went with my suede skirt set quite so well. By the time I'd gotten home, about nine that evening, I was limping as if I'd had foot surgery.

Not exactly filled by the appetizers served at the mixer, I searched my refrigerator for a super quick meal, something that I could start, go sit down for a few minutes, and come back to get after a quick peppermint foot rub. Settling on a couple of beef hot dogs, I sat a water-filled pot on the stove and put them on to boil. I took a quick shower, rubbed my feet a little, and retrieved my hot dogs just as they had begun to split open, just like I like 'em, making a trough for my mustard and relish. Grabbing a bag of chips and a bottle of water, I sauntered to the living room, sank into the couch, and started channel surfing. That's when Terrance started blowing up my phone. To this day, I have no idea how he got my new number. After about three consecutive calls, I switched the phone off and kept watching TV. Ten minutes passed before the pounding on my door started, momentarily scaring the life out of me.

"Deece! December, open the door! Open the door, girl!" I ran to the door but didn't open it.

"You need to leave right now!" I commanded.

"I'm not leaving until you at least tell me why you acting like this!"

"Leave, Terrance!" I warned.

"I ain't going nowhere! I don't care if I gotta sit here all night. You gone come out the house sooner or later." I looked through the peephole and saw that Terrance had taken a seat on the stoop. Not really wanting to call the cops, but wanting him to leave, I sighed heavily as he began to sing the Temptations, "Ain't too Proud to Beg," getting louder and louder with each verse. He put the icing on the cake when he stood up and started doing shuffle, kick, step, and spin moves. Okay. That did it.

I went to the kitchen, picked up that pot of hot dog juice, marched to my front door, opened it, and *splash!* I dumped that water all over Terrance, then shut the door as quickly as I'd opened it.

After a few seconds of choking and spitting, then standing there in total disbelief, he took his cat singing back to his car and pulled off. I hadn't seen the man since . . . until today.

And today's a new day, right?

Seven

Shelley picked me up promptly at 6:30 for the monthly chamber of commerce business mixer. Each account manager was required to attend this function every other month to try to establish new contacts, increase company exposure, and uncover opportunities for placing temps.

I wore a black split-leg pantsuit, accented with silver accessories. I planned on sitting the entire evening, considering the shoes I had on—a pair of silver and rhinestone stilettos with a simple strap across the toes and an ankle wrap that zipped up the heel rather than buckled around. They were beautiful, but these jokers hurt like I don't know what after about twenty minutes of standing.

Tonight's event was being held at the Marriott in downtown Norfolk. It was pleasingly warm outside and what I thought would be the perfect night for a stroll through Town Point Park, with a Stiletto, if I had one. Not the shoe, of course. While I wasn't desperate, I could definitely use a little positive male attention. Maybe I'd meet someone tonight that would be semi-worthy of my company . . . maybe grab an appetizer at Outback, or better yet, sit out on the deck at Joe's Crab Shack, enjoying the breeze off the water, listening to the music that would float over from the park, and watching the *Spirit of Norfolk*, a dinner cruise ship, either drift out or drift in to port. Yeah, that would be nice as long as it didn't require me to walk; my shoes were pinching my pinky toe already.

"Did you bring your business cards?" Shelley asked, pulling into the parking garage.

"Yeah, I brought my business and my personal cards."

"What personal cards?"

"I told you, we needed some cards just for us. I'm tired of scribbling my number on a napkin or having Portia all in my business, screening calls. You know she tells Janice everything!"

"Yeah, but better the office number than your personal number."

"I got the cards printed with the number to this stupid work cell phone, which we have to carry twenty-four hours a day, like we're some kind of doctors."

Janice had assigned each of us a mobile phone so that we could be accessible to her, our clients, and our assigned temps after hours. Very rarely did anybody call, except Janice, that is. She'd call at least once a week just to make sure that we had our phones and were answering. I inadvertently left mine at the office one time, and that was all it took for me.

"I could have been a client calling you," she barked. "Do we need to revisit expectations?"

"I am well aware of what the expectation is. The fact of the matter is, no clients called."

"Don't get smart, December." She paused and folded her arms.

"I'm not trying to be smart, Janice, but there was no negative impact. I normally have the phone. I forgot it one time, and I don't believe that an extended reprimand is warranted."

"Well, until you become the general manager, you don't decide what is warranted. I do."

This was a reminder why I hated working for her. I said nothing more.

"Not being accessible to both our clients and employees is simply not acceptable," she added. "Therefore"—she whipped out a prepared document—"I'm placing you on a written warning for failure to meet job expectations."

I stared at her incredulously for a few seconds, then raised my pen to sign. I would have refused to sign it, but she would have used it later in my evaluation, in the form of "December does not accept responsibility for her actions and has great difficulty accepting feedback." It was easier for me to just sign this petty document.

"So once Janice notices an increase in your phone traffic, how are you going to explain that?" Shelley asked.

"We are at a work event, making contacts. Why wouldn't I give them my work contact numbers? Duh!"

By the time we made it in the ballroom, my feet were screaming for mercy. I would have to hobble, hopefully inconspicuously, to the very closest vacant seat, which I wasted no time doing when we entered. Shelley went to get us drinks while I sat, unable to focus on anything besides the pain in my right pinky toe. Reaching down, I massaged my foot under the table. Would it be too uncouth for me to walk around with my shoes off? I could say that I broke my heel on the way in if anybody asked. But who would ask? People would just take note that I was barefooted like some uncivilized, back woods bama, wouldn't take me seriously, then talk about me behind my back. I dare not embarrass myself or damage my credibility that way. I'd just have to sit here all night.

After twenty-eight and a half minutes of being totally incapacitated by a pair of shoes, I was bored. All the mingling, networking, card exchanging, and whatnot happened as a person worked the room, not nursed a toe. Shelley hadn't made it back yet with my drink, or even a meatball and a cube of cheese. Where was she? Across the way, laughing and working the room, of course. I tried to wave at her to get her attention, but she was engrossed in conversation. Before I could motion for her again, a pair of hands covered my eyes from behind.

The fingertips felt a little calloused, so I knew it was a man. I felt for jewelry. He was single. Then I sniffed for cologne . . . barbeque sauce and Old Spice. Sigh. It was Eddie.

"How you doing there, lady?" he greeted.

"Eddie!" I said, pasting my professional smile on my face. He bent down and kissed my cheek. "I'm great, thanks." He took a seat right beside me. "How's business going?"

"Goin' pretty good." He nodded. "I think I might open up a second store within the next year or so. Gotta find somebody that can run it, you know." He rattled his sausage-link fingers on the table. They were filled with old player-style rings.

"That's good to hear."

"Yeah, things are going real well. I'm looking to hire a couple of your people full time, too. They do a real good job." There was silence between us for a moment before he took it where it always seemed to go. "So what are you doing sitting here all alone, as beautiful as you are? You must have been waiting on me." He chuckled.

"Heh, heh." I laughed politely. "I guess so."

It wasn't that Eddie was a bad guy; I just wasn't attracted to him in the least bit. First of all, he was practically old enough to be my father. Secondly, barbeque sauce and Old Spice aftershave just didn't do it for me. And in my opinion, that potbelly that he carried around wasn't at all becoming. He wasn't the most handsome man, but he didn't look like Otis the security guard from *Martin*, either. He just was not the Stiletto I was looking for.

We were silent again while he assessed the room. Then, without looking at me, he said, "You're not married yet, are you?" Fifty ways to lie ran through my head, but I just couldn't do it straight out. I tried the pause strategy.

"No, . . . at least not yet!" I said, smiling, trying to make it seem that I was possibly engaged, or at least near being engaged. How he interpreted it was up to him, but I didn't lie.

"Who are you seeing these days?" He still looked randomly around the room, as if he couldn't face me directly.

"I, um . . . ran into an old flame the other day, and we're trying to pick up the pieces to see if they can fit together again." That wasn't exactly a lie; I was considering going out with Terrance.

"Who? That apple-headed fella you use ta come by the store with way back when?"

Note to self—Never go to dinner with your boyfriend at your client's establishment. But Eddie wasn't even my client back then. (Had Eddie been eyeing me that long?) Now that he'd mentioned it, Terrance did have a bit of an apple-shaped head.

"That boy ain't no good; he don't want nothin'. I can spot that a mile away. But I guess you have too many stars in your eyes to see clearly."

"Why would you think it was him?" I tried to play it off, but before he could answer, I got a little defensive. "Stars in my eyes? I don't have any stars in my eyes." Did I? Eddie looked at me and chuckled.

"See, what you need is a seasoned and settled man like myself. Somebody that knows how to treat a woman and can take care of you." Finally, he stood up. "Call me when you ready now."

That was my only opportunity to hand out a personal card all evening. I definitely didn't want (or need) to give Eddie one.

These shoes had to go.

Eight

Weekly staff meetings typically meant at least an hour of my day was wasted. The meetings were always scheduled for two hours, but only the first forty—five minutes or so were productive. Oftentimes, during the latter part of the meetings, I'd find myself either doodling or fighting to keep my eyes open.

Janice had listed her agenda on the whiteboard; the last item read "Organizational Update." Wishful thinking had me imagining that she would announce that effective immediately, she'd either be leaving the company or working from the Chesapeake site, or at the very least, she'd been promoted to regional manager and would work from our branch only two days a week.

She opened the meeting with our standard review of some John Maxwell leadership material. This was actually my favorite part of the meeting, helping me to realize my strengths and weaknesses. And John Maxwell was a much better leader than Janice could ever be, even via DVD. Each week, we'd watch a fifteen-to twenty-minute session of John teaching one of his twenty-one leadership laws, followed by us completing a few pages from the complementary workbook, then closing the session with a brief discussion on what we got out of the lesson. Today it was the Law of Intuition. I watched intently, recognizing that area as one I could stand to grow in. It seems I was always blindsided by something I should have seen coming a mile away.

We transitioned to reviewing last week's productivity reports, stack ranking the account managers by performance indicators, first internally, then across sites. My industrial hours were phenomenal, with Eddie currently carrying thirty-nine of our temps. And I'd placed twenty-seven people at the Renaissance as banquet servers, dishwashers, and housemen, which produced the bulk of my numbers. My clerical hours were lacking, though. I jotted a note to myself to make follow-up calls to the local college financial aid and admissions offices. With the fall semester coming up, they would be inundated with student registration activities. Even a temporary lift in my clerical hours performance would make me a shoo-in for the next Star Achiever Award, which came with a five-hundred-dollar payout.

Janice read off the names of the top three performers for last week, with my name being third. I wasn't satisfied with my ranking but was glad I wasn't on the black list. Anyone under eighty percent of hours had to present a detailed action plan on how they would get their performance up to par. That was another one-time-only experience for me. Janice made it such a debasing experience that I swore I'd never be on that list again. She'd call the person into her office, where she'd have Martin Wright, the CEO, on speakerphone to listen in on her verbal berating. For some reason, she thought it was the best way to motivate the staff to get hours up. Obviously, she took extreme pleasure in bringing negative exposure to a person's shortcomings, rather than providing true development through sharing strategies on how hours could be grown.

Next, we reviewed the current issue of the American Staffing Association newsletter, which provided weekly updates of economics, court actions, and regulatory developments relating to the staffing industry. This week Janice wanted to focus on an article that reported a decline in temporary-employee turnover. Our temps had an average of eight-weeks tenure before they secured permanent employment or stopped accepting assignments, while the industry standard was at twelve and a half weeks. Of course, Janice wanted us to be above industry standards.

Portia's voice came across the PA system, alerting Janice to a visitor in the reception area.

"While you guys are brainstorming on some actions we can take, I'm going to step out for a few minutes," Janice stated, rushing to her feet.

When she closed the door behind her, Andre whipped out his cell phone and started sending text messages, I leafed through my new White House/Black Market catalogue, and Troy began singing Rick James's "Super Freak," pounding his fists on the table. To put it plainly, everybody basically went on break. Everyone besides the teacher's pet, that is. Leslie sat at the end of the table, looking like she was taking names. There was a suck-up in every office.

"All right, y'all. Let's pull it back in," I said, standing and moving toward the whiteboard. "How can we increase our temp tenure?"

I listed a couple of my own ideas on the board and spun around just as Janice was making her reentrance. My timing couldn't have been more perfect, because with her walked in the most gorgeous man I'd ever seen in my life. He had no choice but to look at me since I happened to be standing and talking.

He stood about five feet ten, a little on the short side; had warm brown skin; and was impeccably dressed in a charcoal grey suit and tie (perfectly dimpled at the knot), brushed silver cuff links on a smoke blue shirt, and cordovan shoes. The way he had his left eyebrow raised gave him a distinguished, intellectual look. Not a single hair was out of place on his short fro, cut sharp and tight across the front, like Steve Harvey's. A neatly trimmed mustache and goatee framed his smooth lips, and lashes just long enough to bring attention to his eyes pointed out their beautiful shade of brown. I caught all of that in my split-second glance.

Rather than taking a seat, he and Janice stood just inside the doorway, silently observing and allowing me to continue. He lifted one hand to rest his fingers pensively on his chin. I took note that there was no ring on his left hand. I had an impression to make.

"We already ask if they are looking for short-term assignments only, but if you ask more pointed questions in your interviews, you can better uncover the specific goals of your applicants," I said. I nodded as if I had just shared some deep revelation, but it was effective none the less, as evidenced by a head nod from *Mr. Fine* at the door.

No one else gave any type of response, so I continued. "In addition, I think if we take a look at our core competency model and structure, we could probably find several areas that need to be redefined. In keeping with the industry, it is so important that we ensure that our skill set requirements properly align with the fluctuating skill needs of both the job market and the specific requirements of our clients and the tasks and assignments they frequently seek temporary staffing for."

In my mind, I could hear the crowd going wild with cheers; I had knocked the ball out of the park. In reality, the room was absolutely silent. "Well, those were my ideas. Janice, did you want to take it from here?" I said and moved toward my chair.

"Thanks, December." She swiftly transitioned, not bothering to acknowledge my ingenuity and innovative thinking as presented in that huge mouthful I'd impressively spat out. "Team, I want to move to our last agenda item, Organizational Update." She batted her eyes at Stiletto and gave him a knowing smile. "The needs of the business dictate that we have in place a regional manager to oversee the general operations of our Peninsula and Southside Offices." This was the announcement I'd been praying for: she was being promoted out of the Chesapeake office, and *Mr. Fine* was the new boss.

"I'd like to introduce you to my new boss, and the new regional manager, Corinthian Davis." Janice paused as he nodded his head toward us at her introduction, slightly folding his lips inward. "As our branch consistently outperforms the other offices, Mr. Davis will be here for the remainder of this week and next week, making some initial observations before going to our other sites. I expect you all to welcome him and assist him in becoming acclimated to our specific practices. Let's go around the room for initial introductions, and then we will let Mr. Davis have the floor." So she didn't get that job she'd posted for. As bad as I wanted her out of my daily life, I snickered to myself.

Mr. Davis's eyes circled the table as each person stated his or her name, their current role, and said a few words about themselves. He kindly nodded and said, "Nice to meet you," after each one finished . . . except when he got to me.

"I'm December Elliott, senior account manager, and I've been with the company two and a half years, starting here as a temp actually." He gave the response I'd grown accustom to.

"December? Like the month?"

"Exactly." I smiled.

"If you don't mind me asking, how did you get that name?" he asked. I was used to this, too.

"My mother's name is June; my father's name is August. I'm the third of a set of triplets. I have two sisters, April and May. I was delivered seven minutes after May." I shrugged my shoulders as if to say, "There you have it." "December it was."

Andre started coughing to cover his snickering, which Mr. Davis didn't seem to notice. I kicked Andre under the table.

"I think that's the most inimitable anecdote I've ever heard," replied Mr. Davis.

Innamiddible? What the heck did that mean? I couldn't tell if he was making fun of me or not. I guess I deserved it for making up a ridiculous story. To be honest, I don't know why the heck my parents named me December. I liked it, though, because it stuck out in people's minds. I definitely wanted it to stick in Mr. Davis's.

"Welcome to the company. I look forward to working with you," I said. I made a note to myself in my planner to go to a dictionary Web site and look up *innamiddible*.

Sherri Garrett from payroll was the last to speak; then Mr. Davis took the floor.

"Again, I'm Corinthian Paul Davis. Please call me Corey, and, yes, I'm a PK, or preacher's kid, for those of you who aren't familiar with that abbreviation. My parents' names aren't Mary and Joseph, but I do have a brother Lazarus, who was initially reported to be stillborn." He winked at me. Okay, now I felt like a heel for making up my stupid name story.

"So is there a specific reason for your name?" Janice asked flirtatiously. She may as well have had "free booty" tattooed on her forehead.

"Actually, there is. My parents thought they were having a girl, whom they planned to name Love, but after the doctor announced I was a boy, they decided on Corinthian based on the subject matter of First Corinthians, chapter thirteen." I nodded, impressed. "Anyway, I've been with the company for six years and recently relocated here from Chicago. I got a little tired of dealing with the cold weather and wanted to be closer to my parents, who reside in Williamsburg.

"I will be meeting with each of you one-on-one this week to get your opinions on how we can grow our business and discover where it is you want to go, if anywhere, with the company. Please feel free to share with me what I can do to support you in your daily efforts. Don't hesitate to ask questions or just stop to say hello. I'm excited about being here and look forward to building dynamic working relationships with each of you."

"And we're excited about having you, aren't we, team!" Janice chimed shamefully. We respectfully agreed, with varied head gestures, before Janice continued.

"I also have something for you before we close. Mr. Davis just brought these down from Mr. Wright's office." She produced a handful of envelopes and passed one to each of us. Inside was a beautiful card with scripted gold lettering, covered by a translucent overlay, which was an invite to a formal employee appreciation party. "Rather than having our usual Friends and Family Barbeque, Mr. Wright wants to show his appreciation to all

Wright-Way employees by hosting a night of elegance by way of a formal dinner party."

Janice clasped her hands and brought them up to her face, looking completely pleased with herself. Then she continued. "Because it's a formal event, we wanted to give you as much advance notice as possible, to give you an opportunity to get a nice gown or cocktail dress, or a tuxedo for the guys. Some of you will probably need that shopping time, and if you ladies need tips on what to wear, I'll be glad to give you some ideas," she said pretentiously. The ladies at the table all cut their eyes at each other, with offended expressions.

"Right. Because nobody ain't never been to a formal party before but you," Sherri said under her breath, unheard by Janice.

"It's going to be a wonderful evening of dinner and dancing, and there will also be an awards ceremony," Janice added. All branches in our region will be invited, so you will get an opportunity to meet and network with your peers from other sites."

Wow. This event would be a first, and it looked like the company planned to do it every year, as the invitation read "first annual." I was impressed, as was the rest of the group. It would be another three months before the event; I could find something special to wear by then.

Janice ended the meeting and stood alongside Corey as he waited at the door to personally greet each person and shake their hand as they exited. Janice was standing there like she was some kind of bodyguard or something, in other words, blocking.

"Nice to meet you, Corey," I said, extending my hand. When we shook, I felt something shoot up my arm, circle my shoulders, bolt down by torso, split down both legs, and try to break through the toes of my magenta Ferragamo Arabia cork-heel pumps. I didn't let on, though. Never let 'em see you sweat.

"Likewise," he responded, with a slight lift of his brow. I moved on, pretending not to be concerned with him one way or the other. As fine as he was, I was certain that he had his share of advances.

There was a beautiful bouquet of mixed flowers sitting on my desk when I got back from the meeting—tulips, tiger lilies, pink roses, and white carnations, settled in a spray of green leaves and baby's breath. After I inhaled the aroma from each individual blossom, my fingers fumbled with the card. The outside was plain enough, only displaying my name. The card read:

I'd love to see you tonight . . . Wear those shoes that show off those sexy calves. TR

I strutted to Andre's office, fanning my face with the card. He passed me in the hall as he walked an applicant to the reception area.

"Don't forget to call me each morning that you're available for work," Andre told the applicant.

"I won't, and thank you, hear?" replied the woman, who looked to be in her midforties.

"Yes, ma'am. We'll do our best to get you placed as soon as possible," said Andre. He shook his head once the woman left. "That's a shame that she is out having to scrounge for work. I've got to increase my 401(K) contribution."

"What kind of work is she looking for?" I asked.

"Her background is primarily in food service. She used to run a catering business out of her home but lost everything in the Katrina catastrophe and has been here seeking employment ever since. She's desperate for anything right now."

"Let me see her resume." Andre handed me a file folder labeled Geneva Johnson. "Gee Gee's Creole Cookin', huh? You don't have anything for her?"

"Right now all I have are some assembly-line positions." He shook his head before continuing. "I don't believe she has the manual dexterity to perform well in the role. I wish I had something for her."

"How'd she interview?"

"She was great . . . smart, pleasant, articulate. You have anything in your open orders?"

"Not right this second. I might be able to drum something up, though." I thought for a few minutes, contemplating whether or not I should give Eddie a call. The only thing about calling Eddie was, more than he wanted quality temporary employees that would come to work and do a good job, he wanted me.

"So who were the flowers from?" Andre asked, snatching the card from my hand. I snatched it back just as quickly. "You got a man now, huh?"

"Last I checked, I was both single and available." Just as those words escaped my lips, Corey breezed by me from behind. I folded my lips into my mouth, wondering if he'd heard what I said, not that what I said was bad or inappropriate. I just tried to keep my love life out of the ears of my not-so close coworkers. I liked to keep them guessing.

Corey looked back over his shoulder and did that one eyebrow thing, which let me know he'd indeed heard my comment. He turned his head back around, never breaking his stride.

"Why didn't you tell me he was coming?" I said as I smacked Andre in the arm with the folder still in my hand.

"I tried to cue you, but you were so busy rolling your eyes, telling me how single you were, you missed it." He guffawed, then turned to go to his office.

"Hardy har har," I mocked. Secretly, I thought to myself, *Let's see what Mr. Davis does with that bit of information,* but somehow I already knew he had far too much integrity to find himself involved in any type of office scandal. Not that I was scandalous, by any means.

Nine

Clad in a strapless little black dress, I tried on seven different pairs of shoes before I decided on my Manolo Blahnik black ruffled-lace slides, skillfully swiped from the top bidder on eBay three months ago. Generally, I didn't shop eBay, but when I saw Manolo's price for these babies on the Neiman Marcus Web site, suddenly, eBay became a beautiful thing.

After performing an ash check on my heels, I slid into my shoes and accented my outfit with a pair of black crystal earrings and a matching necklace, which was actually nothing more than a strip of ribbon with a tiny crystal bead on both ends held in place by a knot. The ribbon circled my neck twice, then hung down between my shoulder blades. I spun slowly in the mirror, checking myself out from all angles, and noticed that the lace imprint from my half-booty, bad-girl panties was clearly visible in my dress. Right when I slid out of them, the phone rang.

"Hello?"

"Ooh, you need to watch this show that's coming on

TV called *Black Don't Crack,*" Kisha began. "Girl, it's the perfect show for you."

"What is it about? How beautiful black people are, and how gracefully we age?"

"No! About black people rushing to get plastic surgery! I should tape it for you." I rolled my eyes, tempted to just hang up. "On the commercial, this lady that was up there was like, 'Plastic surgery feeds into the historical idea that we're not good enough as women.' Then this other lady was like, 'Why would you even think about erasing any of your blackness?'"

I blew out a huge puff of air. "Kisha, I'm not trying to erase my blackness. My breasts used to be plump and round. Now they're not. What does that have to do with being black? What is wrong with me wanting to main-tain some kind of youthfulness?"

"Implants are not safe," she argued.

"Can we talk about something else?"

"No, I want to talk about this. I don't want to see you do something that you are going to regret later."

"Kisha, I don't want to discuss this with you. Your opinion is clear to me. You don't want me to do it. Okay, I heard you. Now, can I be free to make my own decision? Did I say anything to you when you decided to go get a hole poked in your tongue and keep a metal bar stuck in it?"

"That's not surgery."

"Okay, but that doesn't make it safe to lie in some nasty tattoo shop and let somebody who was not a doc-tor stick a big old needle through your tongue."

"That doesn't even compare. There are millions of people who have their tongue pierced. That's not a good example."

"Maybe it doesn't compare, but it was your decision to make. There are millions of women, I'm sure, who have gotten their breasts done. They aren't all dead and miserable."

"Those things can rupture inside you."

"I know that."

"That stuff inside can kill you."

"No, it won't."

"How you know?"

"'Cause I know."

"Fine then. Go 'head. You wanna kill yourself? Go right ahead."

"Thanks for giving me your permission. Anyway . . ." I paused. "You will never believe who I have a date with tonight."

"First Corinthians, chapter thirteen," she guessed.

"Girl, please. If I did, I'd be speaking to you in tongues right now." We both burst into laughter. "I wish!"

"The barbeque rib man."

"No!"

"Please don't tell me Terrance," she said, objecting. I knew I should have kept it to myself.

"What if it is Terrance?" I tested.

"Why would you even waste your time going out with him again?"

"I don't know. Something to do?"

"If you need something to do, go see a movie," she chided.

"By myself?"

"There is nothing wrong with going to the movies alone."

"I'm not ready to do that yet."

"Okay. Well, go to Barnes & Noble, and get a cup of mocha choca latta something. And sit in one of those chairs and read."

"That is so boring. I can do that at home."

"You can't meet anybody new at home. At least, there

you can meet some intelligent brother who likes to read, too."

"You know what? I'ma do a complete one-hundred-eighty-degree turnaround and start dating outside my race. I'm turning my back on black! I'm going to find me a cute white man. As a matter of fact, that is my new code name for white guys. One-eighty. You know who is a really cute one-eighty?"

"Who?"

"Have you ever seen that show *Judge Alex*? He is cute!"

"*Judge Alex*? No. Who is that?"

"You've never heard of *Judge Alex*? Go to Judgealex. com. I should go on the site and see if I can get on the show. I can just sit in the congregation."

"The congregation? What does he do? Preach while he hears your case?" Kisha laughed; we both did. "You need help."

"What?" I protested. "Can I do anything? You don't want me to get my breasts done, I can't go out with Terrance, I can only date black guys, I can't look for a one-eighty. What you want me to do? Crawl up in a hole and die?"

"I don't want you to die, but you seem like you tryna kill yourself. First, you wanna go up under the knife, instead of being happy with what you got. Then you want to spend time with Mr. Time keeps on ticking into the future. Now you've gone to dating one-eighties. I don't believe you are going to start dating white guys, so I'm just going to throw that one out, but I don't know if I like the fact that you are going out with Terrance again."

"It's just something to do," I assured her.

"Uh-huh."

"Ooh, he's at the door. I'll call you later, when I get back."

"You better bring your grown tail home tonight! You hear me?"

"Yes, ma'am," I said in a mock crying tone. We both laughed. "I'll call you later."

"All right. Have fun."

I hadn't even put on my panties yet, but for some reason, I didn't want to keep Terrance waiting, so I did what any other woman would do: smoothed my dress down, slid in my shoes, and scurried to the door, with no panties on.

"Hey, come on in," I said casually, barely looking at Terrance, then turned to go back to my bedroom. "I'm almost ready. Have a seat."

Terrance's only reaction for the moment was, "Mmmh! Whew!" Properly interpreted, what he actually said was, "Goodgadda mighty! I wish I could get a piece ah dat right now!"

I sifted quickly through my panty collection and picked out what I called my spider thongs; they had three straps that circled my hips and connected in the back like a web. The thirty-eight-dollar price tag was still on them. Really I forgot that I'd even bought them, but they certainly weren't everyday panties. They were some "don't stop, get it, get it" type panties. Not that I planned on giving Terrance anything. After all, this was like a first date all over again, regardless of the many times he'd been in my bed and I'd been in his. Tonight they would just be my "I feel incredibly sexy with this string up my behind" panties.

After I slid into them, I couldn't help but frown. They were a little too tight, making my meat bulge out between the straps. That was so not good. I wasn't going anywhere looking like I had hot dogs strapped around the top of my butt!

I probably had a hundred pairs of underwear, in different styles, colors, and sizes, but I couldn't seem to find the ones that I thought would best complement me in the dress I wore. How did putting on a pair of drawers become so hard? I'm not sure what exactly came over me—maybe frustration, maybe time consciousness, maybe my bad-girl genes—but I decided to live on the edge a little and not wear any panties at all. That would keep a secretive, sexy smile on my face all night.

"Okay. I'm ready." I said as I reappeared in the living room, where I found Terrance browsing my CD collection. I grabbed my Banana Republic three-hole black clutch, which I'd had for at least eight years, but it was too classy to throw out. When I did assess Terrance, dressed in a soft knit grey sweater, neatly tucked into a pair of black slacks, a Kenneth Cole belt circling his waist, with a matching black leather strap watch, and that smooth bald head that would rub up between my breasts, then nuzzle up into my neck, I felt a reaction beneath my dress that I'm ashamed to admit. I had to take a second to rethink that whole no panties thing.

Terrance drove to Sassafras, a picturesque little restaurant in Portsmouth. Its warm color scheme, soft lighting, and live piano accompanying dinner made for an intimate setting, albeit it was a little cramped.

We shared an appetizer of smoked salmon with caviar, shaved portobello mushrooms, red onion, and cucumbers, served on a corn griddle cake. Then we both decided on the red snapper with garlic mashed potatoes and asparagus for our dinner entrees.

Over dinner, Terrance and I reminisced and laughed about old times.

"Why did I let you walk out of my life?" he asked. He lifted my hand and brought it up to his lips. "What I wouldn't give to have you back."

I playfully snatched my hand away. "You know you

don't want me, Terrance," I said, with a giggle. "Stop play-ing."

"Yes, I do. And you want me, too, or else you wouldn't be here." If I was completely honest with myself, I did miss Terrance some. I guess that was what made me go out with him tonight.

"Oh, somebody's got the big head," I teased. He didn't comment right away but only stared at me sexily until I looked away.

"December, you're beautiful." He stared for a few seconds more, then suddenly cleared his throat and flagged the server for the check. Minutes later, he signed the credit card slip, grabbed my hand, and quickly rose from his seat. "Let's get out of here."

His abruptness caught me off guard, and I wasn't sure what to think but went with the flow. We drove in silence down to Virginia Beach's waterfront.

"Let's take a stroll," Terrance whispered. Okay . . . I don't know what he was thinking, but these shoes weren't made for walkin'.

Before I could politely protest, he reached on the floor behind my seat and produced a narrow sandal box, which held a pair of buy-one, get-one sandals. I could spot those suckers a mile away. I started to say some-thing but then decided against it. It wasn't like we were in a relationship. Otherwise, these would be totally un-acceptable.

"I know how you feel about your shoes. Here, put these on," he said. I slid my feet into the thongs and in-stantly felt an uncomfortable pinch between my toes. See, that was exactly why I didn't believe in buying cheap shoes. How in the world could a pair of flip-flops hurt? I kept them on and endured the discomfort until we got to the sand. Then I gave them to him to carry for me.

He cuffed his pants, and we walked barefoot through the sand for a half a mile, hand in hand like lovers, glancing up at the stars and watching the moon reflect off the water's surface.

"So you expect me to believe that you aren't involved with anybody?" I asked after Terrance made that claim.

"I don't have any reason to lie to you, Deece. I've dated a few women since you, but nothing serious. They just weren't you. They couldn't hold a candle to you on their best days."

I knew that those were just lines, but they sounded so good.

"I want you back," he whispered. "I want you back, Deece. And if you just give me one small chance . . . I don't even want you to think about giving me an answer right now. I know I have a lot of proving myself to do, but I can show you better than I can tell you."

Without warning, he grabbed my face and kissed me with such passion that I was again reminded that I'd left my undergarments lying on my bed at home. He placed a trail of kisses from my lips to my earlobe, down my neck, and across my shoulder. I found my hand rubbing that smooth head of his while his hands subtly slid below my waist. "Mmm," he moaned, then reluctantly pulled away from me and said, "Let me get you home."

When we arrived back at my house, he walked me to the door and, like a gentleman, kissed me good night after seeing me in, then walked back to his car. Now that was what surprised me most. He didn't try to get some. We went out twice more over the following few weeks, and (surprisingly) there were no "hit and quit" attempts made. While I didn't know whether to feel respected or rejected, it actually made me think about giving us a second chance. Maybe he had grown and was really ready to settle down.

Ten

As soon as I got to work, my day was slammed. Portia
informed me that Shelley was out sick with a migraine,
which meant not only would I have to cover her interviews, but I'd also have to verify her time sheets along
with mine. Having got that news, I shut my office door
to not be distracted by the general morning chitter-
chatter. There was a sticky note posted to my monitor,
with a toll-free number scribbled on it. I pulled it from
the screen and pasted it to my planner page without giving it much thought, then checked my voice mail.

Shelley had called to let me know where to find her
time sheets, Parkinson's Painting needed two second-
shift painters, and three dishwashers never showed at
Eddie's this morning. Right away, I queried the system
to find a few individuals to replace the no-call no-shows.
After ten calls, I had three guys on the way, or so they
promised. Portia agreed to give Eddie a call on my be-
half to let him know. Then I logged up to begin enter-
ing the previous day's applications into the system.
Interviews weren't scheduled to start until nine thirty,

so I had a little over an hour and a half to key in five apps, start calculating pay hours, and find two painters.

I clicked on my desk CD player, put in Musiq's first album, and concentrated all of my efforts on avoiding becoming overwhelmed and on getting off work on time. Before I realized it, it was near ten. Luckily, the 9:30 applicants had called to reschedule their interview appointments.

Taking a quick break, I logged into my personal e-mail account and scanned the subject lines of a few messages. One in particular caught my attention: a message containing a charity song video clip for Hurricane Katrina victims. As I watched the video, in tears and unable to fathom how I would have handled such tragedy, I was reminded of Geneva Johnson's application. Andre had sent her out on a few housekeeping assignments, in which she had done well, but catering was her passion.

I looked into the system to see if she was currently available for an open assignment and found that she'd just ended her last job two days ago. I jotted her name and number down in my planner, and without a second thought, I gave Eddie a call.

"Eddie's Ribs. How can I help you?" a woman answered, smacking her gum loudly in my ear.

"Hi, Miss Rosa Lee. It's December. Is Eddie around?" I knew that Eddie would ask me on a date, but I had a more pressing purpose.

"Hol' on just a minute, baby," she answered. "Ed-day! Get the phone!" It sounded as if business for Eddie was still going well, as I listened to chatter, laughter, and the sound of forks hitting plates while waiting for him to come to the phone.

"Eddie speakin'," he said, rushed.

"Eddie, it's December," I began.

"What you need, baby doll? I'm busy. You ready to let me take you out yet?"

"Not quite yet, Eddie. But listen, I am trying to place someone who has about twenty years of cooking and catering experience. I thought you might be able to use her. Sounds like your business is going through the roof."

"Yeah, we doin' pretty good down here. Rosa Lee, turn that chicken over for me . . . the chicken! . . . right there!" he yelled. He turned his attention back to the phone. "Yeah, we doin' pretty good right now. You say she got twenty years, uh, cooking experience?"

"Yes, sir. She has a beautiful resume. Short order, catering, gourmet . . ."

"I can use 'er, but what I'ma get out uh it?"

"A great employee and more menu items, for one. Creole and Cajun are her specialties."

"I still cain't get no date, though, huh?"

"Eddie, you know I don't date my clients. Do you want me to lose my job?" I chuckled.

"Oh, I'll take care uh ya now. You know ol' Eddie gone take care uh ya! You won't have to work another day in your life, girl," he said, talking faster than Speedy Gonzales. "I'll let you stay home and take care uh da chi'rn. Ain't got to worry 'bout nothin'."

"Eddie, let me think on that for a while. But in the meantime, when can I send her down?"

"Uh . . . gone and send her down here 'morrow morning. Eight o'clock sharp. I'll have some work for 'er."

"Will do, Eddie. Thank you so much."

"I wont my date now, ya hear me?"

"I hear you." I laughed. Eddie just wasn't going to give up.

I placed my call to Geneva and got her squared away

for her new ongoing assignment. It did my heart good to hear the excitement and gratitude in her voice. I'd been able to send a few dollars to a Katrina relief fund, but this time I really felt like I'd actually helped someone.

Janice swung my door open without knocking. "December, I need to see you in my office please as soon as you wrap up whatever you're working on." I wasn't sure what Janice wanted this morning, but something told me that it wasn't good.

"Sure. I'll be there in about ten minutes. I just need to verify my time sheets."

She glanced at her wrist, pressed her lips together, and raised her brows. That alone let me know that I would have to brace myself for some bull. As soon as she closed the door, I quickly scanned the last few pages of my planner to make sure that I hadn't dropped the ball on any tasks. Not finding anything, I shrugged, thinking that maybe I'd misread her nonverbals.

When I got to her office minutes later, she seemed to be casually talking and laughing with Corey, who sat in one of the chairs in front of her desk, with an ankle resting on the opposite knee. His presence was unexpected, and I tried my best not to ogle him, but he was just like that apple was to Eve, pleasant to the eye and hard to resist! I was glad I'd touched up my make-up before I left my office. Corey caught sight of me in his peripheral, cleared his throat, and straightened his tie, then nodded at Janice.

"Mr. Davis," I acknowledged politely while taking the seat next to him. Then I turned to Janice. "Yes, ma'am?" I crossed my legs and swung my foot slightly, making sure Corey caught sight of my shoes, a pair of aqua-colored open-sided pumps accented with satin braiding. They matched the camisole that peeked out from my off-white capri pantsuit. I put on my most pleasant smile and lifted my pencil to take notes.

"When are you going to get a handheld and get rid of that antiquated book?" Janice asked, smiling just a little too sweetly.

"When they close the FranklinCovey store," I responded. It was a little smart-mouthed, I know, but it was said with a smile to coat my true tone.

"This is so much more of an effective tool," she replied. She lifted her PDA from its cradle, pulled the stylus from the back, and started tapping the screen. "I mean, I have my whole life in here! It keeps up with all my numbers, my appointments, and my reminders," she bragged. "I strongly recommend that you get one." Her tone suddenly became condescending, throwing me off. I felt a slight twinge of panic.

"Have I missed a deadline or something?" I asked. I knew I was on top of my game. What could she be calling me on the carpet for?

"December"—she placed the device back in its cradle, then folded her hands and rested them on her desk—"I was here in the office late last night when a phone call came in for you."

"Right. I saw your message on my desk this morning," I replied. What the heck did that have to do with a handheld?

"I am very concerned about that call," she chided.

"Oh, it was just—" She cut me off midsentence.

"I know what it was. It was an attempt to collect a debt," she stated matter-of-factly. Her lashes batted against each other, as if she was waiting for me to explain myself.

Had I been a white woman, I would have been beyond strawberry or even raspberry red, and more like the color of red grapes. I was trying to think of something to say to redeem the slightest shred of dignity, but nothing came to mind.

"Why are calls like that coming into this office for you?" she asked.

"It was just a small oversight, that's all," I responded, waving my hand in an attempt to minimize the situation. "It won't happen again." I rose from my seat, trying my best to get out of there, but Janice wasn't having it.

"Wait a minute!" she demanded. "I'm not done." Somehow I maintained my composure and took my seat again. "As a member of management, you have a responsibility to lead by example." Her widened eyes expressed both disapproval and reprimand.

Why was she doing this in front of Corey? Why?

"I expect every member of my team to manage both their professional and personal lives, and that includes his or her finances," she added.

My blood was beginning to boil; my personal life, financial or otherwise, was none of her business. Not to mention the fact that this was just another example of her attempt to make herself look good at the expense of making another look bad.

"What do you have to say for yourself?" she said.

"I've already said what I had to say, which was, it was a simple oversight, and it won't happen again." I was seething and embarrassed and close to tears, but thankfully, I was pretty good at not showing my emotions through my expressions.

"See to it that it doesn't. I don't want to have to revisit this situation," she said, then paused for a few seconds, pressing her lips against each other to signify that she meant it, I suppose.

"Is there anything else?" I asked.

"No, other than make sure that time sheets are submitted to payroll by noon." She pasted her fake smile back on her face, satisfied that she had sufficiently humiliated me.

"Of course. After all, it's written in my planner," I stabbed as I exited, smiling just as phonily as she had.

I went straight to Andre's office, closed the door, and began to cry my eyes out. He had no idea what was going on, so my behavior alarmed him. Crying at work simply was not me.

"Deece, what's wrong!" He quickly shuffled through his desk drawer, found a few napkins, and handed them to me. "What's wrong?" With wide-stretched eyes, he searched my face for clues. In my mind, I was trying to talk, but my lips seemed to be glued together. "Is your family okay?" I blew my nose, took a deep breath, and spoke just above a whisper.

"I hate her." Instantly, a look of relief washed over Andre's face. I didn't have to clarify whom I was speaking about; he knew full well I was referring to Janice.

"You need me to beat her down for you?" he asked. I cracked a smile. "'Cause you know I don't play with nobody messin' with my Deece!" he said, rising and jabbing at the air. "I'll take her outta here. Just say the word! I'd be like, 'Whatchu doota mah girl, yo! Whatchu (jab) doota my girl?'" I started to giggle a little, although still terribly upset.

He let silence settle in for about a minute; then I proceeded to tell him the ugly story.

"And the worse part about it was, Corey just sat there and did nothing. He let her openly disgrace me!" Andre didn't comment, shaking his head in disbelief. "I've lost a lot of respect for Mr. Davis," I ended, emphasizing Corey's name.

"Don't let her get you down, Deece. She knows that

was a low blow, and it will come back to her. What goes around comes around. You know that." I nodded my head, knowing he was right, but not really feeling any better about the whole thing, not even part of the thing, for that matter.

"She is what makes a person come to work and just go to shootin' folks!" I took a deep breath, pulled myself together, and prepared to get back to work. "Thanks for listening."

"Anytime, December. It will be all right."

I suffered through the rest of my day, avoiding both Janice and Corey like the plague, shut my computer down at five 'til five, and watched the clock for the last few minutes. Not willing to be there any longer than I had to, I practically ran to my truck. No sooner had I pulled out of the lot than my cell rang, displaying the office number. I didn't know who exactly it was, but I was determined not to answer. They should have called the stupid work cell phone if they had something to say. Janice couldn't make me answer my personal phone. I pressed the *Ignore* key on the phone and stuffed it among a collection of bills stored in the armrest between my driver's and passenger's seats.

And as angry as I was with Janice, deep down, I knew it was my own fault, although she didn't have to do it in front of Corey. Actually, she didn't have to say anything to me at all; a personal call is a personal call, regardless of its nature. If she was going to talk to me about personal calls coming into the office, she needed to address the whole office. I slammed the armrest shut, blocking out the phone and the bills.

To prevent myself from sulking the whole evening, I forced myself to go to the gym and work out my frustration in the kickboxing class. I kicked and punched like never before, mad at Janice, Corey, and myself. My aggressive single and double jabs, uppercuts, and round-houses were so impressive, the instructor approached me right after class.

"Those were some nice kicks you put out tonight," he said, smiling.

"Thanks." I wiped my face and neck with a towel and took a swig of water. "I had some stress to get rid of."

"If you keep working like that, you'll be ripped in no time." He flexed his chest muscles, emphasizing his words. "Six-pack and everything. I'm Rodney, by the way." He extended his hand for a shake.

"I'm December."

"Dee . . . I'm sorry. Say your name once more please," he asked. I repeated it; I was used to having to do that. "Wow, that's very unique."

He paused while we soaked each other in. I was hot, sticky, and sweaty, and I stank, but since I was at the gym, I was sure that that was considered to be sexy (well, maybe not the stank part). And he, standing six feet one in a pair of loose-fitting shorts and fitted T, with defined quads, calves, chest, and arms, was in no way, shape, or form hard on the eyes. His hair was intricately braided in cornrows and neatly edged up, and shiny white teeth (with a small gap between the front two) peeked out from his dark lips.

"So were you, uh, born on Christmas Day or something?" he asked. My lips gave way to a partial smile.

"Something like that." I drank more water but didn't break eye contact.

"So are you a member here?" He was starting his mack.

"Umm . . . Why don't you show me around?" I suggested, although my membership was nearly two years old, and I was more than familiar with the facility.

I let him walk me around for a full half an hour, pointing out things I'd seen a hundred times before.

"You look like you work out pretty regularly," he commented.

"I'm not as faithful as I should be, but I try to stay in shape."

"You did great in the class tonight. I don't think you missed a single step. You should think about taking classes to become an instructor," he proposed.

"You think so?" I crinkled my nose. "I don't know if I could do it for a living."

"So do it part time." He shrugged.

"I might have to look into that."

"Why don't you give me a call, and I can tell you all about the certification process?" he said, assuming that I would accept his number and give him mine. I kept silent for a few seconds purely for effect.

"Do you have a card?" I asked.

"I sure do. Wait right here." He casually strolled to a row of offices down a side hall, stopping along the way to talk to one of his coworkers about an aqua aerobics class. "Call me when you are ready. I'll be glad to help," he said, returning and presenting his card.

RODNEY JACOBS—MANAGER

"That sounds great."

The right corner of his lips turned upward as he offered his hand to properly close the discussion. We shook firmly, but just a hair slower and longer than the usual business shake.

"December . . . I like that," he said. On the inside, I was blushing like an April fool, but on the outside, I kept a straight face. "Maybe I'll see you tomorrow?"

I shrugged. "Maybe."

I disappeared into the ladies' locker room, hopped in the shower, pulled on my bathing suit, and swam a few laps, not caring that allowing my hair to get wet would add an hour to my morning routine the next day. After thirty minutes or so, I got in the hot tub, then the sauna, replaying Janice's words over and over in my head, and wondering how I could show my face in Corey's presence again.

By the time I pulled my weary body into my truck to drive home, my phone showed three missed calls: another from the office, the other two from Shelley. I cut the phone off completely, not feeling like chatting with anybody. Whatever the office wanted could wait until tomorrow.

I showered again to get rid of the chlorine, then practically fell in bed and was asleep before my head even hit the pillow. Even in my sleep, I couldn't escape the horror of the day. I dreamed that Janice and Corey were sitting in the break room, placing crank calls to my desk, asking when they could expect to receive a payment, then bursting into laughter. They called back to back to back, and the more I answered the phone, the more it rang. Just when I had marched to the break room to punch Janice dead in her face, I slowly came to and realized that my home phone was really ringing.

I grappled with the receiver, barely conscious of what I was doing, although I'd only been out for about fifteen minutes.

"Hello," I slurred.

"December."

My eyes immediately popped open. It was Corey. I didn't respond. I could start babbling some crazy words to pretend that I wasn't aware that I was on the phone and just hang up, I thought.

"Hello?" he said. I decided against being a babbling fool; I had already been made a fool of earlier. I sighed inaudibly before answering.

"Yes, I'm here."

"Listen," he began. "I just wanted to check on you and make sure that you were okay."

"I'm fine, Mr. Davis, but I'm asleep. I'll see you tomorrow if you'll be at our site. Thanks for calling. Good night." I didn't give him a chance to respond, although it took me three tries to get the phone back in its cradle.

Tomorrow would be the day that I would make some serious changes to my financial situation. I was going to make sure that what happened today would never ever happen again. First, I was going to call in late for work to give myself the time I needed to call all of my creditors. Then, I was going to contact every single one of them and tell them that I was no longer employed at Wright-Way Staffing.

Eleven

I wasn't sure how I was going to make it through my workday. Rather than calling in, I arrived early, in hopes that I would not run into anyone, parked my car on the far end of the lot, and shut my office door once I got inside. I only tiptoed out once, to make myself a cup of tea, but hurried right back into seclusion. I glanced over at the mini shopping bag from Sephora—my favorite fragrance, bath, and body shop—which sat on my desk, stuffed with all the envelopes that were housed in my armrest the night before. I grimaced just at the sight of them. Coming face-to-face with my finances would be painful, but not nearly as painful as having my mail read by Janice in front of someone.

Taking a deep breath, I pulled out a fresh legal pad and slid my treasured powder blue Louis Vuitton Nails Agenda ballpoint pen from its velvet case. (I guarded that pen with my life, and given the $220 it cost me, I used it every chance I got!) I opened the first envelope, unfolded the letter, and flattened it out on my desk. Wincing at the balance and past-due amounts, I wrote them both down on a fresh sheet of paper, then moved on to the next envelope. By the time I opened envelope five, there was no more fooling myself. I was in deep trouble. So deep that I couldn't bear to go through the remainder of the bills. With a paper clip, I kept the bills I'd already seen together, then put the remainder of them all in a manila folder and placed them in my desk drawer, intending to focus on them during my lunch hour.

I was starting to send e-mails to my clients like crazy, notifying them of our current promotion of a 10 percent discount off of current rates for new assignments, when Shelley's instant message popped up.

ShelleyMac: There?
Deece79: Unfortunately.
ShelleyMac: Girl!!!!!!
Deece79: What?
ShelleyMac: Come over to my office.
Deece79: No, you come over here. Too much can be heard from your office.
ShelleyMac: b right there!

Seconds later, Shelley flew through the door. I didn't even bother to look up.

"What's wrong with you?" she asked, crinkling her nose.

"Nothing." I wasn't convincing, but she let it go.

"You know the wall between my and Janice's office is paper-thin, right?"

"Right." I really wasn't in the mood to gossip. I kept right on typing like she wasn't even there, that is, until I heard what Shelley said next.

"Girl, why did I overhear Corey going off on her!" Immediately, she had my undivided attention.

"About what?"

"I don't even know! Something that happened yesterday. She did something to somebody. I couldn't hear the beginning of the conversation, but he was like, 'I don't support what you did yesterday, and I certainly don't appreciate the way you blindsided me.' Then she said something like, 'It needed to be addressed.'

"Girl, he cut her off and got loud and said, 'You are a piss-poor manager if you couldn't find a better way to do it than that! Now I sat in here and heard your so-called expectations. Now let me tell you mine. You will not belittle and embarrass another employee in this building. This is not the first time I've gotten that feedback regarding your management style, and I am not going to stand for it. Now I have to do some damage control to make sure that we aren't at risk of losing a quality employee because you thought it fitting to show your behind, and if you think I can't see past your vindictive behavior, you had better reevaluate your thinking processes!'"

"Whoa!" I commented, somewhat regaining respect for Corey.

"It was as quiet as a mouse after that. She didn't open her mouth. Well, if she did, I couldn't hear what she said. I saw her in the bathroom a few minutes later, and her eyes were all red like she had been crying. Girl, talking about how her allergies were bothering her." I couldn't help but giggle. Shelley continued. "Yeah, it was allergies all right."

I debated whether I should tell Shelley that I knew exactly what that conversation was about, but before I could decide, she said something else that shocked me.

"And you know, she tried to give him some."

"What! When!"

"No sooner had he got off the plane and ever since then."

"Wait. How do you know?"

"I just told you, I can hear everything that goes on in her office. She was in there on the phone, telling somebody that she invited him over for a nightcap about three times, but he has always had a meeting or something to go to. She was saying, 'He said no this time, but you know I love dark meat, and I know just how to get it.' Now I have heard of a little office romance, but she's involved in straight-up office ho-mance!"

Two taps on the door startled both of us and abruptly ended our discussion. Corey peered in.

"Good morning, ladies," he said. A fresh wave of embarrassment washed over me as I had instant flashbacks from the day before. "December, do you have a few minutes?"

"Sure," I responded respectfully. Shelley got up and headed for the door.

"Just drop the folder off at my desk once you've completed your portion of the spreadsheet," said Shelley. We were good about mentioning pretend projects at the drop of a hat.

"I may not be able to get to it until tomorrow morning, since I have client meetings this afternoon, but I'll just shoot you an e-mail to let you know when you can expect it," I responded.

She closed the door behind her while Corey took a seat.

"How are you doing today?" he asked, testing the waters.

"I'm fine, thank you, Mr. Davis."

He chuckled, looking up at the ceiling. "So how long am I going to be Mr. Davis?" Getting no response from me other than a blank stare, he continued. "Listen, I wanted to talk with you a little bit about what happened yesterday." I bit my bottom lip and kept silent, never taking my eyes away from his. "First of all, I want you to know that I had no idea of what Janice was going to say to you yesterday. She caught me in passing, apparently, after she'd asked you to come to her office, and asked if I had a couple of minutes to sit in on a conversation she needed to have with one of her direct reports. I had no idea it would be you and was totally blindsided as to what it was about."

He searched my eyes for acceptance of his explanation thus far, but my face was like stone. "Secondly," he added, "I do not agree with or support a style of management that belittles others and attempts to strip them of their dignity. I am very concerned about her management style and why she chose to handle the situation that way."

He paused again, and this time I acknowledged his statement with a slight nod. He went on. "Finally, and please let this stay between me and you, I placed her on corrective action, as I found her behavior to be totally unacceptable."

It was very difficult for me to keep my cheeks from rising, but somehow I managed to hide my elation. "I want you to know, December, that I value you as a Wright-Way employee and appreciate your contributions. Even if your performance was substandard, you did not deserve what she did. Moreover, and most impressive, you remained professional."

"Thank you, Mr. Davis, for coming to speak to me about it. I was a little distraught yesterday when I left, but I feel much better now knowing that your management style does not mirror or support Ms. Wheeler's."

"You're welcome. Can you stop with the formalities now?" he said, rising and walking to the door. He turned back just before opening it. "And one more thing, Ms. Elliott." He emphasized my name. "You look stunning today." That time I did blush. He disappeared before I could respond. Seconds later, an instant-message dialogue box appeared.

ShelleyMac: Potatoes?
Deece79: No.
ShelleyMac: Her @*!# got wrote up!

Twelve

I'd been to the gym just about every day since meeting Rodney. He'd check me out while I did my Nautilus reps; I'd check him out while he worked the free weights. We were giving each other lots of eye rhythm between sets. After about eight weeks of this subtle flirting, he finally asked me out to dinner on the upcoming Sunday.

"How about lunch on Saturday instead?" I negotiated, still wanting to be a little reserved and not wanting him to take my company too seriously. At this point, I didn't know where things were headed with me and Terrance, but at the same time, I didn't want to limit my options, especially with this buff brother.

"That'll work. I don't have to be at work until five, so is twelve cool?"

"Twelve is perfect. Why don't we meet here at the gym?" I wasn't quite ready to let Rodney know where I lived, although if he really wanted to know, I'm certain all he had to do was look in a file cabinet or click in the gym's database. But then again, I lived in one of those hard-to-find, back in the cut spots, which generally required step-by-step instructions to get to.

"What? You scared to let me know where you live or something?"

"No, my momma and them be acting crazy when I bring guys over," I said, without cracking a smile. He looked as if he was searching for words but couldn't find them quickly enough. "I'm just kidding." I elbowed him playfully. "Seriously, I just prefer to meet in a public place for now."

"Oh, that's cool, that's cool." He folded his bottom lip into his mouth while giving me an admiring stare. "So, I'll see you here then." I nodded, trying not to smile.

When Saturday came, there was absolutely nothing to smile about. I arrived at the gym a little before noon, dressed in a black A-line skirt with white flowered stitching and a halter-style white knit sweater. My diamond-studded Chanel logo necklace rested between my collarbones, and I carried my black and white Chanel purse, with matching white with black trim thong slides on my feet. I had wrapped my hair with a foam mousse the night before, and it now now lay neat and flat against my head. I'd been sitting idly in my car for about ten minutes, listening to some Anthony Hamilton and thinking about making a quick run to the gas station, when Rodney called my cell.

"Where are you?" he asked.

"At the gym, waiting on you. Are you here?"

"I'm about two minutes away. I'll pull up to the door. See you in a few."

I checked my visor mirror to make sure I still had on lip gloss and looked like a dream, which I did, grabbed my purse and shades, secured my vehicle, and walked through the lot to the sidewalk. I could feel the very earth tremble beneath my feet as a car approached me from behind, thumping bass amplified at one hundred times what it needed to be. The blue Chevy Caprice pulled up to the curb, and in a quick glance, I saw a brother, with dark glasses and a high mountain of nappy hair exploding through a sun visor, which he had on upside down, get out of the driver's side. He had on a wife beater, with another T-shirt on top. His arms were in the sleeves, but the rest of the T-shirt was pulled back behind his head and around his neck.

"'Sup!" he said above the volume of Petey Pablo blasting from the car. As he approached the sidewalk, he stopped in front of the car, squatted just a bit, yanked a towel from off his shoulder, and spun it around in the air, singing along with the song's chorus. The waistline of a pair of black basketball shorts circled his butt, exposing a portion of his navy and light blue boxers. On his feet, he wore ankle socks with Adidas flip-flops. I acknowledged him with a head bob, then looked toward the parking lot entrance, expecting to see Rodney any second, although I had no idea what kind of car he drove. I spotted a silver Mazda coming through the lot and heading for the front. Its driver resembled Rodney from a distance. Assuming that it was him, I pulled my purse up on my shoulder, ready to hop in the truck and ride.

The Caprice driver was obviously sucked into the groove of his music and began doing several deep, doggish pelvic thrusts, a slowed-down, rhythmic, and far more sexual version of John Witherspoon's "Bang! Bang! Bang!" Now, normally, I didn't give guys like that any type of attention, because thug brothers just don't appeal to me. I'm not against any sistah that is looking for a thug for a mate; I'm just saying the thug life is not for me. But what made me do a double take was what he said to me next.

"You gone stand there all day, or are we going to lunch?" he asked, jerking his shoulders up and down, still dancing. I squinted at him; then my eyebrows shot up to my hairline. The small gap in his front teeth was unmistakable. *What the . . . ?*

In one second flat, I thought twenty complete thoughts:

What in the world? I know you don't expect me to get in that car! What is that on top of your head? Why are you dressed like that? Is that how you dress? You have got to be kidding me! Where do you think you are taking me, looking like that? Can you turn that mess down!

Should I, or shouldn't I? Girl, get in your car, and go home. It's just lunch.

Am I desperate? We're just friends. It's not a real date. Could I be a ride or die chick . . . in my Coco Chanel? Suppose I see somebody I know. I should drive. Don't be stuck-up, December. Live a little; show some versatility. This one time won't kill you.

"I didn't recognize you," I exclaimed, with a confused smile. Rodney wrapped his arms around me in a friendly hug. At least he smelled good.

"Yeah. This is how I roll when I ain't workin'."

I should drive, I thought again as he opened the car door for me. Against my better judgment, I got in, anyway, and right away found the volume control, not caring that Chris Tucker's character in *Rush Hour* gave clear instructions to never touch a black man's stereo.

"Too loud for you, huh?" Rodney didn't seem to mind the adjustment.

"A little bit. So where are we going?" I asked, struggling to be a good sport and not show my disapproval of his appearance.

"Wherever you want to go." He shrugged.

You can take me to the next row and drop me off at my car.

"Umm . . . how about . . ." I couldn't think of a single place where I wanted to be seen with Rodney, with him looking the way he did. With his hair sticking up all over his head and his flip-flops and socks, he had the whole House Shoe thing going.

Think, December. Think!

"How about Jillian's?" I suggested, figuring it was my best choice since it was a restaurant, slash arcade, slash billiards hall, slash sports bar, and at this time of day, it would probably be pretty slow.

"Cool. Let's ride!" I literally thought I'd been shot as the car backfired when he, without warning, put it in gear and jammed on the gas, slamming me into my seat. Before we reached the end of the block, he started feening for bass. "I gotta turn this up a little bit," he said. *Little* is a relative word, by the way.

So there I was, riding shotgun in a backfiring Caprice, with a knotty-headed Petey impersonator yelling obscenities out the window. I tried to inconspicuously slide down as far as I could in the seat, silently cursing at myself for not driving. This was not the Rodney I'd been previously exposed to. Rodney calmed down a bit once we entered the restaurant, but even with his practically perfect physique, his appearance was still embarrassing. When we got to Jillian's, the first thing I did was ask the hostess if she had anything for a headache. She kept looking back and forth between both of us; she had to be thinking, *Now how did this couple end up together?*

We decided on Grilled Chicken Nachos as an appetizer, and I selected the Honey Mustard Spinach Salad, while Rodney ordered the Cheeseburger Philly with fries.

"So have you given any more thought to becoming an instructor?" he asked.

"Some." I shrugged. "I'm spending so much time at

the gym these days. It probably wouldn't hurt to add it to my repertoire of talents. What exactly is the process?"

He picked up a saucer, loaded it with nachos, and thoughtfully served me before serving himself. How considerate. Too bad his head looked like it was on fire.

"You would have to complete about five hundred hours of comprehensive course study. You'll have to learn about client evaluations, anatomy, physiology, and nutrition. Do an internship, which you can do at the gym. You'd be looking at about six months of study time." I was impressed at his knowledge, but again . . . too bad his head looked like it was on fire.

"What about tuition?" The price he quoted me made me choke on the tortilla chip I had in my mouth. If I had that kind of money, my breasts would be like pa-dow!

"Most programs offer some kind of financial assistance or payment plan to make it more affordable." He paused for a minute to swallow some soda. "If you're serious, the gym would even pick up a portion of the tuition." That made my eyes pop.

"Really?"

"Yeah. There's some stipulations, though. You would need to be an employee, first of all. That's a given. Then you have to work a certain amount of hours, fill out some paperwork, you know, some preliminary stuff."

"Guess I'd be working for you then, huh?"

"You got it."

"I don't know about all that," I teased. "It's bad enough you boss us around in your class."

"I'm just doing what I do, baby." He lifted his arms as if to say, "This is me," exposing the curly tufts of hair in his armpits.

We finished our meals, then walked to the arcade side. On the way over, this god-awful odor slapped me in the face. I quickly looked around, noticed we were passing the bathrooms, then quickened my pace to get out of that vicinity.

"Whew! Somebody really got sick in here," I commented, fanning my hand across my nose. We walked on, and the odor hit me again. "What in the world!" I looked around frantically like I was being chased by a murderer.

"I can't front," Rodney began as he rubbed his stomach. "Those nachos, man."

Oh . . . my . . . God. I looked at him, but I was totally speechless. What could be said? If I opened my mouth, that smell would get in it.

"Let's race!" he said, heading over to a set of motorcycles.

I let him walk in front of me, hoping that the cloud of funk would follow him and dissolve before I got over to where he was. When I finally made it over, the air seemed to be clear. I hiked up my skirt, straddled my bike, and waited for him to start the race. The screen counted down to zero, and just as the flag dropped, Rodney cut one so loud, I swore it was the sound of the bikes virtually taking off, and when it wafted over to my nose, I froze and slid clean off the machine and onto the floor.

"What are you doing?" he exclaimed, glancing back and forth between the game screen and me. I knew this only because my eyes were stuck open. Luckily, I had sense enough to hold my skirt down when I fell. "December! Come on!" Someone from the Jillian's staff noticed me lying on the floor and hurried over.

"Ma'am, are you okay?" said the staff member. Rodney was still racing. "Ma'am? Ma'am, do you need me to call an ambulance?" I looked up at a name badge, which, once my eyes came into focus, I saw read STEPHANIE.

Then I saw her hand fly up to her nose and her eyebrows crinkle.

"No, I'm okay," I said as I shook my head, coming out of a daze. Stephanie helped me up off the floor, while Rodney sat leaning into curves and letting out bombs all at the same time. "I'm just going to go sit over here," I said, pointing to a nearby booth.

"Are you sure you're all right?" Stephanie asekd. I nodded as she escorted me to the booth.

"As long as I stay over here, I will be."

"I'll get you some water," she offered. While she was gone, Rodney finished his race and started toward me.

"Uh-uh, uh-uh!" I retorted. "Stay over there!"

He threw his head back and laughed, turned around, and headed toward the virtual bowling games. I didn't know how I'd make it home without dying!

I'd never see Rodney outside of the gym again!

Thirteen

"Did you see that e-mail from Janice?" Andre asked. "She wants to meet with us at one o'clock."

"Us who?" I glanced down at my watch, which read 12:50. "I'm about to go to the mall," I declared.

"Us, me and you. That's who. You may as well forget about that midday mall trip. You don't need to spend any money, anyway."

"How do you know I wasn't going to pay a bill?"

"December, we've already talked about this. I told you to pay your bills online. You know if you go to the mall, you are going to be tempted to buy something, if it's nothing more than a pretzel and a medium lemonade." Andre knew me too well; I wasn't fooling him one bit. Not to mention the fact that I was really trying to go to Arden B. to see if they'd gotten any new long-length pants in.

"Anyway"—I rolled my eyes—"what does she want to see us about?"

"Some special task force project. Open the e-mail." He came around my desk and looked over my shoulder as I scanned my in-box, looking for Janice's note. It said nothing more than what Andre had already stated to me. "Walk me to the break room so I can grab a soda before we go in there," he said, reaching for his wallet, then fingering out a dollar. "You want something?"

"Nah, I'm good. I have some change." I opened my top drawer and fished a few coins out to get some M&M'S or something.

"You know you have to track that, right?"

Frustrated, I tossed the money back in the drawer. Andre was getting on my last nerve with that "watch every single penny" crap. I didn't need any candy, anyway.

A few minutes later we both were seated in front of Janice, who was on the phone. There was a sandwich bag of baby carrots and celery chunks open on her desk, alongside a bottle of Crystal Light.

"My two superstars just walked in," she said while beaming at us like some kind of proud mother hen. I would have cut my eyes at Andre, but she was looking right at us. "I'm going to go ahead and get with Michelle about that this afternoon . . . right . . . right. Well, I have to run. My two stars are waiting on me." She gave us the sunbeam look again. It could mean nothing but tricks. I was sure of it. She hung up and directed her attention toward us.

"Hi, guys," she practically sang. "You two are so awesome. You know that, right?" She popped a carrot into her mouth.

"That's a lot of butter you're rubbing on," Andre responded. "The only thing I know that gets this much butter is the Thanksgiving Day turkey, right before it goes into the oven." Janice burst into false laughter.

"You're so funny, Andre," she said, tilting her head

toward him and batting her lashes. "And how are you, December?"

"Good, thanks. And you?" I tried to smile cordially, but I don't know if I pulled it off.

"Better now that you two are here!" She paused momentarily, her eyes bouncing back and forth between us. If I didn't know any better, I would have thought it was Christmas, and she had some wonderful present for us that we'd been begging for all year. "I wanted to meet with both of you because I need two strong leaders to take on a project this month, and I can't trust it to anyone else. It may require some extra hours, but I promise you that you will be compensated when recognition time comes." I sat diplomatically silent, waiting for her to continue. It wasn't like we could refuse the work. "You know I take care of my people," she added.

"We are always excited about taking on opportunities that provide professional development, Janice," said Andre. I was tempted to kick him with the point of one of my Jimmy Choo Peony leather boots, but I'd paid too much for them. "What exactly are we taking on?"

"Well, you know we've been exploring strategies to increase our average employee tenure, and, December, Corey and I were discussing your idea of examining and restructuring the basic core competencies for our industrial, clerical, and legal applicants. I don't believe we've redefined those requirements in a few years, so that was both an exceptional and innovative suggestion," she said, nodding toward me. "After coming out of the quarterly planning meeting last week, one of the action items this office left the table with was to implement your recommendation, December, and realign our expectations in order to position and retain the best temps to meet our clients' needs."

"I'm glad the company was able to see the value in my idea," I responded. At that point, I felt pretty good about my recommendation being reviewed and accepted. It showed through a slight smile.

"And who better to take on the task of the competency restructuring than the person who birthed the vision?" said Janice. She paused momentarily, gloating for me. "I would like the two of you to work together on this project as, Andre, you bring wonderful insight and industry experience to the table, proven in the way you lead the region in new accounts month after month."

"How will this impact our daily responsibilities?" I asked, concerned about how lately she'd been allowing the appointment team to overbook interviews. Some days, we could barely take a break, and then we were still expected to do our usual number of established client contacts as well as cold call to potential new clients.

"You will only do interviews during the morning hours for the next several weeks so that you can focus on this project in the latter part of the day. As far as established and potential customer contacts, your teammates will pick that up for you. I blocked out conference room B for the rest of the month to give you both the necessary space and solitude that you'll need to be successful with this project. And, of course, whatever tools you need, just let me know and I'll make sure you're taken care of."

She stacked four large binders on her desk, which contained the current competencies, skill sets, and practices. "Go ahead and take these with you now, spend the rest of the afternoon and tomorrow reviewing them, and maybe by Friday you can start the beginning phases of the restructuring," she suggested. "What questions do you have for me?"

Andre looked at me and did a mock introduction.

"I'm Andre O'Neal, and I'll be working in close quarters with you for the next few weeks. And you are?" I pushed his extended hand away in jest.

"No questions," I answered. "I'll include a status update on my weekly activity report."

"I know you will," Janice said and winked. "You're so efficient!" Okay. I'd had enough.

"Anything else?" I asked.

"Nope. You guys have a lot on your plates, but I know you will do well." We both rose to leave; Andre heaved the binders into his arms. "Let me know what you need."

"Will do. Open or closed?" Andre asked, referring to her office door.

"Pull it closed for me please, Andre. Thanks."

We stood outside of Janice's door, eyeing each other for a moment.

"What is she going to get out of this?" I asked, knowing Janice did nothing that didn't somehow, someway, have a huge payout in it for her.

"A promotion out of this office if we're lucky." Andre chuckled. "Let me check my schedule for open appointments and get my day cleared off for tomorrow," he said.

"Yeah, me, too," I agreed. As soon as Andre slid into his office, I hotfooted it to the mall. I was supposed to see Terrance tonight, and I was going to have something for his eyes to behold!

Fourteen

Terrance and I had been seeing each other again for nearly three months. I was still a little intimidated about letting him fully into my space, trying not to be the same fool twice, but at the same time, still seeking the fun, excitement, attention, and affection of a relationship. I guess I felt a little safe where Terrance was concerned because we had so much history. Not all of it was pleasant, of course, but there had been some good times.

I was still protective of my goodies but was feeling super frisky tonight. Terrance and I had planned on just staying in at his place and watching a few good DVDs or cable movies over some Chinese takeout, but I had something else in mind. On my bed I laid out the items that I'd bought from the store: a pair of long white gloves, some white thigh highs, and a two-inch wide piece of white ribbon. I then dug through my panty drawer and found a white thong, a pair of boy leg briefs, and a matching strapless bra. I put all of those pieces on, then went to my closet and pulled on a tight-fitting all white jogging suit, covered it up with a looser-fitting black jogging suit, and then put on a crazy pair of white Baby Phat pumps.

I overdid my eyes and lips in white-makeup and placed a white headband on my head to keep my hair out of my face. Tucking the black lightbulb I'd picked up at the mall into my bag, I headed for Terrance's, calling him on the way and expressing that I wanted to shoot a little pool tonight.

"Pool?" he asked. "You don't even like pool."

"I know, but tonight I thought I'd try it again and see how well I do. As a matter of fact, I just want to see you play."

"Let me see if I got this right." He chuckled. "You want to come over and spend the evening watching me play pool by myself."

"Yeah, pretty much. I mean, you look so sexy the way you lick your lips and slide the cue stick between your fingers. I just wanna watch."

"I don't know about all that, Deece. I really don't feel like standing up at the table tonight."

"Do it for me. I'll make it worth your while," I coaxed.

"We'll see when you get here."

I pulled up to his place ten minutes later and rang the bell. He opened the door and burst into laughter.

"What in the world do you have on?"

"You won't be laughing long."

I took him by the hand and led him upstairs to his pool room. It was perfectly dark there. Oh yeah, this was going to be fun! I flipped the light on, quickly changed the bulb to the black lightbulb, and pretty much disappeared from his sight—other than the white that highlighted my face, hair, hands, and feet.

"I'll tell you what we're gonna do," I said as I grabbed

a cue stick from the rack and handed it to him. "For every ball you sink, a little bit of this is gonna come off."

Terrance nodded his head and chuckled. "Okay." He wasted no time racking the balls. "Forget what I said about not wanting to shoot pool tonight."

"Mm-hmm," I moaned seductively. Right before he cracked the set of balls, I moved toward the stereo in the corner and fumbled my way through starting his CD player, not knowing what he had loaded. The room filled with the sounds of some romantic favorites from a *Body & Soul* collection.

I stood across the table from him as he began to call shots as best he could in the alternate lighting. When the first ball sank, I fully removed my black jacket, revealing the white one underneath. The second ball dropped, and I removed the dark pants. I was now glowing from head to toe like the Ghost of Christmas Past. Quickly, he sank the third ball, then waited for my response. I unzipped my jacket, exposing the contrast of my glowing bra against my skin, which was dramatically darkened by the black light. He let out a groan, which let me know he was pleased with what he saw. The next ball hit the pocket, and I fully removed my white jacket, better highlighting my figure in the bra, gloves, and pants. When the next ball dropped, I removed the white pants, and I thought he inhaled all the air in the room through his teeth. Another ball hit. I removed the boy leg briefs slowly and seductively, revealing the skimpy thong beneath, while in the background Johnny Gill cried out, *"My, my, my."*

"Mmh!" Terrance exclaimed and called his next shot. By the time he'd pocketed all the balls, there was nothing left on me but the ribbon I had tied around my neck and the thong. I had been strategic in my positioning and had stayed my distance the entire game, but now, with all the balls cleared away, he approached me slowly and wrapped his arms around me, then let his hands explore my flesh.

Gently lifting me up, he sat me on the edge of the pool table, and I wrapped my legs around his back. He began kissing me all over, taking me to a familiar place that I'd not been to in a very long time. Together, we slid back onto the pool table. My eyes closed, and I began to give myself to the moment and to his kisses, which had become more and more passionate. My body trembled in anticipation of what I knew Terrance was going to put on me, but then he became Denzel Washington . . . in a way that I couldn't appreciate.

"Ssss Tiffany girl . . ."

My eyes popped wide open, and I pushed him off of me. This was a scene right out of Spike Lee's *Mo' Better Blues*, when Denzel's character, in heated sexual confusion, mixed those two women's names up.

"Tiffany!" I screeched.

"Deece, I'm . . . Deece . . ." He was taking slaps upside the head as I struggled with all my might to get off the pool table.

"December, wait a minute. I didn't mean that. I just—"

"You just called me someone else's name! That's what you just did!" I screamed. In a fit of tears, I collected whatever clothes I could find, which, of course, was all the white stuff, pulled the pants and jacket on as best I could, and ran out of the room and down the steps. Terrance was right behind me, trying to calm me down, but knew better than to try to grab me.

"December, just wait a minute! Please!" I spun around, angrier than a swarm of hornets whose nest had been disturbed.

"Wait for what, Terrance? Wait for you to tell me that you're sorry!" I spat. "Well, I don't want to hear it! And you know what the sad part is? If you were to say to me, right now, that you're sorry, that would be the most honest thing you've *ever* said to me."

I yanked the front door open, virtually flew to my truck, and sped off down the street, but at the end of the block, I pulled over to the side of the road to get myself together, not wanting to kill myself on the way home. A number of emotions washed over me: shame, embarrassment, anger, frustration, and a few more I didn't even recognize. The only thing I could be glad about was things didn't go as far as they could have, and as far as I was willing to let them go tonight. I guess I could salvage a little of my dignity from that fact.

I dug my cell out of my purse and dialed Kisha's number.

"Hello," she answered, sounding incoherent.

"You're asleep?" I could tell that she was but knew that she'd wake up if I asked her to.

"Um . . . I had just dozed off. What's up? Are you okay?" she asked, detecting the misery in my voice.

"Yeah . . . I'm okay. I just needed someone to talk to right quick." Then out of the blue, I wished I hadn't called at all.

"Okay. I'm up. What happened?"

"That's okay. Go ahead to sleep. I'll tell you about it tomorrow."

"No, go 'head. I'm up now," she insisted.

"Uh-uh. I'll call you tomorrow. Go back to sleep. I feel a little better."

She sighed. "All right, girl. Call me back if you need to." After I hung up with Kisha, I turned the phone off altogether, anticipating that Terrance would call.

I drove home in silence, reliving what had happened and wondering what had possessed me to let Terrance back into my life.

Once I got home, I went into my second bedroom and pulled a box off the closet shelf that contained photos of me and Terrance, along with cards, dried flowers, and other relationship knickknacks. I didn't even look inside the box; I just walked it straight to the dumpster, threw it inside, and never looked back.

Fifteen

I received roses every single day for ten working days straight after black-light pool night. I hadn't shared with Andre or Shelley that I'd been seeing Terrance, so no one had a clue about who the roses were from and why I was suddenly getting an abundance of them. They made their assumptions, but I neither confirmed nor denied them. Even Janice brought her nosy, round tail in my office, inquiring.

"Mmmmm! Somebody is really in love with you, huh?"

I didn't give her the satisfaction of even commenting. It was common knowledge that if any woman in that office had a man and Janice knew about it, she was going to find a way to have sex with him. She seemed to not even care about her reputation and even had a picture of the *Sex and the City* girls posted up in her office, with her name posted under Samantha's chin. Anybody who watched the show, even a little, knew that Samantha was the one who considered herself the most sexually liberated, but in my opinion, she was the ho of the

show. Janice stating to the office that she was like Samantha was saying a whole lot.

Thomas Graham, who was the branch manager in
Richmond, had found himself caught up with her, and
his wife came storming into the office one day, ready to
beat Janice down. Christina Graham demanded to see
Janice, creating a huge scene in front of a lobby full of
applicants. She was calling Janice all kinds of names and
screaming every obscenity she could think of. One thing
I can say about Janice is, she ain't no fool. She stayed in
her office the entire day and called her brother to escort
her to her car when she got ready to leave that evening.

"Who is this mystery man that is spending eighty dollars a day on roses on you? You must have done something really well," she nudged, giving me a knowing
look.

I kept silent and tapped my fingers against my lips.

"It will come out sooner or later!" she said before
leaving.

I threw myself totally into my work over the next two
months, intensely focusing on the competency rewrite
project and spending countless extra hours in the office, despite my exempt-level position. Some nights I was
there up until eight o'clock, working without Andre, just
losing myself in the task at hand. I even forgot about my
little infatuation with Corey. Other than working out
and shopping, I allowed work to absorb all of my time.

It was about seven o'clock one evening, and I was still
sitting at my desk, reviewing a stack of statistical reports,
doing a study on age ranges and tenure, when Corey
waltzed in.

"December, you sure are burning the candle on both
ends here lately."

"Just trying to stay on top of this project," I responded. He watched me silently for a few seconds, leaning against the door frame.

"Do you want to run with me to get something to eat? I'll be here for a few more hours myself."

"No thanks. I'm fine." I gave no thought to what he'd said, not even bothering to look up. I was just totally not interested at the moment.

"Can I bring you something back?" he offered. This time I did look up. I ran my hands through my hair and let out a sigh.

"You know what? I could use a break." I opened my bottom file-cabinet drawer and retrieved my purse. "Where were you thinking of going?"

"Mmm, how about Panera Bread?" he suggested. "They have a mean turkey and artichoke panini. Get that with a cup of French onion soup, and you have some good eating."

"Okay. That sounds great." I pulled on my jacket, and we walked out to his Mercedes SUV. "Nice truck," I commented.

"Thanks." He walked to the passenger's side and let me in, then got in himself. The radio was tuned to 95.7, which featured classic and current R & B. Anita Baker's "Same Ole Love" was playing, which always made me think of skating at the roller rink, without a care in the world. In my mind, I was doing a cross step and spin, gliding past other skaters, taking a minivacation from the reality of being engrossed in work.

Other than Anita singing, there were no other voices during the ride, there or back.

"You mind if I eat in your office?" he asked as we stepped back into the building.

"Not at all. I guess I could use the evening company."

The conversation was general and pleasant as he shared a few things about himself in terms of his career path and how he saw the company growing. I turned the conversation in a more personal direction, not to be nosy, but simply because I didn't think the question was too invasive.

"Do you have kids?" I asked. He shook his head as he bit into his sandwich. He swallowed, then responded verbally.

"I had a baby girl, but she passed away when she was five. Got hit by a car. She would have been fifteen this year."

"Corey, I am so sorry to hear that." I gasped, almost regretting that I'd asked.

"Thanks." He reached for his wallet and pulled out a picture of a beautiful little girl with huge Afro puffs. She was sitting on the floor, looking up at the ceiling above her head, which was obviously where the camera had been placed. Her white dress was fanned out all around her in a circle and complemented her sparkling white baby teeth. I nearly broke out in tears at just the thought that he'd lost her.

"What's her name?" I asked softly.

"Octavia." He pressed his lips to the photo and stared at it himself for a few seconds.

"She's beautiful."

"Yeah, that was my angel. Still is." He put the wallet back in his pocket. "How about you? You have any children?"

"No. I'd like to one day, but I try to stay focused on my priorities. You know, first comes love, then comes marriage, then comes the baby . . ."

"In the baby carriage," he finished while I let out a giggle.

"I can't really seem to get the love part right," I shared.

"Oh really? Who would know it with all the flower deliveries you were getting at one time."

"They were doghouse flowers," I commented, flicking my hand in the air. "They meant absolutely nothing. I would one day like to get flowers from a man just because. I take that back. Not one day. I would like to consistently, you know, every now and then, on a regular basis, get flowers from a man when he hasn't done anything wrong. He hasn't slept with anybody, forgotten to come home or forgotten it was my birthday, or called me out of my name. He's not scared that I'm going to walk out of his life, and he hasn't busted my lip open. Not that all of those things have happened to me, but generally speaking, those seem to be the reasons why men give flowers. I would like to get some just because he finds me worthy of them." I sighed a little louder than I intended to.

"You are worthy," he stated, without looking up from his food. "It just takes us knuckleheaded guys a little while to figure out how to let women know that." He balled up the paper wrapping from his sandwich, tossed it in a nearby wastebasket, then rose from his seat.

"Thanks for accommodating me." he added. "I know you didn't plan on wasting time shooting the breeze, but I appreciate your attention."

"I enjoyed your company, Corey," I said sincerely and without motive.

"You're doing a great job, by the way."

I smiled. "Thanks."

"And, as your regional manager, I'm insisting that you get out of here. You don't need to be here this late in the evening, anyway. As a matter of fact, don't come in tomorrow until ten."

"Janice is going to have a cow."

"You let me worry about Janice," he said, with his brows raised.

"Yes, sir." And with that, I put away my reports, logged out of my computer, and went home, feeling better than I had in a long time.

When I did get to work the next morning, at ten on the dot, there was an arrangement of tulips on my desk, with a card that read simply: *You are worthy.*

When the usual questions arose about who they were from, I said nothing. I now respected Corey too much to put his name in the rumor mill. And somehow I knew that he trusted me to keep both our conversation and the fact that he'd sent the flowers confidential.

Sixteen

The night of the first annual Employee Appreciation Awards event would be one that I'd never forget. I couldn't remember a time when I'd looked so incredibly stunning, not that I didn't look my best every day. I'd had my hair micro-braided and swept the tiny braids up in a high bun, with tendrils cascading down each side of my head, at my ears. Thin strands of silver hung from my earlobes, and I'd followed the step-by-step instructions listed in the latest issue of *Essence* magazine to apply my make-up flawlessly. My eyes were alluring, brows perfectly shaped, lips full and inviting, and skin unbelievably smoothed, with a foundation so light and closely matched, I couldn't even tell I'd put it on. Halle, Jada, or Beyoncé had nothing on me tonight. The next time *Essence* was on a search for the world's most beautiful women, I was going to send my picture. I wore a fitted sparkling silver gown with a fluted hemline and cowl-neck that lay just off my shoulders. It seemed to be made purely of glitter, but the dress was nothing short of dynamic! My French-pedicured toes were clearly seen through a pair of clear T-strap thong sandals with three-inch heels, which would allow me to comfortably socialize all night.

Although I initially had my reservations about the event being held at the Virginia Air & Space Center, the setting couldn't have been more perfect. Midroom, round tables had been set up and were elegantly covered with white tablecloths, topped with gold balloon centerpieces and formal place settings. There was a stage area, where a pianist sat off to the side, along with a five-piece live band, creating melodies that enveloped the dining area in amazing acoustical perfection. The lighting was dim, creating a striking after-five atmosphere, and against the backdrop of massive windows displaying the Hampton River waterfront, it was actually kind of romantic.

Walking the room, I scanned the crowd for any staff members from my branch, or more specifically Andre and Shelley. I sampled delicacies from several appetizer stations, which were strategically positioned between exhibits. There was an assortment of fruits, cheeses, and fresh vegetables, of course, and a variety of flaky, meat-filled pastry bundles; bacon-wrapped turkey brochettes; mini chicken, shrimp, and steak shish kebabs; sun-dried tomato and wild mushroom quiches; and this decadent cinnamon and pecan Brie. Servers walked the room, offering glasses of wine. I was highly impressed with Wright-Way and how they'd seemingly gone all out for this appreciation event. In the past, all we had got was a burnt-up hot dog and a cold generic soda at the employee picnic.

After a few minutes of looking and speaking to various employees from other branches, I spotted Andre standing next to an ice sculpture of the company's logo, chatting with a woman with rich, brown glowing skin,

who favored India.Arie. Her hair was in natural tendrils. They weren't even twists. They were just segments
sticking up all over the place, with the healthy and radiant sheen I'd been trying to achieve all my life. Her
dress looked like she had found a super-sized off-white
trouser sock, cut the foot part off of it, stepped inside,
and pulled it up over her breasts. The hemline, which
was right at her ankles, was trimmed with small wooden
beads. She didn't have an ounce of fat, a wrinkle, bulge,
or indentation anywhere. Her shoes were a pair of
strappy brown stilettos that were the same color as her
skin, therefore, practically invisible. I had to hand it to
her: she was bad. All of a sudden, feeling like an ugly
duckling, I discarded my plate of cheese balls and
chicken chunks on a stick and sucked my stomach in.
No more skipping gym sessions for me. As a matter of
fact, I was going to turn Billy Blanks on as soon as I got
home.

Andre spotted me before I got to him and waved me
over.

"Hey, December, you look great," he began. "This is
Monique McGlone from Richmond."

"Hi, Monique. It's nice to finally meet you and put a
face to the name." I was very familiar with her name
from the cross-site performance reports. "I'm December Elliott."

"December!" she repeated as if she suddenly remembered me from high school. "Likewise," she said, with a
smile. For some narrow-minded reason, I expected her
to have an accent of some sort, but her dialect was no
different than my own. "That is a beautiful gown," she
commented.

"Thanks, but I have to tell you, you look remark-
able!" I was intrigued and most jealous of the way her
breasts sat firm and round beneath her sheath. Did she

even have on a bra... or panties, for that matter? I looked away, toward the band, before she caught me staring.

"Oh, girl, please. If you only knew where I got this dress from," she replied, flipping her hand in the air, then leaning in closely to my ear. "I made this thing when I got off work today."

"What? You made it?" I said. So it really was a sock.

"Shhh. . . ." She winked. "I get tired of spending my money on a whole bunch of dry-clean-only stuff. You'd be surprised at how quick and easy it is to make something."

"I don't know, Monique. Sewing is not exactly my strength," I replied.

"Stick with me, and you'll be a pro before long. I mean, we already run neck and neck on the hours report." She laughed.

"Let's grab a seat, ladies," Andre recommended, pointing to his watch. "It's about time for the program to start." Shelley appeared out of nowhere, out of breath.

"I didn't think I was going to make it. That girl took forever with my hair," Shelley panted. Her hair had been straw set and fell in beautiful spirals around her face. She wore an elegant chocolate-colored gown with gold beading, with a pair of gold shoes. "Do I look okay? I didn't know about this dress."

"You look amazing," Andre answered, then introduced Shelley and Monique. They exchanged smiles and handshakes briefly; then Andre escorted us to a table in the middle of the room, where about four individuals were already seated. I almost protested, wanting to sit with our office group, but then thought about some advice Corey had given me about taking advantage of my networking opportunities.

Andre, being a perfect gentleman, held our chairs

out as we were seated—first Monique's, then mine, then Shelley's—and finally seated himself beside Monique. He nudged me beneath the table and gestured his head toward the door, where Janice was making her entrance, dressed in some sequined, eggplant-colored, mother of the bride–looking getup. I nearly choked on my ice water. She made her way across the room, grinning and flirting with every man she could. *Sickening, just sickening.* She noticed our group and immediately approached our table.

"How are my superstars?" Janice said, with a wide smile, to me and Andre, draping an arm around each of our shoulders. "December! You look fantastic! Oh and you got your hair done!"

"Excuse me?" Andre grabbed my elbow to keep me from standing.

"Hi. I'm Janice Wheeler," Janice said, turning to Monique. "And you are?"

"Monique McGlone, from the Richmond branch."

"So you report to Thomas Graham. I remember when Thomas worked for me! I helped him to get that branch manager role," Janice bragged. *Yeah, and I remember when Mrs. Graham came looking for you, behind you sleeping with her man,* I wanted to add. Needless to say, I didn't.

"Monique, did you know that you are sitting at the table with a couple of Wright-Way celebrities?" Janice said as she eyed me and Andre knowingly. "But, you're quite a performer yourself, aren't you? I saw your stats for last week. You're doing a great job. Let me know if there is anything I can do to help you get a lift in your numbers."

"Thanks. And what is it that you do in the company?" asked Monique. *Good one, Monique. Let her know that she ain't nobody.*

Janice had clearly taken offense. "You've not been with

the company very long, have you?" she asked, through a patronizing smile. "I'm the general manager. I'll have to talk to Thomas about communicating to his team the company's key players." She patted Monique's shoulder, then circled around to the other individuals seated with us. Once she was gone, Monique looked at me.

"You three work directly for her?" asked Monique.

"Yep," we all said in unison.

"I'm so sorry," Monique said and giggled.

"So are we," Shelley added.

After dinner and before the dance party, Martin Wright took the podium to give away the last award for the evening, which was an all-expense-paid six-night, seven-day trip for two to Cancun, Mexico. I had already received two awards, one for highest number of employees retained and one for being in the top five of increased hours percentage. I felt like a movie star as my name was called and I was applauded by my peers, as was everyone who'd received any type of recognition that night.

Mr. Wright cleared his throat at the microphone and tapped on a wine-glass with a fork to get everyone's attention.

"As the CEO and founder of Wright-Way Staffing, I am so honored to be surrounded by such a dynamic group of professionals, who have taken this company to the next level. I want to personally congratulate each person who has come up on stage tonight and received an award, as well as those who maybe were not recognized tonight but made worthy contributions to the company's bottom line. I hope that I have shown you here tonight, with great food, great drinks, and a great celebration, how much I truly appreciate the hard work you put in every day to make this company one of the most successful in the Hampton Roads and Richmond areas. Please give yourselves a round of applause." We all stood clapping and cheering for a good thirty seconds or so. Once we quieted, he continued.

"Now I am especially pleased to be able to give away a trip tonight. . . ." He paused while the live band suddenly interrupted with some upbeat Latin music, causing an eruption of cheers from the audience. "We have seen such an enormous lift in production and overall profits due to this individual's contributions, a trip to Cancun is almost a small honor. I tried to make it a trip to London, but the board wouldn't approve it." He chuckled, and we did the same to appease him. At that, he took a small piece of paper from his suit pocket and began reading a brief description of the winner's contributions.

"I challenged each of my branches to create a strategy to increase the average temporary employee tenure, knowing that if we could improve in just that one area, it would make such a significant impact to our clients and profits and would allow us to corner the market in our regional areas. While several different ideas were presented and came across my desk, there was one particular strategy, suggested by one particular employee, that allowed us to pave the way and prepare to experience what we anticipate to be phenomenal success over the next twelve months. This individual realized that our employee core competency structure was far outdated. . . ."

My heart stopped beating. Actually, it didn't, but I could now hear it beating more than I could hear him talking. I heard him say other words, like *innovative* and *thumb on the business,* and *sharp eye, industry changes,* and *total restructuring*. "Please help me congratulate the winner of an all-expense-paid trip for two to Cancun, Mexico . . . Ms. . . . Janice . . . Wheeler!"

This time my heart did stop beating.

I fought back hot tears as I watched Janice strut up to the stage area, sprinkling thank-yous and blowing kisses along the way. She tightly embraced Mr. Wright, who rocked her from side to side in jubilation, then kissed her cheek. He took the mike again.

"Janice, you are such an incredible talent and asset to our business. It is because of you that Wright-Way Staffing has become the staffing agency of choice in this entire region. I want you to enjoy that trip to Cancun and have a margarita or two for me!" Janice threw her head back in laughter as Mr. Wright placed a hand on his stomach, held the other in the air, and did a few cha-cha moves.

"Deece, I am so sorry," I saw Andre mouth.

I left shortly after that.

Seventeen

I had spent the rest of the night crying, sulking, moping, and more importantly, rehearsing exactly what I was going to say to Janice when I saw her again. I even dreamed at least three times about knocking her slam out. The initial shock was over, and now it was time for me to confront her about her conniving, trifling, back-stabbing, trip-stealing management style. Not that I expected she'd lose the trip as a result of it, but I had to get this off my chest.

I first put on a Donna Karan eggshell-colored linen two-piece suit. It gave me a long, elegant, but professional look; it said class and style. *Nah, too wimpy.* I tried a chocolate pantsuit, then a navy one, then three black suits before deciding on a black Esprit power suit, with black Prada pumps. It said everything that I wanted to be today: angry, mean, confrontational, and cutthroat . . . revengeful. Instead of wearing the standard corporate America white blouse, I opted for a sleeveless black spandex mock turtleneck.

I pulled my braids straight back into a chignon, leaving no strands or tendrils. I lightly dusted my face with powder, drew attention to my eyes with a little mascara (I wanted her to see and feel the daggers when they shot forth), and coated my lips with a clear matte gloss. My earrings were simple silver balls, nothing dangling or fancy. Then I topped off my look with my nonprescription black-framed glasses. They gave me the intelligent, executive look. I looked like one of the CIA's best employees. My whole persona reeked with so much power, if I turned around a few times, my clothes would fly off to reveal a full-fledged Wonder Woman costume underneath.

On the drive to work, I had to turn on something to keep my energy boosted, but all I could put my hands on was Destiny's Child's *Survivor*.

"Thought I could zubba without you, but I'm zubba! Zubba dubba dubba da da da, but I'm zubba!" I sang, slurring the words, most familiar with the chorus part of the song. "I wish I could dis you on the radio . . . I'll straight take off my Christianity. . . ." I kept the fire burning. The song played a full three times before I switched to the radio, just in time to catch LL Cool J's "Momma Said Knock You Out." I pumped one fist wildly in the air, remembering all my Billy Blanks moves while I chanted the chorus.

Pulling into the lot, I rehearsed my words once more in my head while my eyes scanned for Janice's car, a late-model black BMW 6 Series coupe, which I didn't see anywhere. I was a little early, and I probably didn't need to be so anxious, anyway.

Portia started in on me when I walked by her desk. "What? You got an interview today or something?" I didn't even give a response but walked coolly to my desk.

Every time the thought of confronting Janice crossed my mind, I felt my stomach leap a little. I could admit that confrontation was not my strong suit, especially not with Janice, but it was going to be do or die today. After all, what was the worst that could happen? She wouldn't be able to fire me, because I would be respectful rather than insubordinate. I had gotten all of my insubordinate comments worked out of my system this morning in the mirror. It was hard for me to focus on work because every two minutes, I'd glance out the window, waiting for Janice to pull in.

After about thirty minutes, I finally asked Portia whether Janice was coming in at all.

"She called and said she'd be in by twelve. Why? Do you need to leave or something? I can let her know for you."

"No thanks." I strolled down to Corey's office just to chat a bit, but he wasn't in yet, either. I guess the only person who was really excited about getting to work today was me. On my way back to my office is where I ran into Shelley, who grabbed my arm and practically dragged me down the hallway.

"Girrrl!" she said, with clenched teeth and stretched eyes.

"What?" Shelley didn't respond but led me quickly out into the back parking lot.

"Have you seen Janice today?" she then asked.

"No. She called and said she would be in around twelve. Why?"

"Girl, after you left, Janice got buck wild! She got sooooo drunk." She paused for a moment and took note of my suit. "Where are you going today? To an usher board meeting or something? You look like Sister Elliott." We both burst into laughter; then she continued.

"After she won that trip, she started drinking like a fish and dancing all crazy with everybody. She was doing the Butt, the Shake, and the Huck-a-Buck!" Shelley did a few hoochie-fied dance moves to demonstrate Janice's behavior. "Just making a fool of herself!"

"Okay, and?"

"She got so drunk that she went to the bathroom, pulled down her clothes, and tried to sit on the toilet but fell down in the stall, peed all over the floor and on herself, threw up everywhere, and couldn't get up!"

"She fell with her clothes still down?" I gasped.

"Yes! Clothes down, booty out, stank, and pissy!"

"What! How did she get up or out, or whatever?"

"Monique and I went to the bathroom and heard all this grunting coming from the back corner. At first, we kind of ignored it because we figured somebody was just having a hard time taking care of their business, but then she started saying, 'Hey. Who is that? Can you help me?' So Monique and I walked back there and, girl! I think I'm going to have nightmares for a long time. I had to turn my head."

"Wait a minute. How did she fall over on the floor in a stall? The stall is only so big," I reasoned.

"She was in the handicapped stall, all sprawled out, legs gapped wide open."

"Ugh!" I shut my eyes and turned my head away at just the thought of that visual. "So y'all had to help her pull her wet drawers up?"

"We tried, but we couldn't lift her up! She was too heavy and drunk! I stayed there with her, trying not to throw up myself, while Monique went to find help. And guess who she came back with?"

"Who?" It was me who now had the stretched eyes.

"Mr. Wright, Corinthian Davis, Andre O'Neal, and Thomas Graham." Shelley counted on her fingers, emphasizing the names. As much as I didn't like Janice, I was horrified for her sake. "They had to go in there, lift her up off the floor, pull her clothes up, and walk her out of the bathroom." I shook my head, totally speechless. Now I almost would have given away a trip to Cancun to see that with my own two eyes.

"That is why she is so late today. She is hung over," Shelly added.

"I know I am not supposed to find pleasure in other people's misfortunes, but that is what she gets."

"And if you would have seen Mr. Wright . . . He was burgundy when he came out of there. He looked just like a boiled lobster."

"What about Corey?"

"You know how he is, always a gentleman, but he was looking so disgusted. And then, after they sat her down, she says to Corey, 'If I get a room, can you come take care of me tonight? You can see I got the goods,' and started bucking her hips in the chair." My jaw literally hit the ground.

"What did he say?"

"He looked at Mr. Wright and said, 'Mr. Wright, thank you for an unforgettable evening. I'll see you in the morning.' Then Mr. Wright looked at me and Monique and said, 'Can you ladies stay here with her until I secure a room for her next door?' So he got her a room at the Raddison. He, Thomas, and Andre took her over there."

"That is unbelievable."

"Well, believe it, 'cause it's true."

"Why didn't you call me and tell me last night?"

"Because I knew you weren't going to answer your phone after seeing how Janice stole that trip to Cancun! After all that work you and Andre did, she stood up there and took the credit for it. Wasn't the whole thing your idea?"

"Yeah, it was," I said, becoming angry all over again.

"I came up with that suggestion in that meeting when Corey was initially introduced, remember?"

"So you made the suggestion, worked on the project, and completed the restructuring, and Janice got the trip?" Shelley shook her head. "When are you quitting?" she teased. We both laughed, then went back into the office.

"Good morning, Mr. Davis," Shelley chimed as we passed his office.

"Good morning." He barely looked up as he spoke. He looked tired and worn out. I hoped that it wasn't due to him nursing Janice all night.

"Corey, will you have a few minutes today? I'd like to talk to you about something," I said. I glanced at his monitor and saw that he was replying to an email from Mr. Wright regarding Janice's behavior and what action needed to be taken. I couldn't read the entire thing, but I saw the word *termination* in bold. Janice terminated? That was highly unlikely, because rumor had it that she had done Mr. Wright more than a few "favors."

"Sure, December. What time were you thinking?" said Corey.

"Any time before Janice gets in," I replied.

"Okay. Give me about a half an hour. I'll stop by your office." He glanced up for a split second. "You look nice today," he added.

"What's on your mind?" Corey asked as he took a seat and crossed one ankle over his knee, leaned back in his chair, and huffed out a sigh. That was a sign to me that he was exasperated and probably could do without what I was going to say.

"Corey, I'm not exactly sure how I want to start this conversation, but I'll do my best not to take too much of your time."

"Okay," he said, more as a question than anything else.

"I feel that my talents and contributions to Wright-Way have not only been overlooked, but they've also been stolen, for lack of a better word, and used to further another individual's career."

"What specifically has caused you to feel this way?"

"Last night I watched my manager take full credit and a reward for work that she did not do. Work that was mine, from idea conception to implementation. Work that I slaved over for several weeks, ensuring that the end product was one that would be appreciated and valuable to the company. And last night I found out that my work was so appreciated and so valuable that the company is sending Janice on an all-expense-paid trip to Cancun to thank me." I paused to give Corey a chance to respond. He was silent for several seconds, studying my face.

"I'm sorry to hear that you feel cheated, December. At the same time, ultimately, the responsibility of the project fell on Janice's shoulders as the general manager. I hope that you understand that anytime you are working in a subordinate situation, the person functioning in the superior role does receive credit for the contributions of the employees he or she manages. My personal advice to you would be to carefully document your work to make sure that you receive credit for a job well done."

I blinked back tears, not that I had expected him to jump up, rant and rave, and say, "Oh, I'm going to see what we can do about that! She won't be going to Virginia Beach, let alone Mexico!" Well, maybe I had in my imagination.

"Now what I will do is talk to her," Corey continued, "and uncover specifically what her level of involvement was throughout this entire project. I'm most concerned that if what you are saying is true, that it may cause a negative ripple in morale, not just where you are concerned, but also of the entire staff, creating an environment where everyone will think twice about taking on additional responsibilities or special projects." He paused momentarily. "I also think that it is important that you share your views with Janice so she will realize the impact of her actions."

Those were the words I was waiting to hear.

Janice looked a hot mess when she made it into the office. Her frock was a super homely, kindergarten teacher–looking red jumper dress, layered over a white T-shirt. The dress had tulips embroidered across the front and a high waistline, which made her look pregnant. Her feet were out in the open in a pair of black Coach ABBI sandals with the dog leash clip detailing. (They were so cute. I had planned on getting a pair, but suddenly, I didn't want them anymore.) Her hair was wet, as if she had just stepped out of the shower, hanging in sloppy, water-matted tendrils around her shoulders, and was pushed back with a black knit headband. In about an hour, that mess would be dry and fully transformed into a bird's nest of frizzy curls. She hid her eyes behind a pair of Coach Daisy retro sunglasses. She looked better fit to be frolicking around the park with some grandchildren or something than to come to work. I was surprised that there wasn't a little froufrou puppy peeking out of the weaved basket–style purse she carried on her arm.

I waited about an hour, to allow her to get settled, before I psyched myself into going to talk to her. Before going, I asked myself what exactly I expected to accomplish by confronting her and concluded that I just needed to let her know that I was not to be taken advantage of.

"Janice, do you have a few minutes? I'd really like to discuss something with you," I said in a tone that suggested that I wasn't there to chitchat, but instead had a serious concern. Or so I thought.

"Uh . . . yeah. Come on in." She was hammering away at her keyboard and barely gave me any eye contact. I sat and waited patiently for her to give me her undivided attention. She began drafting aloud whatever she was working on between sips on a can of Slim-Fast. "Please . . . Cc me on . . . your . . . response to . . . Pat. . . ." She continued to type, then addressed me without looking.

"What is it?"

"Janice, I'd like to have your full consideration and would appreciate it if you could direct your attention solely toward me." *Mistake!* (Although she did stop typing and looked at me.)

"You don't decide my priorities. I am the general manager, and I know what I need to give attention to and when I need to give it. If you were on my level, you'd understand that. Don't you ever try to tell me where to put my focus." She pursed her lips and blinked her eyes rapidly.

I didn't say a single word but rose from my seat slowly, then, without warning, jumped across her desk and tried to choke the pure life out of that woman . . . and then I woke up from my daydream.

I didn't say a single word but sat there like a dummy, waiting another four minutes until she finished with her "priority." I think she intentionally took her time, to make her point that she considered me a lowly peon. Finally, she stopped typing and glanced at her watch.

"I have a conference call in about six minutes. What

is it?" she said. Okay. Clearly, this wasn't going to go well, but I was in it now.

"Janice, I wanted to talk to you about how you view my contributions made to the company, because I feel grossly unappreciated." I kept my tone even and professional.

"Well, while I feel that you add value to the company, you do have opportunity areas that you should give some thought to."

"I realize that there are some areas where room for improvement exists, but I am more specifically talking about my efforts on the core competency rewrite project. I can't help but feel that I was not fairly recognized for a project that I birthed, developed, and implemented, and to be honest with you, it was very difficult for me to watch you receive an honor for a project, my project, that you had very little input on." While I spoke, she spun her chair away from me and dug my employee record out of a file cabinet.

"Let me ask you a question, December," she said snidely. She opened the file folder and pulled out a document. "Do you remember signing this document when you started with the company?" She flipped to a sheet of paper bearing my signature on the bottom and slid it across the desk at me.

"This document, if you can recall, in short says that any idea, strategies, or proposals that you present as an employee become the property of the company," she said. "So I am completely confused as to why you would refer to the rewrite project as *your* project. I am even more confused about how you feel justified walking into my office to question me about recognition for work that falls within the scope of your job description."

She slid me a copy of my job description, which also had my signature on it, then continued. "If you read item number twelve, you will see that the creation and implementation of new business strategies is an expectation of your role."

She snatched both documents from the desk, stuffed them back in the folder, then made her closing statement. "I believe that I am most confused"—she folded her arms across her chest—"about the fact that you don't seem to understand that as a general manager, I own every project in this office, regardless of your perception of my contributions to its success. *You,*" she said, pointing, "report to me, not the other way around." She blinked even more rapidly than before.

I was infuriated but speechless at the same time. I guess she had told me. She left no room for a response. There was silence for a good ten seconds, while we had a staring contest. Then she dismissed me by simply saying, "Excuse me. I have work to do."

I walked out, feeling more defeated than ever before, even in my power suit and Prada shoes, which were now painfully scrubbing the backs of my heels with every step. I was going to have to find another job.

Eighteen

My truck was filled to the brim with food and other party paraphernalia for Shelley's book shower. Her guest list had grown from a few close friends to nearly fifty people, who would all crowd my living room with gifts for Shelley. Normally, I would have served frozen meatballs drowned in barbeque sauce, chicken wingettes, potato chips, deviled eggs, and a fruit tray; however, Corey (and Janice, only because of Shelley's invite) were coming. So my menu was kicked up a few notches to Santa Fe chicken wraps, apricot almond bruschetta with melted Brie, peppered herb cheese balls, and shrimp cocktail with tomato marmalade. Instead of the standard, run-of-the-mill congratulatory sheet cake, I opted for fresh sweet peaches with a scoop of frozen vanilla yogurt topped with raspberry sauce.

Now, I couldn't serve food like that on paper plates, so I purchased the clear plastic plates that resembled glass and the clear cutlery to match. My guests would be served Pecan Stream Chenin Blanc wine or sparkling bottled water. Of course, I owned only one set of six wineglasses, so I picked up a few new sets along with the cases of water.

Shelley had already arrived and was waiting for me by the time I got home with the food and my raped checkbook. She stepped out of her truck in a pair of raggedy jeans, a worn-out T-shirt, and house shoes. A pink hair bonnet, hiding a variety of bendable rollers, covered her head.

"Please tell me you haven't been anywhere else looking like that," I said.

"No, I came straight from home," she replied, helping me to tote trays inside. "I brought clothes to change into."

"That's a relief!" My condo had been professionally cleaned, including the windows, and was absolutely immaculate and 100 percent dust free. Shelley immediately took notice.

"Wow! It is super clean in here."

"As opposed to what? Super dirty?"

"You know what I mean. It's just extra clean today."

"Well, it's not every day that my girl gets picked up by a publisher. And it's really not every day that Corey comes over." I winked.

"Here. I brought you this." Shelley handed me a magazine once we sat the food down. "I got it in the mail today and knew it was for you."

The main heading read: NEED SOME EXTRA CASH? FIND $2000 IN YOUR CLOSET!

Before you go through the hassle of getting a loan, that cash may be right at your fingertips!

"I'm telling you, if you got rid of all those shoes, you wouldn't be scrambling from paycheck to paycheck," Shelley said.

"Ouch. That hurt, Shelley." I tossed the magazine on the countertop.

"I'm not trying to hurt you. I'm only trying to help."

"Mm-hmm. Well, right now you can help me bring the rest of the food and stuff in."

It took us only minutes to get the food set up and eloquently arranged; all we had to do pretty much was uncover it.

"This food looks good, but . . . What is it?" Shelley asked. She sampled the apricot Brie while I unpacked and rinsed the wineglasses, then set them out on the bar.

For the money I paid for it, the spread needed to do more than look good; it needed to physically jump up and make its own introductions. "Chicken wraps, shrimp, cheese balls, and whatever you are stuffing in your mouth." I slapped her hand playfully. "Stick those waters in the fridge, please. We have about an hour before people should start arriving. I'm going to go get in the shower."

"Deece, thank you for throwing this party for me." She grabbed me in a tight sisterly embrace. "It's so wonderful to have a friend like you to celebrate my successes with."

"You're so welcome. I'm proud of you, if I haven't told you already." I had told her that at least four times, but one more time didn't hurt. "Now let go of me so I can get dressed. You know I have to look extra good tonight."

"I don't know why. You won't even consider dating Corey as long as he's the boss."

"That doesn't mean I don't want to give him something to think about, now does it?" I sauntered to the linen closet and got fresh towels for Shelley. "If you need a plastic cap for your hair, look under the sink." At that, I disappeared into my room. Right before I got in the tub, my cell rang, displaying Corey's number.

"Hello," I answered, trying to sound unfazed.

"Hi, December. It's Corey."

"Oh, hi," I responded, pretending not to have known it was him.

"Listen, I seem to have lost the directions to your place. Can you give me directions from Diamond Estates?"

"So you are coming?"

"Yes, I'm looking forward to being there, but I can't stay long."

"What gift did you decide on?"

"I took your recommendation and bought a case of paper."

"Good choice." I gave him the directions and ended the call. I was looking forward to seeing Corey outside of the normal, everyday work environment, even though I anticipated that his demeanor would still be highly professional.

It was forty-five minutes later when the first guests began to arrive. I was still trying to wiggle into my clothes, a pair of white cuffed capris and a red, single-sleeved, one-shouldered knit top. "Shelley, get the door!" I yelled as I inserted the posts to a pair of white hoop earrings into my lobes. Instead of choosing white shoes, I selected my black, Kate Spade, wedge-heeled, braided-leather sandals, which had white striping in the heels, then touched up my toes with a coat of clear polish.

When I came out, Shelley introduced me to her mother, Ann and her aunt Barbara. I embraced both of them and showed them where they could put Shelley's gifts.

"You have a beautiful home," Shelley's mom commented, adoring my suede rug.

"This old place?" I waved a dismissive hand but felt

quite smug inside. "You ladies can just have a seat anywhere you choose. What can I get you to drink?"

"You got some Olde English, baby? I'ma little thirsty,"
Shelley's aunt said. *Old English? Isn't that a furniture polish?* I thought, but refrained from saying it.

"No, ma'am. I have some sparkling water and some
wine," I offered.

"Where we at? The wedding where Jesus performed
his first miracle?" Barbara said. She shook her head full
of stringy, Jheri-curled tendrils and pursed her lips.
"Lawd, I'ma have to go to the sto'."

"Don't start that stuff, Barbara, now," Shelley's mother
chastised. I couldn't help but giggle while I looked in
the fridge for other beverage choices. There were a
couple of Coronas left over from a book club meeting
I'd hosted several weeks back. I offered that as an alter-
native.

"Ms. Barbara, I have a Corona, if you'd like that."

Barbara looked disappointed and answered in a defeated tone, "Yeah, gimme that if that's all you got. I guess
that's gon' hafta do. I thought we was comin' to a sho'nuff
party." Shelley looked mortified and jumped to answer
the chiming door, letting in several more guests.

I was busy in the kitchen, warming up the wraps,
when the doorbell rang again.

"Shelley!" I heard Janice's voice before I saw her and
rolled my eyes. Next, I heard Andre's voice.

"Hey, Shelley," he said. Andre and Janice coming together? Couldn't be.

Janice rounded the corner from the foyer and entered the living-room area and spoke to Ann and Barbara and the other guests before spotting me across the
room.

"Hi, December!" she chirped. She looked around, with

wide eyes, absorbing every piece of decor and color that she could. "This is a cute place you have. It reminds me of the place I rented when I was back in college."

She was starting up already. I came to the conclusion that Janice didn't have a mother. She couldn't have had one, 'cause mommas teach their kids better than that. Why Shelley made me give her a rude, condescending behind an invite, I just didn't know. So what if she would have been the only person in the office not to be invited? The good thing about Janice being there, though, was she was on my turf. I'd whup her hind parts if I had to . . . well, that is, if I could fight. I could at least get a good soap-opera slap in if she got too far out of line.

"Respect my house, Janice," I said firmly, giving her a caveat.

"What? What do you mean? I was just saying . . ." She threw her hands up, trying to put on her usual "I wasn't trying to be insulting" act. I raised one eyebrow and gave her my most stoic look, daring her to say another word. "Well, um . . . Can I have a glass of wine please?"

"Sure, you can. Have a seat, and I'll bring it to you." She turned and quickly found a seat.

"You can put the claws away," Andre said, coming to stand beside me.

"She can get away with that stuff in the office, but she's on my stomping grounds now. She better act like she's got some sense!" I huffed. "And, by the way, what are you doing coming in with her?" I asked as I poured a few glasses of wine and loaded them onto a serving tray. I hadn't noticed Andre's lack of response until I glanced up and saw that he was looking like the cat that swallowed the canary. "Andre O'Neal!"

"What?" he asked, trying to claim innocence.

"What?" I mocked in my best impression of him. "We'll talk later."

A slew of other guests arrived before Corey made his appearance, looking finer than ever. He was very casually dressed in loose-fitting, drawstring-waist khaki-colored pants, with a matching loose-fitting shirt with a wife beater underneath. He had a pair of brown sandals on his feet and looked as if he had just flown in from Jamaica. After cordially speaking and adding his gift to the others, neatly arranged in the corner, he approached the bar and greeted me.

"December," he said, with a nod.

"Mr. Davis. I'm glad you could make it," I responded coolly. His eyes grazed over me gently before he lifted a plate and began to sample from the platters.

"The food looks really good." He bit into a shrimp. "It's far better than my usual cuisine of lunch meat and ramen noodles." He chuckled.

"Sounds like you could use a home-cooked meal every now and then," I replied. Before Corey could respond, I noticed that a brawl seemed to be breaking out in the living room.

"I don't know who you thank you are, chile, but don't slip up and make me hafta show you who I am!" Barbara was pointing a finger at Janice. Barbara had already drank both Coronas and was on her second glass of wine. "Chile, you liable to get your half white tail beat outta frame up in front of these good folks!" Ann was trying to calm Barbara down, while the other guests were snickering as Janice seemed to sink deeper into a corner of the couch.

"Oh, she's in there trying to grandstand," I concluded.

"I bet Janice hasn't got a good beat down in a long time."

Corey chuckled at my statements, piled more food on his plate, then took a seat on a nearby bar stool. I casually took a seat beside him and gestured Shelley to start opening gifts. She continued chatting with her guests.

"This is a great place you have here," Corey commented.

"Thank you. It's humble, but it's home."

"Did you do your own decorating? The mixture of browns is very warm and inviting." I nodded my head as I swallowed a gulp of water. He pointed to a nearby photo of me, Kisha, and one of her friends that'd we'd taken on my last visit to Atlanta. "Is that you with your sisters?"

"My sisters? No, I don't have any sisters," I quickly responded, taking another swig of water.

"Oh." He leaned back, crossing his arms over his chest, and raised his eyebrows. "I could have sworn you told me you were the third of three triplets." I nearly spit the water across the room, then burst into giggles, embarrassed.

"Corey, I am so sorry. I made that story up."

"Uh-huh." He nodded and bit into his bottom lip.

"I just get so many questions about my name, that's all. People are always curious about how it came about, and saying, 'I don't know,' just got kind of boring." I shrugged. "I'm actually an only child. My parents live in Africa. My dad works for the U.S. Embassy." I pointed to a large photo of my parents, dressed in African garb standing in the midst of a village marketplace. Corey was silent for a few more seconds as he looked at the photo, then turned to me and, in a voice just a hair above a whisper, blew me away.

"So were you making up the part about you being single and available?"

"Deece, come make a toast so I can open the gifts," Shelley said, running to me and grabbing my wrist.

"Uh . . . Can't you get your mom to do it?" I asked. "I'm sure she'd be glad to."

"But you're the hostess," she debated. "Please? I just don't want to start ripping boxes open." Talk about bad timing. "Come on, Deece! It would mean a lot to me."

"All right, all right! Quit your whining," I said. I placed my bottled water on the floor, beneath my chair, and stood. "I'll be back," I said, looking at Corey. He turned toward the bar, popped another cheese ball in his mouth, and gave me a slight nod.

"Ladies and gentleman!" I said. The room quieted before I continued. "As you know, there is an author among us, and I want to thank you all for coming to join in this celebration in Shelley's honor. Shelley has received a book deal from some big-time publisher in New York, and although I get to work with her every day, I am honored to be in her presence tonight." I bowed my head slightly in Shelley's direction. "We want to make a toast to Shelley tonight, so please raise your glasses or your bottles. Shelley, we are very proud of you and wish you much success in your writing career and know that this is just the beginning of something wonderful. I look forward to seeing your work in actual book form, not sheets and sheets of paper off the printer and stacks of photos." I paused while the group laughed. "And, I say, may we see you on the best sellers list! Hear! Hear!"

There was the sound of clinking glasses and bottles throughout the room and then silence as Shelley prepared to talk a little bit about her project, which was a coffee-table book about interior design. She then began opening boxes of all sizes. I really wanted to go back and talk to Corey, but, of course, I had to play hostess by collecting torn paper, handing Shelley the next gift, and writing down what she'd received and from whom for thank-you cards later.

Shelley was just getting started when Janice slinked her way from the couch over to Corey. *Tramp on the prowl*, I thought. That thought caused me to think about Andre's guilty look when I asked him about them arriving together. Maybe he had a sincere interest in Janice; I hoped not. Especially with the way she was trying to be all over Corey. She sat where I'd been sitting just moments ago and started chatting, laughing, and practically falling into Corey's lap. He seemed to be cordial enough, entertaining whatever she said, occasionally nodding and chuckling. Oh, if I could be a fly on the bar.

By the end of the night, Shelley had received several gift cards to an office supply store; a new laser printer; a flat-screen monitor; ink cartridges; pencils; ink pens; reams and reams of paper; journals; mood music; plot, character, and setting development books; sticky notes; desk accessories; and a bottle of pain reliever. Little by little, the guests trickled out, leaving Shelley, Andre, and me to clean up. Corey had slipped out while Shelley was opening packages. I never did get to chat with him like I'd wanted to.

I pulled a box of trash bags out of the cabinet while Shelley ran dishwater for the glasses, and Andre began gathering folding chairs from the living room.

"So, Andre, what was with you two arriving together?" I asked.

"It was nothing. We bumped into each other leaving the mall, after shopping for Shelley's gift. She asked if I wanted to ride with her, I said no thanks, and consequently, we arrived here at the same time." He shrugged it off.

"Yeah, right. I heard the Hampton branch needs a new manager," Shelley threw in.

"So have I," he responded. "And what are you saying in saying that? It's obvious that we didn't come together, because we would have had to leave together, right? Janice is gone. How would I get home if I didn't have my own car?"

"Oh yeah," Shelley answered.

Thirty minutes later, we had my place in pre-party condition. Andre and I helped Shelley load her gifts into her truck.

"Where'd you park?" she asked Andre.

"Way down there," he said, pointing toward the end of the block.

"Do you want a ride to your car?" asked Shelley.

"Nah, I'm going to take the trash out for December and move those folding chairs to the utility room," replied Andre.

"Okay. Well thanks for everything," said Shelley. She hugged us both, hopped into her truck, and sped off.

No sooner had she got around the corner than Andre turned to me and said, "I need you to give me a ride home."

Nineteen

"You'd better not breathe a word of this to anybody," Andre instructed. I pinched my lips with my fingers, indicating that my lips were sealed. I had to hear this story. "Not to Shelley, not to your friend Kisha, not to your momma. Don't even have a little talk with Jesus."

"Andre, as much stuff as you have on me, I can't even think about betraying your confidence."

"All right. Well, you know that there is an opening in Hampton right? Both the manager and the account rep walked out. Actually, Steve, who was the manager, officially quit, but Pat just got fed up with Janice and left."

"I heard something about her walking out, but you know me. I don't really get into the details. What I want to know is, why were there only two people staffed at the branch in the first place?"

"Janice couldn't control the turnover there. You know how she manages, poorly, and the Hampton branch got sick of it. Both sales guys quit, then one of the account reps, which left only Steve and Pat. Janice wouldn't allow Steve to hire anybody, and she was taking her pure sweet time filling those open slots, but at the same time demanding that the Hampton branch produce hours, as if it were fully staffed. Steve got burned out, put in his two weeks notice, and packed up. That just left Pat there all by herself."

"But didn't Steve quit like two months ago?"

"Yep."

"Pat was there working by herself for two months?"

"Yep."

"So Pat was there trying to build new accounts, maintain the existing accounts, answer the phone, do interviews, calculate payroll, take and fill job orders, do phone calls, and enter applications all by herself?" Andre nodded slowly as I drove. "And Janice didn't make any moves to staff the office? What sense did that make?"

"I don't know, but as I understand it, Pat asked to meet with her one day to discuss her concerns about being overloaded with work, and more importantly, her feeling unsafe in the office all day by herself. In a nutshell, Janice told her to love it or leave it."

"What?" I said disbelievingly.

"Pat told her that with the kind of applicants she was getting, ex-cons, felons, and the like, that she didn't feel safe being the only person there, and then add being a female on top of it. Then she brought up the fact that the office was understaffed, and there was no way she could produce hours without being better supported. Janice's response to her was that until she could get the office to produce at least one thousand hours a week, she wasn't adding any additional staff."

"Now that is crazy! So Janice was willing to take on the responsibility if something were to happen to Pat in the office all by herself?"

"Janice told her nothing like that had ever happened before, and she'd been in the business for twenty years.

So, the next day, Pat came to work all by herself and dropped the office keys in the drop box. Quit without saying a word."

"I can't much blame her. I thought I felt devalued!" I paused for a minute, then remembered that I was taking Andre home. "What does all that have to do with you sleeping with the enemy?" Andre chuckled.

"I just went in her office last week around six o'clock to talk to her about the potential of me being considered for the branch manager position in Hampton, and she came at a brother . . . hard."

"Y'all did the huck-a-buck in the office! You nasty!" I turned my nose up.

"How am I nasty? I'm a man. She offered it, so—"

"So you just take anything anybody gives you, with her dumpy little self? Looking like the dough boy's momma!"

"December, you gotta admit, Janice is not an ugly woman. I mean, she might be carrying an extra pound or two and got a big ol' jelly booty, but she's not ugly. She was like, 'I got something you can get before you get to Hampton.' Next thing I know, she was all bent over the top of her desk and was like come and get it, so I spanked it." Andre drew his hand back, then swung it down quickly in a spanking motion. "Pow! Wiggle, wiggle, pow! Wiggle, wiggle, pow!"

"I cannot even believe that I am having this conversation with you." I laughed, though I was disgusted. "What about protection? Please tell me you happened to have some."

"Oh, homegirl pulled a condom straight out of her pocka-book."

"Andre Demetrius O'Neal! You ought to be ashamed of yourself!"

"Oh, don't even try it, Deece, 'cause if your boy Corey

came at you, you know you would be pulling the panties down."

"Corey?" I tried to cover my surprise. "Corinthian Davis? Corey?" He'd caught me off guard with that one. I had tried to keep my whole attraction to Corey to myself.

"You like him. You know you do. I see it all in your face whenever that man comes around. You about had a fit when Janice sat by him tonight. Now say it ain't so," he challenged. I couldn't even think of a word to respond with. "Go 'head and try to deny it."

"What's that got to do with you poking Janice?" I defended. "Anyway, what is in it for her? 'Cause she don't do nothing that is not some strategic chess power move that is going to be for her benefit. Nothing!" I pulled into Andre's driveway, where his car sat, cold.

"I don't know. All I know is I hadn't had none since Monique and I stop seeing each other, and that's been a minute. Janice was offering; I was taking."

"Get out my truck," I said, playfully angry.

"Thanks for the ride." He grinned, hopped out, and slammed the truck door.

Twenty

I was pleasantly surprised to find an e-mail from Monique amongst my usual in-box messages. Skipping past the messages from Janice, my everyday coworkers, and even Corey, I clicked on Monique's message first.

Hi December,
Hope everything is going well with you. I saw your stats last month. Great job! That's a great photo of you on the company Web site.
Congrats and keep in touch!
Monique

I didn't think twice about clicking on reply.

Hi Monique!
It is so good to hear from you. Thanks for your kind words regarding my last month's numbers. You know the name of the game: hours, hours, hours!
I have to tell you again that you were so stunning

at the party! What is your secret for keeping your skin so radiant? And that gorgeous sheen to your hair? How do you do it!
Talk to you soon,
Deece

I wanted to also type, "And how in the world did you fit into that sock dress?" but I thought she might take offense.

Not ready to get to work just yet, I pulled the financing brochure from CPS out of the back of my planner. It wasn't that I hadn't read over it at least a dozen times, but it kept calling out to me, suggesting that I had missed something. Flipping to the back, I studied the payment matrix again. The smallest loan amount would give me a payment of fifty-two dollars a month for forty-eight months. That was just thirteen dollars a week. I could afford thirteen bucks. All I had to do was sacrifice one Chick-fil-A combo, a cup of coffee from Starbucks, and three trips to the break room snack machine per week. I could do that. Although the smallest loan would not fully cover the cost of my surgery, I could pay some of it in cash and split the balance on my cards. My mouse found its way to the Internet Explorer icon, then to the address bar, and I typed in the URL listed on the back of the brochure.

The site opened with images of faces of beautiful women with varying degrees of smiles, obviously pleased with their decisions to have their bodies altered in some way. Its headers read: CONFIDENCE: ENJOY THE CONFIDENCE THAT COMES FROM LOOKING YOUR BEST! AFFORDABLE: NOW YOU CAN HAVE THE COSMETIC PROCEDURE YOU'VE ALWAYS DREAMED OF BUT NEVER THOUGHT YOU COULD AFFORD. I was instantly more encouraged to have my procedures done. Talk about effective marketing strategies and tapping into buyers' emotions. I skipped over the introductory stuff and looked for the *Apply Now* link and clicked on it. That particular page indicated right up front that cash was the best way to pay. Yeah, yeah, yeah. It next stated that many customers who choose to pay cash acquired their funds through one or a combination of the following:

MONEY IN SAVINGS OR INVESTMENT ACCOUNTS

I had $138.15 in saving. And investments? What exactly were they again? I jotted a note to myself to become more financially savvy.

MONEY BORROWED FROM A 401(K) PLAN

I underlined the note I just made to become more financially savvy.

MONEY BORROWED FROM A LIFE INSURANCE POLICY

Would Wright-Way actually let me borrow money from my company-paid life insurance? Second note to self: *Review life insurance policy.*

MONEY BORROWED FROM FRIENDS OR RELATIVES

Yeah, right. I didn't have those kinds of friends. Well, I take that back. They would probably help me if I maybe needed to pay a bill real bad or would loan me some lunch money or something, but they weren't paying for new boobs.

ADVANCE OR LOAN FROM AN EMPLOYER

And have Janice in my business? No way.

MONEY FROM A TAX REFUND

Tax refund? No such thing for a single adult with no dependants.

PRESURGERY INSTALLMENT PLAN

In other words, layaway. I gave that option some thought. I was more of an instant gratification person, though. And . . . layaway at thirteen dollars a week would take too long. Plus layaway payments were generally much higher, with shorter terms than credit. Maybe if I saved fifty dollars a week . . . okay, twenty-five dollars. So knock out two trips to Chick-fil-A, two cups of coffee, and five break room trips. Totally doable. That would give me one hundred dollars per month times . . .

My e-mail in-box indicator chimed, notifying me of a new message. It was from Monique. I stopped my calculations to read her response.

Hi December,
I normally don't share my beauty secrets, but for you . . . I guess it'll be okay. ☺
For my skin, I make my own brown-sugar body scrub. It's pretty simple. All you do is take about a cup of brown sugar, mix it with some fresh-squeezed orange juice (about half the orange), and a cup of olive oil. Rub it on in the shower, then rinse it off. The sugar gets rid of dead skin, the orange juice tightens, and the oil locks in moisture. And there you have it—beautiful, silky smooth (not to mention sweet), glowing skin.
   Now, as for my hair, I deep condition it with warm shea butter every two weeks. I just rub some on, cover my hair with a plastic cap, and sit under the dryer for fifteen or twenty minutes. It's been the best thing I've EVER done for my hair.
   Let me know how these work for you if you try them.
Monique
PS: Here is my own little disclaimer . . . If you break out in hives, bumps, or itchy patches, you can't sue me. LOL! Seriously, you should be fine unless you are allergic to any of the ingredients.

Brown sugar and orange juice? Opening a new Web browser, I plugged *brown sugar, orange juice, scrubs,* and *skin* into the search box and struck the Enter key. (I'd come back to the breast augmentation financing alternatives page later.) Several brown sugar results were produced that seemed to validate Monique's regimen. I scanned through quite a few pages, becoming more and more convinced that my skin could have a rich, smooth glow just like hers. Orange juice as a tightener got me to thinking. I wondered if orange juice could tighten the skin on my breasts.

Not that I was looking that hard, but Monique's breasts were beyond perfect that night. Dr. Patrick's words played back in my head. *We'd cut away the extra skin right along here.* It wasn't that much extra skin, was it? I pulled the neckline of my sweater forward and peeped down at each breast. They didn't look so bad. Granted, I had on one of my better bras. Maybe brown sugar and orange juice would be a miracle cure. It wouldn't be as immediately gratifying as surgery, I thought, but it was, undeniably, less expensive. All I needed was the ingredients and a bowl or something to mix the concoction and keep it in. Something made of plastic, with a sealable lid, that could sit on the edge of the tub and look pretty at the same time.

I flipped back to the financing page, where I had not started to put in my personal information yet, and instead went to the Tupperware Web site to look for containers. Lucky for me, there was a huge banner midpage linking to their Last Chance section, where several items were on sale for 40 percent off. In just a few minutes, I found a set of three cute little bowls, colored in tangerine, kiwi, and mixed berry (i.e., orange, green, and pink), that would be perfect. They were on sale for only $12.50 (plus shipping and handling) and had a full lifetime warranty. The only bad thing about it was, I wanted to make the scrub tonight, not in three or four days, when the bowls arrived. I closed out of the site. Wal-Mart would have something.

I peeked back in my sweater again, visualizing my soon to be skintight breasts. Janice walked right in and caught me, and I jumped, letting go of my sweater. Having just got back from Cancun, she was three shades darker than her normal light cappuccino complexion, with sunburned skin peeling from her forehead.

"What are you doing?" she asked, looking perplexed. "Admiring yourself?"

"No, I had a paper clip in my mouth, and it fell down my shirt." I pretended to search and dig for, then shake free, the clip that wasn't there.

"Why is your door closed? You need to let some air in here." She swung the door open fully, then sat down. "Ahh! That's better!"

"Just trying to concentrate on my deliverables." Since Janice had come to my office alone, she probably didn't want much of anything. She pulled her belittling shenanigans only in front of other people. "So how was your trip?" I asked, trying to hide my sarcasm and bitterness.

"Oh . . . my . . . God! It was wonderful!" She leaned back and closed her eyes, transporting herself back to the vacation my hard work had paid for. I quickly stuck my tongue out while her eyes were shut and nearly got caught doing so. "I ended up taking my mom. You know she's been going through so much since she had that mild stroke a few months ago."

I really had nothing against Janice's mom and wanted to show sympathy, but honestly, I didn't know her mom from a can of paint and really didn't care if she lived or died, not that I would wish death on anybody's mom. Okay. Maybe I did, somewhere in my heart, care if the woman died, but I really didn't care that she got to go to Cancun and I didn't. The least Janice could have done was take me. I would have ditched her as soon as the plane hit the ground, though.

"Cancun has to be the closest thing to heaven," she continued.

While she went on about snorkeling and sunbathing, my thoughts drifted off to making my grocery list. I wondered if navel oranges would produce better results. Or should I use California oranges? Suppose I used lemon juice instead. Wouldn't that be like rubbing lemonade on my skin? I guess I would taste pretty good.

"So the cruise was actually pretty disappointing after she got sick. . . . ."

I'd e-mail Monique back and ask her how often she did her scrub. Were Monique's breasts real? Maybe she'd got a little lift and fill herself. Nah, she was too natural of a woman, from what I could tell. I mean, anybody walking around with their hair all over their head like Oon-Fufu and rubbing olive oil and sugar on their body, dressed in a sock with beads on it, probably wasn't down with plastic surgery.

"And I brought you something," Janice sang. I guess I was supposed to jump up and down and start clapping my hands like a little show monkey or something.

"Thanks for thinking of me, Janice," I said nonchalantly.

"Boy! Nothing excites you, does it?"

"I'm sorry. I was just thinking about some follow-up calls I need to make in a little while." From a large shopping bag, she pulled a rectangular package wrapped in black tissue paper and embellished with a lei made of small white and brown shells and tied around it like a ribbon. I took it and laid it on my desk, then turned to my computer to enter a job order.

"You're not going to open it?" She was almost offended.

"Um . . . I'd rather open it when I get home so I have a true opportunity to look at and appreciate it. When I'm at work, I can't do that, because I'm too distracted by work. Then the gift kinda gets tossed to the side, and I don't want to do that, you know?" Oh, I was good.

"Always thinking about work." She gave me her best patronizing look. "And that's why you're my superstar! Well, enjoy it. I'm sure you're going to love it." She stood to leave but stopped in the doorway. "Just so you know, that is a special gift." She winked. "Everybody else got a key ring, well, except Andre. I brought him a little something special, too."

"Thanks," I said, forcing a smile. *Yeah, I know what kind of gift you have for Andre.*

"I just thought I'd let you know that. You know how haters are. But you and Andre deserve it. Let me know what you think of it!"

Regardless of what it was, it would hardly compare to living in paradise for a whole week.

"I will."

I unwrapped the gift shortly after Janice left my office, to find a photo album that held 4 x 6 prints. The unique cover was made of a piece of thin wood covered in clear shellac and had some sort of twine attached to its front, which spelled out Mexico. I actually thought it was kind of cute . . . until I looked on the back and saw that Janice had inadvertently left the price tag on it.

It read, "Three for ten dollars."

Twenty-One

*Financing Alternatives—Your Solution for Financing
Your Dreams!*

Ms. Elliot,

*We recently received your loan application for your
anticipated cosmetic surgery procedures.*

*As much as we'd like to assist you in achieving the
body you've longed for, unfortunately, we simply cannot
approve your request at this time.*

*This decision comes after a careful review of your
credit report, which reflects adverse payment history with
various other creditors.*

*If you feel this decision has been made in error, please
feel free to give us a call to personally discuss your situation with one of our highly trained credit specialists, who
will gladly take a more in-depth look at your application.*

*If we have made an error in our decision making, we
sincerely apologize and look forward to financing your
dream of a more beautiful you.*

Respectfully,

Sharmaine Bennette

Account Manager

I crumpled the letter and threw it into the trash can on my way inside the gym. I knew I had a few late payments here and there on a few accounts, but fine. They didn't have to help me. I'd find a way to do it myself. There had to be a way for me to make some extra cash.

Not feeling like being in the Body Pump class tonight, I signed the treadmill waiting list, then made my way over to the Nautilus equipment. After a few reps of leg extensions, thigh abductors squeezes, and sitting crunches, my treadmill was ready. Several TVs were facing the treadmills, tuned to various stations. Directly in front of me, the latter part of *Seinfeld* was playing, followed by an infomercial for real estate investing. I'd seen it twenty times before but this time was forced to give attention to it. Person after person gave his or her testimony of how the program had changed their individual lives.

> *I never dreamed that my net worth would be 1.2 million dollars, but today I own nine properties, which are producing an astounding amount of residual income. And it was so incredibly easy. All I did was follow the step-by-step instructions in the book, and before I knew it, I was walking away from the closing table with more money than I had made all year working full time as a customer service manager. I'll never work for another company again.*
>
> *Before I bought the You Can Own It! program, I was so behind on my bills, and my credit was just terrible. I had received an eviction notice and didn't know how I was going to explain to my wife and kids that in three weeks we were going to have to move out of our apartment and into the street. I was sitting up late one night, after my family went to bed, because I couldn't sleep not knowing where we would go, when I came across the program on TV. I decided to take a chance, and it was the best thing I've ever done! In less than thirty days, I had*

found a beautiful home for me and my family. Since then I've bought three other properties, and right now we are living in a six-bedroom, four-bath home, with a pool and recreation room for the kids. Buying this program was the answer to my prayers.

The testimonials seemed pretty convincing, and the program was being offered at no risk for ten dollars, giving me thirty days to review. After that, it would cost fifty dollars a month for six months to pay for it fully. If I could buy a property, then turn around and sell it in thirty days, like the people on TV did, six fifty-dollar payments would be a piece of cake. I kept jogging, chanting the toll-free number to myself, making a mental note to call them once I got home.

I moved away from the TVs and onto the elliptical machine and began cycling. The more I pushed forward, the more pessimistic I felt about buying the real estate investment program. I mean, did I really want to spend my evenings looking at properties, filling out paperwork, and trying to buy houses, then turn around and sell them? Plus, it was going to cost me three hundred and something dollars. I needed something simpler . . . and cheaper.

Maybe I could sell icebergs. That was simple and cheap enough; all I needed was some flavored drink mix, some sugar, and some paper cups. I could freeze the cups in the morning, before I went to work, then open my door to the neighborhood kids when I got home in the afternoons. Perhaps I was being a little juvenile. It would be different if I had a kid or something that I could hide behind, all in the name of teaching my child something about entrepreneurship. Icebergs? *Okay, December. Pull it together and grow up.*

I could look into selling Your Beautiful You products. I was forever running into some woman, who had on too much make-up, asking me if I was interested in a wonderful business opportunity that could supplement my income or replace my current job. These ladies would pour the compliments on thick, too, not that I didn't think I was worthy of them, but I knew they were just sales tactics. I wasn't really interested in packing my truck up with cosmetics, going to someone's home, entertaining all night, then hoping they'd buy some lipstick. Maybe I could just take orders from a catalogue. How hard could that be? I'd look into it later.

I could always strip. I'd have my surgery money in no time. Nah. I'd be willing to become the laughingstock of the neighborhood by selling icebergs out my backdoor before I'd start stripping.

On my way home, I stopped by the post office to pick up a package from the American Association for Aerobics and Fitness Professionals, then visited a smoothie bar and ordered myself a large strawberry, banana, and pineapple protein shake. While the girl behind the counter prepared my order, I opened the package, skipped over a few cover documents, and pulled out a certificate.

This certificate is awarded to December Elliott in recognition of her satisfactory completion of the prescribed course Aerobics Instructor—Step and Kickboxing for Group Exercise & Personal Trainer.

I had no current plans to teach classes, but I was still proud of myself, even though I'd be making monthly tuition payments for a good while. With a huge grin on my face, I forked over six bucks for my shake and headed home.

Twenty-Two

User Name: Deece79
Password: xxxxxxxx

*Welcome back, December! There have been 313,619 jobs
added in the past 14 days.*
Number of times your résumé has been viewed: 22
Number of employment matches: 6
To view these matches click here.

*Below are the jobs posted within the past 24 hours that
match your skills and background.*

Sales Manager/Account Manager	*Norfolk, VA*
Account Executive	*Virginia Beach, VA*
Managers Needed/$250,000 yr. Potential	*Norfolk, VA*
Community Relations Manager	*Chesapeake, VA*
Customer Service Coordinator	*Hampton, VA*
Assistant Store Manager	*Virginia Beach, VA*

I viewed all six positions, which were supposed to match my skill set, and for one reason or another, was disappointed with all of them—mostly for salary reasons. All of them would cause me to suffer a significant decrease in income, and with my debt as out of control as it was, I couldn't afford to make less money.

After visiting four other job sites, I applied for seven more jobs. They weren't dream jobs but anything had to be better than continuing at Wright-Way, or more accurately said, anything had to be better than working for Janice. If I didn't have so many bills to pay, I would be very tempted to do what Pat did: Just go to work one day and quit.

Bored, I surfed from one site to another, looking for nothing in particular, then challenged myself to go to a debt reduction Web site. After reading some basic information about reduction strategies, I opened my desk drawer and grabbed my folder full of bills, turned to my computer again, and plugged in all of my credit card balances, interest rates, and minimum payment amounts. Taking a deep breath, I clicked on *Calculate* and nearly passed out. It would take me forty-one years and ten months to get out of debt. I now realized what finance people meant when they said if a person is in debt, he or she is a slave.

This sucked. It more than sucked. It was downright depressing. Forty-one years and ten months from now, I'd be almost seventy years old.

I needed an escape. Nothing elaborate, nothing fancy, no white sandy beaches required, just an escape from my current reality. I needed a girlfriend trip. I called Kisha.

"Hey," she answered after three rings.

"What are you doing next weekend?"

"Nothing," she replied.

"Good. I'm coming down there. I need a girlfriend getaway."

"Okay. Come on."

"I'm serious." I made a few clicks to a travel Web site and began pricing a ticket to Atlanta.

"Okay. Me, too. You know you are welcome to come down anytime. I've been telling you to come down here for three months, anyway."

"Can you pick me up from the airport?"

"Of course. What time are you going to get here?"

"Hold on. I'm checking now." I paused for a few seconds. "If I leave here at six thirty, I will land there by eight, on Friday night. Then I'll fly out on Sunday night at ten. No wait. I'm going to request that Monday off and make it a three-day weekend." I hit Alt/tab and shot an e-mail to Janice, requesting a personal day, stating that I had a very important appointment that I'd just received notification of and it could not be missed.

"Eight will be perfect. We can go to Cafe Intermezzos and have dessert out on the patio. I'll be there. What do you want to do when you get here?"

"Cry."

"Cry? For what? What's wrong?" Kisha asked, concerned.

"I don't know. I just need to get away for a minute, that's all. We don't have to do anything special. I'm just going to throw some clothes in a bag and crash for the weekend."

"That's fine with me. I'll get the guest room ready."

"Thanks, Kisha," I said dismally. "All right. Let me get back to work. I'll call you later."

Before we got off the phone, I'd booked my flight, which was fairly inexpensive from Norfolk, so I used my VISA CheckCard to purchase the ticket, rather than adding it to any of my current card balances. I made a vow to myself that this would be my last little piece of luxury before I began my plight to free myself from debt's prison. No more shopping sprees; no cruise in November, even priced as a low $219; no more designer purses; no more buying more than what I actually needed; and no more shoes!

With my new commitment to not do any more major shopping, I'd never been so excited about buying oranges, sugar, olive oil, and bowls before in my life. I deemed these four items as necessities because even though I wouldn't be spending money at Sephora anymore, I still needed to take care of and pamper myself. With my homemade scrub, I'd be saving a ton of money. Not to mention tightening my skin and avoiding surgical procedure costs.

As soon as I got in the truck, I reached behind the passenger's seat to get my "walking in Wal-Mart after work" shoes, which was a pair of clear mini-heeled flip-flops. I kept them in the truck for times just like this, when I needed to get my dogs out of the shoes of the day. I also had an alternate pair in the truck, for the days I had on panty hose, because everybody knows that wearing panty hose and flip-flops is about as country as a plaid living-room couch sitting on the front porch as patio furniture.

I unbuckled the ankle straps of my brown sandals. These straps were actually separate from the sandals altogether and were made like pieces of a chain. The heel had to be inserted in the last link of the chain; then the rest of the chain came up the back of my heel and around my ankle. Those bad boys were hot, but they hurt like I don't know what by the end of the day.

Thank goodness for flip-flops. They were actually good for something.

In the produce section at Wal-Mart, I studied the different oranges, picking them up, squeezing them, smelling their skins, rolling them in my palms, trying to decide whether to buy loose or bagged. I finally settled on a bag of nicely colored, fresh-smelling seedless California navels.

In the sugar aisle, I found dark brown sugar and light brown sugar—in a box, in a bag, and lightly packed. The olive oil aisle was no better. There was regular, virgin, extra-virgin, fresh cold-pressed (as opposed to hot-pressed?), light-tasting, better for bread, better for salads, and so on. After several minutes, I picked a large bottle of extra-virgin. How were olives virgins, anyway? . . . And how exactly did they become extra-virgin? I felt like an extra virgin; I couldn't remember the last time I . . .

"What's up, girl?" Terrance had crept up behind me and wrapped his arms around my waist.

"Boy, get off of me," I snapped.

"Oh, it's like that now?" He rocked back on his heels and crossed his arms over his chest. He was dressed in a slate blue Nike jogging suit, with matching shoes that had probably never seen a track, gym, or court.

"It's like it's always been. You're always making a bunch of empty promises that you have no intentions of keeping. You are nothing but a liar."

"Nah, it ain't like that." He moved closer to me to let a woman with two kids by. "I mean, I just be having a lot on my mind, man."

"Man? Do I look like a man to you? I must look like a fool to you, 'cause that's what you keep taking me for. Oh, I forgot. You love me and want me and all that crap, but you can't remember my name, and I look and feel like Tiffany to you!"

I'd dipped my head so hard, my braids fell from the loose pinup style I'd arranged and cascaded around my shoulders. I didn't mean to, but I started crying right there in the store. I quickly pulled myself together and used my hands to blend my tears into my make-up. Terrance tried to pull me to him, but I yanked away and pushed my shopping cart down the aisle. He followed right behind.

"What you crying for?" he said.

That was a good question. Why was I crying? Why did I let Terrance waltz back into my life after his track record proved to me that he really wasn't interested in me? He didn't want anything: not a relationship, not a marriage, not a future. He just wanted sex on his terms. He was just like the flip-flops I had on my feet: they made a lot of noise, but they weren't really much of anything. I spun around quickly.

"Get gone," I spat, "'fore I spray you with this fake mace!" I fumbled through my purse for my keys, which had pepper spray attached to them.

"Deece, you know I be working and stuff. . . ."

He obviously didn't remember his hot dog water bath, because if he had, that memory would have caused him to leave me alone. He didn't get another word out for breaking out in a fit of coughs from the face full of pepper spray I delivered. I coughed a few times myself but kept moving, only glancing back once. He was bent over, fanning his face wildly and gasping for air. I sped to the water aisle, desperately tore the plastic from a case of twenty-four one-liter bottles, and gulped down an entire bottle, then placed the open case in my cart.

Taking two minutes to breathe and calm down, I noticed that I was right in front of the aluminum foil, sandwich bags, and storage bowls. They happened to be on the same aisle as the water. Without a lengthy deliberation, I grabbed a package of four bowls and moved toward the health and beauty aids section. Really, I was ready to go, but I didn't want to risk running into Terrance at the registers or in the parking lot. It would be more difficult for him to locate me in the store.

While I was looking for nothing in particular on the lotion aisle, Monique's recipe for shiny hair ran across my mind. I began picking up various shea butter products and reading the labels. All of them boasted of being able to work wonders for skin. If I mixed this with the brown sugar, I wondered what kind of concoction I'd have. Taking the top off of a jar of 100 percent pure shea butter, I first smelled it (ugh!), then stuck my finger in it to test its consistency (a little hard, but nothing that a few minutes in the microwave couldn't fix). I tossed it in the cart, along with a large jar of cocoa butter, planning on melting both butters down and mixing them up. Hopefully, the cocoa scent would tone down that awful old smell of the shea butter, and the shea would tone down the heavy chocolate smell from the cocoa butter. At any rate, I planned on being one smooth, shining, radiant, chocolate/orange-smelling sister.

After my shower and body scrub, followed by a shea and cocoa butter slathering, I fell totally in love with myself. My skin was so smooth, I couldn't believe it. I stood in front of my full-length mirror in my bedroom and examined every inch of my body, pleased with what I saw. On the other hand, I had so much butter on my body, I could have been thrown in a frying pan, toasted on both sides, and served as a grilled cheese sandwich.

I slipped into an oversized T-shirt and white socks, and some big ol' "he ain't gettin' none tonight" bloomers; poured myself a glass of wine; sank into my chaise; and picked up the magazine that Shelley had brought me the night of the party. Flipping to page fifty-seven, I began reading the cover article.

Need Some Extra Cash? Find $2000 In Your Closet! Chances are, you have hundreds of dollars of clothes just hanging in your closet. By simply taking inventory and selling on consignment some of the things in your closet that you may not have even thought about all year, you can find yourself with quite a bit of cash on hand. Follow these easy steps, and before you know it, you will be on your way to the bank!

The article gave instructions to sort my clothes into four piles: Love It, Like It, Hate It, and Unsure. Then it went on to say I could keep my Love It and Like It piles, but I should send the other two to the consignment shop. Hmmm. I went to my bedroom closet, picked out a few random items, and tried to estimate what I could get for them. A Bebe rhinestone-studded T-shirt had to be good for at least fifteen bucks. I was sure that my sweatshirt that I got from Michael Jordan's restaurant in Chicago back in 1996 was worth a couple hundred dollars because the restaurant didn't exist anymore (well, maybe on eBay it would be). I took out a Vera Wang silk beaded blouse, which I had actually gotten for a little of nothing because it had a tiny (but completely repairable) hole in the back seam. The $248 tag was still on it. If it sold for that, that would be easy money, with no effort. Maybe consignment was the way to go.

I went to my second bedroom and scanned my shoes. Now, here is where the big money was. Three hundred sixty-five different boxes were staring me in the face, all stacked neatly against one wall. In looking at just a few

boxes, I calculated nearly $1200. Granted, they would
have to sell for what I thought they were worth. I began
randomly pulling down and opening boxes, oohing and
aahing at the varied shoes I'd bought over the years. Before I could get too emotionally involved, however, I
pulled myself away; went to the foyer, where I'd dropped
my work bag; and retrieved the manila folder that had
all of my bills—opened, unfolded, and viewed—and a
printout of the matrix from the online debt tool, with
all my numbers plugged in. I grabbed a box of pushpins
from my desk, then went back to the bedroom.

"This means war," I said to my shoes, but more to myself. I began tacking the bills up on the wall opposite
the shoe boxes. It was by having the bills in my sight
that I planned on garnering the strength I would need
to sell my prized possessions—my shoes.

Twenty-Three

It was right at nine o'clock when my doorbell rang.

"This better not be Terrance," I said out loud, rising from the sea of shoes and boxes I now had scattered all over the room. I took the phone with me to the door, ready to call the police if it was him. Looking through the peephole, my eyes became as wide as dessert plates. It was Corey! I couldn't open the door with what I had on: my big bloomers and T-shirt.

"Uh . . . just a minute," I called.

I ran to my bedroom, snatching my night scarf off my head on the way, quickly filed through a variety of pajamas I had hanging in my closet, and tried to pick a pair that wouldn't look like I was trying to be impressive, but wouldn't make me look like Granny Magoo, either. I opted for a sky blue brushed-silk shorts set with satin trim. The shorts weren't so short that they showed my cheeks, but they definitely said, "You caught me relaxing at home." They did showcase my now well-sculpted thighs. I hadn't really noticed how effective my workouts had been until now. And then, with my fresh sugar scrub and butter rub, my muscle tone was more defined and glowing.

I pulled a few braids out from the ball I kept them in at night, let them fall by my ears, then cracked the door.

"Corey?" I said. I felt like I was on a soap opera. . . .

> *"December, I've been waiting for a woman like you all my life, and I just can't let you leave me for Michael." (He drops to one knee). "Marry me, December. Don't say no."*
>
> *"But, Corey, what about—"*
>
> *"Please don't say it. Don't say anything . . . but yes."*
>
> *I pause pensively while the show's background piano theme begins to play; then we fade into a commercial.*

Okay, back to reality.

"May I come in? I promise I won't be long," he said. His eyes stayed respectfully above my shoulders as he stepped in. He looked as if he'd not too long ago left the office. His shirt was still tucked neatly inside a pair of navy slacks; the sleeves were rolled to just below his elbows; while he still had on a tie, it had been loosened; and the top button of his shirt was undone. His feet were still in his black slip-on Cole Haans.

"Have a seat. Can I get you something to drink?" I asked rhetorically while I made my way to the kitchen. "I wasn't expecting anyone tonight and certainly never expected that you would be here." I started to pull down two wineglasses, but then thought that it might send the wrong message. I grabbed two bottled waters instead, returned to the living room, and sat across from him on the chaise after handing him a bottle.

"December, I know that I've crossed boundaries by coming here at this hour, especially unannounced. However, I didn't want to let this wait until morning." He cleared his throat before he continued. "I know we've had conversations about a few of your concerns here of late, and I am very concerned about your perception of Wright-Way and its ability to support your goals in terms of professional growth and development."

"Okay . . . ?" I shrugged. What had happened after I'd left work today that had him ringing my doorbell?

"Let me just get to the point. In retrospect, I think your concerns as shared with me foreshadowed recent events and I may not have been as attentive as I needed to be. But it's come to my attention that you are seeking other employment, outside of the company."

Silence hung in the air. I felt like if I spoke next, I'd be at a disadvantage. But by keeping my thoughts to myself, he had no clue what I was thinking. Option B, definitely.

He continued "You are an exceptionally talented and valuable employee, which, I believe, I have shared with you on more than one occasion. While I realize that there have been a few things that have been very upsetting to you, I failed to recognize how much impact those things have had. What I'm trying to say is, I'd really hate to see you leave the company. Losing you, especially to a competitor, would be an incredible loss for Wright-Way, both from a personal and performance standpoint. I'd like to hear from you what can be done to have you reconsider the possibility of your leaving."

I gave his statements some thought, then became slowly infuriated at his unmitigated gall to crack my door at nine o'clock at night to ask me not to quit my job so he could keep performance up. I stared at him incredulously through narrowed eyes, shaking my head.

"Mr. Davis, I believe it's time for you to leave." I rose slowly and deliberately from the chaise, walked to my front door, and folded my arms. He remained seated, watching me, with a partially shocked look on his face, then sighed, slapped his hands on his knees, and stood. His steps toward the door were measured, and his eyes were directed at the floor, as he seemed to contemplate saying something further. When he reached me, he stared into my eyes. I was certain that the defiant look on my face dared him to say another word. Nonetheless, he took a chance and spoke.

"We really don't want to see you go, and I had to at least ask if there was a retention opportunity."

"I cannot believe that you are so numbers conscious that you have brought yourself to my personal living space to pretend that you are concerned about me. Do you really want to know what you can do to keep me, Corey?" I spat. "Well, you can start by getting rid of that overly pompous, self-righteous, condescending, stank. . . ."

Corey grabbed me and kissed me fully on the mouth, inhaling any other adjectives I was ready to spew to describe Janice. Whatever words I had not already said slid totally and completely from my mind. My eyes fluttered closed, and my body gave in to the strength of his arms, the solidness of his chest, the feel of his goatee against my chin, and the potency of his kiss. I literally got weak in the knees, and this man had to hold me up.

He pulled back gently. "It's not about the numbers," he whispered. "It's not about performance. I'm in love with you, December."

His brows furrowed as he looked directly into my eyes. I was too intimidated by the intensity of his gaze, so I turned my head toward the living room, looking away. With his index finger on my chin, he turned my head back toward him.

"You're an incredible woman. Beautiful, professional, intellectual, alluring, stimulating . . . And I've had to pre-

tend not to notice. I've had to struggle with my attraction to you for too long. And while I have suppressed my
desires and respected professional and ethical boundaries, I can't just sit back and just let you disappear on
me." He paused for several seconds. "I didn't come
here to ask you not to leave the company. I came to ask
you not to leave me."

I stood silently, at a total loss for words, feeling a
gamut of emotions that I couldn't rightfully describe.

He went on. "If you decide to leave the company, I
can say that as your manager, it will be a significant loss,
but personally, I can't say that I'll be completely sad-
dened to see you go. I hope you understand what I
mean when I say that."

He moved in and kissed me on the cheek, then
leaned back and studied my eyes once more. With one
hand now resting on the doorknob, he said, "I better
go," and let himself out.

Twenty-Four

Shelley popped into my office, ready to give me the latest on what she'd overheard through the walls.

"December, you will never guess . . ." She stopped abruptly, then eyed me suspiciously. "What'd you do last night?"

"Nothing." The glow I wore just couldn't be hidden (and it wasn't from the brown sugar, either).

"Yes, you did," she insisted. "Why are you looking like that?"

"Like what?" I responded, innocently straightening a stack of files on the corner of my desk.

"You broke your dry spell!" Her eyes widened. "You been glowing like that for a whole week now. Get up. Let me see if you are walking funny."

"Shelley, cut it out. Who would I break my dry spell with? Andre? You know I'm not seeing anyone." There was no way I could share with her that I was still floating from a kiss that was nearly a week old now.

"I heard Andre is doin' the do with Janice," she said knowingly.

"Girl, you know you can't believe everything you hear." I kept my response nonchalant, to not give any indication as to what I knew and what Andre had shared with me in confidence.

"I think it's true," she went on. "You haven't noticed that she is always in his office?" she asked, emphasizing "always."

"As long as she stays out of mine, that's fine with me." No sooner had I let that slip from my lips than my door swung open. Speak of the devil. A devil who didn't believe in knocking first.

"Good morning, ladies," Janice sang. "What are you two working on?"

"Just reviewing our daily tasks, that's all," I replied.

"Well, good. Because, December, I need to see you at ten thirty in my office," replied Janice. She smiled. "So make sure that your schedule is clear. Shelley, can you pick up any interviews that come in for her?"

"Sure, Janice, I'd be glad to," replied Shelley.

"Great. I'll see you then." Janice winked. "Shelley, can you walk with me over to finance? I need you to help me with some records over there. I've been looking for some trending information. . . ." Her voice trailed off as Shelley escorted her down the hall.

My stomach had instantly started turning flips. What in the world did she want with me now? *Think, December. Think!* I knew I'd not gotten any more phone calls, because I'd called all of my creditors and had given them each my cell phone number and asked them to delete my work number altogether. While they had me on the phone, I had made them all promises to pay each bill each week until they were all current, which I had done. She couldn't have known that Corey was at my house earlier this week. I hadn't shared it with anyone, and I knew beyond a shadow of a doubt that he wouldn't share it. I hadn't put her name on the wall in the men's room, although I was responsible for it being written in permanent marker in the ladies' room, with a few choice descriptions, but no one could prove that I'd done it. I wasn't even a suspect. I concluded that she'd gotten wind of the same information that Corey had gotten and was ready to, in some way, rake me over the coals. Well, this time I'd be ready.

I opened up the word processing software on my computer, and my fingers got to work.

To: Janice Wheeler
From: December Elliott
Cc: Corinthian Davis
Re: Resignation

Ms. Wheeler,
    While I have thoroughly enjoyed working for Wright-Way Staffing, it is necessary that I make a career path decision that will better align with both my personal and professional goals.
    After long and careful thought about various factors, I have finalized my decision to resign from Wright-Way Staffing, effective immediately.
    I regret leaving the productive relationships that I've built and maintained during my tenure; however, this change is most beneficial to my long-term career goals and personal objectives.
    I am ever grateful for the professional growth and development I've experienced while working under your leadership, and I wish you and the entire Wright-Way staff many years of professional success.
Sincerely,
December Elliott

I'd flip hamburgers and scoop ice cream before I tolerated one more of her demeaning and berating incidents. Peeking out into the hallway, I saw that there was no one near the group printer, or even out of their offices. I quickly sent the document to the printer and scurried to pick it up before it could be seen by anyone.

Satisfied and ready, I tucked three copies into a manila folder and placed the folder under my planner, which I'd take to this "meeting." Oh, I was going to fix her little red wagon.

It was only a little past eight. I had about two and a half hours to land a new job. Ignoring the list of tasks I was to complete that morning, I started applying for jobs like crazy. If I qualified for it, I applied. By the time 10:00 A.M. rolled around, I had, with a few clicks of a mouse, responded to twenty-two job postings.

There was a box under my desk of various knick-knacks with the company's logo on them that were used to put together goodie bags for prospective clients. I dumped the items into my bottom desk drawer, then filled the box with my personal items: a photo of me, Shelley, Andre, and Monique at the employee appreciation dinner; a cup that I kept pencils and pens in; a desk lamp from home; a box of personalized stationery; a coffee mug with my name on it; a small vase, in which I was supposed to put a flower every week, which had been empty for months now; a collection of dusty birthday cards given to me by my coworkers last year; a stack of CDs; and my CD player. Not caring if anyone was looking, but at the same time trying to be inconspicuous, I took the box out to my truck. With fifteen minutes left in my Wright-Way career, I changed my voice mail greeting to the standard automated one rather than my personal voice, scanned my hard drive for any personal files that I needed to save on my thumb drive or delete, then went onto the Internet to delete my site visits history.

Two minutes left. I decided to have a moment of silence, or in other words, pray.

Lord, be with me while I go in here to this meeting. Please help me not to knock the stank offa this woman, although she could use a litte destanking, but I'll let You handle that. Amen. Oh yeah, please help me to find another job real real, fast! Amen.

There was boldness in every step of my mid-morning stroll to the showdown. On my way, I tried to create a snappy statement that I could use when I delivered my resignation.

Janice: I'm putting you on notice.

Me: No, you aren't, because I'm putting you (I slap my resignation on the desk) on. . . .

Okay, I couldn't think of anything to add to the end of that statement.

Janice: I expect you to fix this immediately.

Me: And I expect you (I slap my resignation on the desk) to find my replacement!

Hmmm . . . wasn't quite sharp enough.

Janice: I am appalled that I even have to have this conversation with you.

Me: And I am appalled that I've worked for you this long. (slap my resignation on the desk.)

No Good. Generally, I had no problem being smart-mouthed, but it just wasn't flowing today.

Janice: You've dropped the ball on one too many projects.

Me: And you've dropped your drawers one too many . . .

Okay. Forget it. I would just remain respectful and deliver my resignation like I had some professional sense. It would be bad enough that I'd never be able to utilize Wright-Way as a reference since I wasn't giving two weeks notice.

* * *

Like the time before, Corey was seated in Janice's office when I got there. That meant he knew exactly what was going on and obviously supported it, based on the conversation we'd had before. We made unexpressive eye contact, but I couldn't help but think about our interaction earlier in the week, wondering how it would play into his reaction if Janice started going off on me.

"Have a seat, December," Janice said. She was smiling, but there was nothing unusual about that. "I'm sure you're wondering why I asked you to this meeting." I gave a single nod as my response. "I wanted to talk to you about your past work performance as it relates to your career path." She pulled out the same folder she'd smacked on the table in times past. "I keep a very close eye on my business and on the performance statistics of those who report directly to me."

I was just waiting for her to crack one comment; my hand was trembling in anticipation of whisking my resignation out.

"December, month after month, you've led the company in billable hours, even when taking on additional responsibilities, like the rewrite project, demonstrating your strong multitasking skills. When I review what it takes in order to accomplish a feat like that, I have to look at your ability to interview candidates effectively and fit them in assignments for which they are best suited, to maintain client relationships, and to be proactive in forecasting their staffing needs, as well as to balance various administrative duties, all of which you do extremely well. As you know, the Hampton branch has all but shut down and is in dire need of strong leadership in the way of a branch manager."

She paused momentarily. "I've had a few discussions with Corey regarding the qualifications of several individuals who have expressed interest in that particular role. I was somewhat disappointed that you had not come forward, seeking upward mobility in that regard. Nonetheless, both Corey and I believe that without seeking external talent, you are best suited to take on the branch manager role and get Hampton's performance where it needs to be."

"What are you saying, Janice?" I asked. Stunned and suspicious, I needed clarity.

"I'd like to offer you the branch manager role for the Hampton branch," said Janice. She waited for my response, which took me a few seconds to think up. I glanced over at Corey. How long had he known this? He had to know just a few nights ago, when he came to my house. Maybe they hadn't made the decision yet.

"What would it mean in terms of salary and compensation?" I asked.

"I'm glad you asked," Janice replied. "I'm sure you will be pleased with your base, and of course, you will have an hours incentive. I was able to get you started on the high side of the salary quartile for this role, given your successful track record."

She handed me an offer letter, which outlined what my new salary would be. My eyes nearly popped out of my head; it was almost double what I was currently making. I studied the paper while I did a number of calculations in my head, seeing a glimmer of light at the end of my debt tunnel. *Play it cool, Deece. Play it cool.*

"I certainly appreciate both of you recognizing my talents and considering me for the role," I said and paused for effect. "Please allow me some time to think the offer over and get back to you. I'd like to sleep on it, if you don't mind."

For a fleeting moment, Janice looked surprised, then pasted her smile back on. "Of course," she replied.

Thanking them both, I strolled back to my office, with a sense of accomplishment and worth. When I passed Andre's office, there was a sudden knot in my stomach. *Oh my God.* How was he going to feel about me getting a promotion that I didn't even post for? I wondered if he'd already been declined. Or was he banking on booty calls? I didn't know whether I should say something to him or not. If I did, and he didn't know, it would be a shock to him. If I didn't, and he did know, he might perceive my not saying anything as avoidance. With that in mind, I detoured to Corey's office to ask if the other candidates had been declined.

"We've not notified the other individuals as of yet, because you have not accepted nor declined the role. Please keep that information to yourself. I know I can trust you to do just that," Corey stated. "And by the way, congratulations. You deserve it."

"Thanks, Corey." I smiled.

Twenty-Five

Kisha, looking more radiant than the last time I'd seen her, pulled up just as I stepped out of the airport. She jumped out of the car, with her long, straight hair flying off her shoulders. We screamed each other's names on sight, then embraced.

"How long were you waiting?" she asked, bogarting her way into a line of traffic.

"I had just walked out. You were right on time." I settled into the leather seat of her Acura and turned the stereo up. "You are forever listening to Alicia."

"That's my girl." She snapped her fingers and sang a line or two. "You hungry?"

"Not really, but I do have reason to celebrate, so drive somewhere, anywhere, 'cause drinks are on me!"

"What? You're engaged?"

"Let's not be ridiculous. The man just kissed me practically the day before yesterday."

"You pregnant?"

"Don't make me get back on the next plane outta here," I threatened. "How in the world would I be pregnant? I'll say this. Having sex better be like riding a bike, something you never forget how to do." We both burst into laughter.

"Speaking of sex, have you heard of jade eggs? I want to get me some."

"Jade eggs? What the heck is that?" I asked.

"These little egg-shaped things that are supposed to make you able to do kung fu with your coochie."

"What!"

"They are supposed to help you exercise and strengthen your muscles."

"Wait a minute, wait a minute," I said, waving my hand, in a fit of giggles. "You mean to tell me you stick an egg up your tail, and all of a sudden you are doing magic?"

"Stop laughing and listen," Kisha said, fighting laughs herself. "It says if you work with them for a while, you'll be able to lift ten pounds."

"Ten pounds! You let me find out you can lift ten pounds from between your legs! Girl, your man ain't gon' *ever* get rid of you!"

"Let me find a man first. When I do find him, I'll be ready!"

"I'ma have to starting calling you G.I. Joe!"

"G.I. Joe? Why?"

"'Cause you 'bout to have kung fu grip!"

We laughed the rest of the way to the restaurant, where I shared with her the news of my promotion over slices of lemon cake and celebratory champagne.

"So you are going to take it?" Kisha asked.

"Heck, yeah! Why wouldn't I? I'd still be working for Janice, but I'd hardly ever see her, because I'll be in a different office. I will be doing pretty much what I do right now but making almost twice as much money, with a much higher bonus payout structure. I'll have a staff under me that I can delegate responsibilities to; the upward mobility will look great on my resume; I'll be able to pay off my bills a lot sooner; and as a bonus, I'll be able to see Corey a little more freely, without hawks watching. I can't think of one reason not to take it."

Kisha lifted her glass toward me. "Well, here's to you. Do your thang, girl!"

Just as our glasses made contact, my cell phone rang. I glanced at the number and saw it was Corey. As tempted as I was to talk to him, before I answered, I remembered one of the rules that I'd read over and over in the various dating handbooks: Don't always be available; that will drive him crazy. The last time I didn't follow the rules; it only resulted in my having a broken heart. Reminded of that, I pressed the OFF button.

"He can leave a message," I stated, raising my glass to my lips, taking another sip of champagne. "So tomorrow we have to go shopping to celebrate!"

Again Kisha lifted her glass and began to sing. "All my ladies making money. Throw your glass up at me!"

For the next two days, using every dollar of available credit I had and my entire paycheck, I gave new meaning to the expression "shop 'til you drop." There was nothing that I saw and wanted that I wasn't worthy of and didn't get for myself. I picked up four new power suits in black, navy, cream, and tan. I couldn't get the suits without getting the shoes: a pair of tan Mizrahis; black open-toe pumps from Hollywould, with beautiful stones across the top; a Christian Lacroix silver stiletto bootie; and a Jimmy Choo flat for the days when my feet really didn't feel up to the challenge of heels. If I was going to be the boss, I had to look the part.

Coach had their Legacy Leather Flap business bag

on sale, which I purchased to stylishly and professionally carry the new laptop I'd picked up. I finally got my right-hand diamond, a beautiful swiggle of vertically placed stones set in white gold. Kisha helped me pick out a PDA (maybe it was time to let the Franklin Covey go), and I had about ten other random items that all celebrated me.

Before Kisha took me to the airport, I logged onto her computer and ordered us both a set of kung fu eggs to close my trip out properly. By the time Monday night rolled around, I had to purchase another piece of luggage to be able to get my things home.

Unlocking my front door, I was exhausted, but in a good way. Good relaxation, great friends, excellent shopping . . . phenomenal weekend!

Twenty-Six

My initial feeling when I cracked my eyes the next day was disorientation. It took a few seconds for me to remember where I was. Shortly after, my feelings turned to panic; the clock read seven after eight.

"Oh snap! I'm late!" In an instant I was wide awake and on my way to the shower. And fifteen minutes later, I was fully dressed, had on my new jewelry, and was hopping on one foot to the truck as I pushed my other foot into a leather sling back. I applied my make-up at every traffic light and finished with lip gloss as I sped into the office parking lot, nearly running over both Janice and Andre. Andre was toting a copy-paper box in one hand and several flat NOW HIRING signs in the other. Janice also had a box, which held stacks of blank applications, temp time-sheets, I-9 forms, and tax credit sheets. They both looked surprised to see me, judging by their vanishing smiles. I could admit that it did look a bit bad for me, the newest branch manager (although I'd not officially accepted yet) to be late for work. They walked across the lot to Andre's car but seemed to keep their eyes on me as I whipped my truck into the closest parking space and jumped out.

"Good morning," I sang, slipping into my butter yellow suit jacket, then freeing my braids from its collar. I felt around my neckline to ensure that my new O-shaped diamond pendant was properly adjusted at the opening of my blouse, to catch the sun's rays.

"Good morning," they both responded, but with a lot less enthusiasm. They were eyeing me dubiously. My eyes bounced back and forth between the two of them. Were they on their way to a rendezvous or something?

"Why are you two looking at me like that?" I asked.

They both looked at each other in silence; then Janice spoke. "Why don't you head on over, and I'll come by this afternoon to sit with you and help you get some things situated." She patted Andre on the shoulder and smiled at him, with a hint of sexual devilment in her eyes. She was just straight-up nasty.

"Great" replied Andre." I'll see you this afternoon. See you later, Deece."

I quickly waved my hand, wondering if either of them had taken note of or been blinded by my right-hand diamond. Andre seated himself in his vehicle, then pulled off, tapping his horn twice.

"How are you doing this morning?" I asked Janice. I beamed, walking around to the back of my truck, ready to retrieve my workbag, which had been there since Friday. When I looked up at Janice, I couldn't read her expression accurately. It seemed to be a mixture of confusion, skepticism, and hatred. She stood motionless, with her arms folded across her chest.

"What do you need, December?" she asked sharply.

"What do you mean, what do I need?" Perplexed, I crinkled my brows.

"Didn't you already get your things?" she huffed in annoyance.

"What things? What are you talking about?"

"I got your resignation," she said firmly, with a look of contempt.

"My resignation?" My heart stopped beating.

"Yes, your resignation. You know, the one you so kindly left on the desk, in a folder, after you cleaned out your office and removed your personal greeting from your voice mail?" she asked rhetorically. "The one that said, 'Effective immediately, I resign.'" She threw her hands in the air, marking quotations. "That resignation."

Oh my God, oh my God, oh my God. Right away my legs turned to noodles, my head began to hurt, and I couldn't think. My eyes blinked rapidly as I searched every crevice of my mind for something to say.

"Janice, I . . . I . . ." *Oh my God.* There was nothing I could say. I was going to be sick. Tears welled rapidly and began to sting my eyes. I cleared my throat and tried to speak without trembling. It didn't exactly work. "I, umm . . . I thought I left . . . my . . . my umbrella underneath my desk, and I just came to get it."

"I'll take a look for you. You can stay here," she responded in her nastiest tone.

I took offense at her forcing me to stand outside. What was I? Some kind of criminal now, who couldn't be trusted to come in the building? She spun on her heels while a thousand thoughts ran through my mind. How had I been so careless to have left that folder? I didn't put it in my bag? And why had I insisted on taking my things out to the car? My mind flashed back to how my office looked when I left on Friday. It was as neat as a pin, with no sign that I occupied that space daily.

"Hold it together. Hold it together," I coached myself out loud. I took a series of deep breaths until Janice reappeared. I thought about dropping to my knees, not caring about the eighteen-dollar designer hose I had on, to begin begging, crying, and pleading, and claiming that I hadn't typed that resignation, and that my very scriptive and unique signature had been forged. The only thing that stopped me was the knowledge that it would not result in my getting the promotion, keeping my current role, or having a job at Wright-Way, period. Even if it were to work, I couldn't even begin to imagine how miserable Janice would make life at work for me. I'd be permanently listed on every single slot of her Employees to Mock and Belittle list. She definitely would never consider me again for a promotion, especially one that I didn't even post for.

How did I let this happen? Suddenly, my necklace felt like a noose, my ring had the pressure of a sprung mousetrap, and the Isaac Mizrahis I wore began to squeeze my feet in a vicelike grip.

"There was no umbrella there," she said, pausing and looking at me with such poison in her eyes, I had to look just past her, pretending to see something behind her head. "Your final pay stub will be mailed to you." The finality in her voice suggested that I remove myself from company property immediately.

"Okay. Thanks for checking." She turned to go back in the building while I climbed into my truck, drove to a neighboring lot, and began to cry like a hungry newborn baby.

After several minutes of just sitting, with tears and snot trailing down my face and onto my clothes, I turned my phone on, dialed Corey's number, and trembling, held the phone to my ear. His voice mail immediately picked up, stating that he would be in Richmond for the week. Right after I hung up, the chime of my phone indicated that I had new voice mail messages from the weekend that I had not yet checked. Not yet in a state to drive, I pressed the appropriate keys to get into my voice mail.

"December, call me as soon as you get this message," Corey requested. *"I am in receipt of your resignation, and I am very surprised that you would deliver it like this. This doesn't line up with your usual level of profes-sionalism."* He let out a heavy sigh. *"Call me imme-diately, and let me know what is going on."* My mind raced back to Friday night and my decision to ignore Corey's call and, on top of that, cut the phone off altogether for the entire weekend.

"Girl! You didn't tell me you were making a power move like that! Call me!" I deleted Shelley's message.

"December, this is Corinthian. Since I've not heard back from you, I guess we have no choice but to accept your resignation. I would have appreciated a call back, at the very least." He paused for a moment, then spoke again, with a hint of guilt in his tone. *"I hope I am not the cause of your very sudden decision to leave. I sincerely apologize. I should have used better judgment."* Again there were several seconds of silence. *"Well, at any rate, I wish you much luck and success in your future professional endeavors, and I have enjoyed work-ing with you. Please let me know if there is anything I can do to assist you."* With tears welling again, I skipped to the next message.

"Deece, what in the world happened? I can't believe you quit without saying anything to a brotha!" Andre began. *"I thought we were better than that. You could have at least said bye or called me or sent me an e-mail or something. Anyway, I was offered the branch manager*

position today for Hampton. It starts right away, so as soon as I gather my things from Chesapeake, I'll be heading to the big chair on the other side. Call me so we can get together and celebrate on me. All right hit me back." I think that was the part that twisted the knife I'd stabbed in my own back.

It was a miracle that I made it home in one piece; I'd barely been able to see through the overflow of tears, not to mention that I could hardly remember where I lived. As soon as I stepped inside my door, I sank to the floor and cried even more profusely. Why hadn't I just accepted that job right away? There was nothing to think about. And, in the snap of a finger, due to one extremely careless and stupid mistake, I'd managed to blow my much-needed promotion and throw my job away. Then, to top it all off, I was in a whole lot more debt than I was just a few days ago, with no means to pay off any of it.

Never even bothering to get off the floor, I lay right there in the foyer at nine thirty in the morning, in a three-hundred-and-some-odd-dollar suit, and cried myself to sleep.

Twenty-Seven

"Thank you," I said and shook my interviewer's hand and left the office, disappointed, knowing I wouldn't get the field sales executive position, but at the same time, not really wanting it. The position consisted of handing out flyers in random parking lots, as well as making cold calls to area residents and trying to set up appointments for home demonstrations for an exorbitantly priced knife set. Who bought knives like that? I thought people just went to the store if they needed knives. Greg, my interviewer, knew I was way overqualified and showed great hesitancy in hiring me based on that fact.

"With your level of skill and talent, I just don't think you would be fulfilled in this role," he'd said. "I could see you getting bored very quickly, thus becoming un-enthused about the product and unmotivated to sell it." He was absolutely right, but I was absolutely desperate. I could successfully make phone calls and cut through a piece of rope with a kitchen knife! Nonetheless, he didn't make me an offer. "Let me review your resume a little further and give it more thought." In other words, "Don't call us; we'll call you."

I'd been on nine other interviews within the past three weeks and just wasn't coming up with anything. I had to work somewhere and could not understand why that dream job just wasn't falling out of the sky. Well, actually, it had, but I quit before I could accept.

After another two weeks of moping, checking the Internet for new job postings, buying the newspaper, and circling ads, I was at my wit's end. I was going to have to make a real power move, not a stupid, "I quit my job by mistake" power move. I hadn't even told Shelley or Andre what had really happened. Guess my pride got in the way. But faking the funk, like everything was going fantastically well, was getting harder and harder to do. Not to mention, it was stressful. In reality, I was becoming more and more familiar with the theme song to *Good Times*. Especially the "scratchin' and surviving" part. Ain't we lucky we got 'em? Who wrote that line?

Through a series of gasps and sobs, I did tell Kisha of my misfortune. She suggested I take all my purchases back and offered to send me some emergency cash. Before I could adamantly refuse (although I offered a little tiny bit of resistance), she had gone online and wired me a thousand dollars, no stipulations or promissory note attached. That had been twenty-two days ago, and while I was being extremely careful with the money, a grand only goes so far.

When I got home, I took a seat at my desk and whipped out a sheet of paper, grabbed a pen, and began listing on one side components of my new power strategy. When I finished, my list read:

1) *Find a job*
2) *Take ATL stuff back to stores before it's too late*

3) *Finish sorting through shoes and take to consignment shop*

4) *Sort through clothes and take to consignment shop*

5) ~~*Ask other friends for money*~~

6) ~~*Ask my parents for money*~~

7) ~~*Sell my house*~~

Number one was a given. But where I would find work in the next few days was beyond me at this point. I had seemingly searched all over the city, but to no avail. Number two should have been done on the same day that I found out I quit my job, but I had dragged my feet, thinking that I would be employed by now, could reimburse Kisha, plus a little extra as a thank-you, and could still enjoy my purchases. Number three was going to be harder than I'd thought. Every time I started to go through my shoes, they all started talking to me, reminding me of when and why I bought them and why I shouldn't let them go. Same thing with number four. Plus, I needed clothes to interview in. Regarding numbers five and six, I was too ashamed to beg for money from my friends, and I could hear my father now.

"December, how many times do your mother and I have to dig you out of a financial trap? I told you the last time that that was the last time. You're not a little girl. You're not even a big girl; you are a full-grown woman now. Grow up, and stop being so frivolous with your finances."

If I were to tell him how I happened not to have a job, he would get at me twice as hard for typing the resignation up in the first place in preparation to quit my job without securing other employment. Back to the list.

Number seven? No! That was out of the question.

Maybe I could start some kind of business. I flipped the paper over and made a list of what I could possibly do working for myself. My completed list read:

1) ~~Baby-sit kids~~
2) ~~Sell real estate~~
3) ~~Sell make-up~~
4) ~~Sell diet pills~~
5) *Utilize my personal trainer certification*

Regarding number one, I could deal with a child or two for a couple of hours, but all day, every day? No way. As for number two, I just didn't feel up to selling stuff unless I absolutely had to. That goes for numbers three and four as well. I don't even know why I wrote those three things down. As for number five, I did earn a certificate that qualified me as a personal trainer, and all it was doing was collecting dust and getting old, but I was spending more and more time at the gym these days.

Just thinking about the hours I'd put in at the gym made me get up and strip out of my interview suit. Standing there in my panties and bra, I did an assessment in the mirror. I'd never been fat, but months back I did have a tiny roll or two, which was now gone. My thighs were tighter and well-sculpted, and my butt was like POW! Come to think of it, I had noticed that some of my older suits were slipping a little.

"Hi! I'm December Elliott, and I am so glad you are joining me for the Shake Down, my new cardiovascular program, which will have you looking like a million bucks in no time! Get ready to burn some fat and have some fun!" I spoke to the mirror in my most upbeat motivational voice. My imagination started running away with me as I began to perform kicks and jabs, talking out loud to my pretend TV audience.

"Come on. Just one more set. Kick! Punch! Knee! Hook! Now other side. You can do it. Yeah! Feel that burn, baby. Now twist your hips. That's it! Four more, now three . . ." Just as I was getting ready to do a one-minute turbo sprint, I caught the reflection of the mailman rolling by in his truck. That crashed my daydream, broke my momentum, and brought me back to the present, knowing that he'd just dropped off a ton of bills, reminder letters, and delinquency notices.

Without wasting another minute, I threw on my lavender and navy Nike yoga pants, cami, and matching shoes; dug through a stack of mail for my certificate; and headed for the gym. On the way, I gave Rodney a call. I knew he needed help; on several occasions, he had been forced to cancel classes due to not having an instructor.

"Rodney speaking," he answered right away.

"Hey, Rodney." I said. "I'm on my way to see you. I need to talk to you about something."

"Okay," he said, with hesitancy in his voice. "What's going on?"

"I'll tell you when I get there." I hadn't told Rodney that I'd received my certification. After that whole date mishap, I'd tried pretty much to steer clear of him but stayed cordial in passing. I was still having flashbacks every time I stopped to fill up my gas tank. "I'll be there in a few minutes."

I couldn't believe that I was actually going to apply for a job as a fitness trainer. It would at least help me to try to make ends meet (or at least come a little bit closer together) until something else came through. If someone had told me five months ago, or even five weeks ago, that I'd be doing this, I would have never believed it.

"What's up, Deece? You ready to start teaching classes yet?" Rodney asked when I walked into his office. His head was tilted downward as he shuffled through some files on his desk.

"Actually, yes. That is what I wanted to talk to you

about. I've decided to pursue a fitness career full time."
He instantly stopped looking through the stack of files
and looked at me instead.

"You're kidding, right?"

"Nope, I'm as serious as a heart attack. I've been having such a great time working out, and the results are
clear. I'm ready to do it as a career. I'm tired of the office grind," I said in my most believable tone. I just
couldn't bring myself to tell him that I was mistakenly
unemployed.

"Deece, you know you need to be certified first."

I whipped out my certificate from my shoulder bag
and presented it to him. "Yes, I know." I nodded. "When
can I start?"

"When did you get this?" he asked in amazement.

"Look at the date."

"And you are just now coming to me?" he asked after
several seconds of reviewing the certificate.

"I had to clear some other things off my plate first."

"I do need some instructors. Are you serious?" He
searched my face for the slightest hint of gaming.

"I'll start right now if you let me," I said, without batting an eye.

He stared for a few more seconds, then, convinced,
pulled an employment application out of his drawer
and slid it across his desk toward me. I wasted no time
filling it with ink and giving him a copy of my Social Security card and driver's license so that he could make
copies for my employee file.

"It must be my lucky day," he said, shaking his head
in disbelief before leaving the room to make copies.
When he returned, he quickly reviewed with me employee guidelines, basic benefits, and my salary, which
absolutely sucked. I'd barely have enough money after
taxes to make my mortgage payment. I couldn't even

think about lights, water, cable, cell phone, shopping, or even eating, for that matter. The good part was, Rodney said it wasn't too late to get partial reimbursement for my certification tuition.

As I left the gym, the urge to shop for new workout clothes hit me right away, but then, so did the reality that I didn't have any money. I had plenty of gear at home and tennis shoes to match every single outfit. I'd be just fine. A small sense of accomplishment came over me. It wasn't the best job, but it was a job. I could put a check mark on one of my list items.

1) ☑ Find a job

"Come on, Deece. You can do it," I coached myself, knowing that my Atlanta purchases needed to go back to the store. I had to be strong. No matter how badly I wanted to hold on to the merchandise, it all had to go back. Really, I hadn't even had an opportunity to enjoy most of it, seeing how I became unemployed right after I got the stuff home. I never even opened the laptop or PDA boxes. The suits were still in their bags, although they'd been folded up and stuffed in my suitcase. I had worn the jewelry, but the store had a sixty-day return policy. I had a few more days to get it back. The shoes . . . oh, the shoes . . . not the shoes. Yes, the shoes, too. "Take 'em back, Deece!" I commanded myself. "Okay, okay, okay!" I answered back.

Fortunately, most of my purchases had been made at stores that had locations nationwide. With partial reluctance and partial excitement, I returned every single item that I could. Every time they swiped my card in reverse, a feeling that I couldn't describe washed over me, like a wave of relief or a release of built-up pressure. And each time it happened, I felt better and better. By the time I'd returned my last item, I felt exhilarated, like the richest woman in the world.

As for the purchases I'd made that didn't have stores in my area, as soon as I got back home I went online, located the stores' customer-service numbers, and called each of them to get permission to return the merchandise and their exact returns shipping addresses. I spent the next hour or so neatly packing those items into boxes, along with my receipt copies, and labeling the boxes to to send them to their respective stores.

2) ☑ *Take ATL stuff back to stores before it's too late*

While my momentum was in high gear, I went to my second bedroom and selected ten boxes of shoes to take to the consignment shop. Ten was a pretty low number in comparison to the almost four hundred pairs I had in total, but I had to break myself in easy. I started with the pairs that hurt my feet the worst, and even then, it was hard, but I stuck to my guns. I loaded the boxes into two large shopping bags and took them to the truck.

Next, I attacked my closet, pulling out several outfits that were now too big for me. Shorts, halter tops, dresses, evening gowns, and everything in between were now piled in a huge heap on my bed, and I had just gotten started. As I folded each garment and placed it into one of four shopping bags, my emotions stirred, trying to convince me to keep the items, but I resisted. All four bags were toted to the truck to join the shoes.

I visited and interviewed five different shops before settling on one that I thought could move my items the quickest, and at the best prices: the Sequel Consignment Boutique. First off, there were luxury cars parked in the lot outside of the building. What that said to me was, the Sequel was more of an upscale boutique rather than a glorified thrift store.

Once inside, I was greeted by a very slim young lady

clothed in a pair of black dress slacks coupled with a tight-fitting black turtleneck. A black and charcoal grey Fendi belt with a chrome buckle circled her waist, and a pair of Fendi black suede boots covered her feet. Two more women, also in all black, came from behind a door marked EMPLOYEES ONLY. Together, the three of them looked chic. I liked that.

Before asking any questions about their guidelines, I browsed the shop to get a feel for how they priced their clothes and to find out if they had a dedicated designer section, and if most of their garments were fashionable, well-kept, and well-presented. I especially checked out the shoe section, because used shoes could really look beat-up, dirty, and run over. I was pleased with everything I saw. On my way back toward the counter, an exquisite Christian Dior vintage blouse caught my eye. It would go perfect with my Citizens cropped jeans . . . if they weren't in the back of my truck.

"Excuse me," I said, trying to get the attention of one of the three ladies. The girl that initially greeted me didn't hesitate to offer her services.

"Yes, ma'am?" She smiled.

"I have quite a few things that I'd like to place in your store. Can you tell me about your terms and conditions?"

"Sure," she sang. "We offer a sixty/forty split of the selling price to consignors, and seventy/thirty if your item sells for more than three hundred dollars." I nodded attentively while she continued. "Our consignment period is for ninety days. During the first thirty days, we will attempt to sell your items at the price we'll set together. After that, they will go on sale for 20 percent off. After sixty days, the price will be dropped to 40 percent off. If we are unable to sell your items after ninety days, you can either pick them up if you'd like them back or donate them to the store." She raised her eyebrows as she shrugged. "That's pretty much it."

"How often do you pay your consignors?"

"We write checks to our consignors on the fifteenth of the month for items sold in the last calendar month." So if my items sold right away, I could have money in less than thirty days.

"Do you have time to price my items with me today?" I smiled, seeing how this might really work out well for me.

"Ah . . . give me just a minute, and I'll get the manager for you. Katherine?" she called.

Katherine walked over and pleasantly introduced herself as the store owner as she shook my hand and swung a head full of blond curls out of her face. After a few minutes of chatting with me, she walked me to my truck to help me bring in my bags.

"My, you have quite a few things here!" she commented.

"And this is just the tip of the iceberg. If things go well, I may be bringing you stock for a long time."

We went through the EMPLOYEES ONLY door, where there were a couple more dressed-in-black employees, hanging, steaming, and tagging garments. They all stopped when Katherine and I walked in, and they came over to help assess each piece while Katherine took a seat at a computer to enter and track my things. They had an awesome online process that would allow me to log on to see if my items had sold or not. It took the rest of the afternoon to go through the four bags and ten pairs of shoes, but when I left, I knew I'd found a great home for my former clothes. And if they sold at the prices we'd agreed upon, I'd have a pretty nice piece of change.

Twenty-Eight

Working out all day was a lot less stressful than staffing and dealing with Janice. Despite Rodney's social etiquette deficiency, he was great to work for, my schedule was as flexible as a contortionist's backbone, and I was in the best shape of my life, developing muscles that I'd never used before. The only downside was the pay. My bills were still severely behind, and I'd only sold a few things through the consignment shop so far. After a long night of contemplation about what I could do, I picked up the phone and called Andre. I was long overdue on catching up with him, anyway.

"Deece!" he said. I had to admit, it was good to hear his voice. "What's going on with you, girl? I mean, you just dropped everybody when you dropped Wright-Way, huh?"

"I didn't mean to Andre. I've just been really busy, that's all."

"Too busy to return my phone calls? Busy doing what?"

"If I told you, you wouldn't even believe me." I sighed. "Congratulations on your promotion, by the way."

"Thanks, but try me," he challenged.

"Promise me, you won't get mad first," I said, thinking about how I was offered the branch manager position before him.

"Deece, you know me better than that. Come on. I was gonna whup up on Janice for you, remember?"

"All right. Remember that day that I came to the building and you and Janice were going to your car?"

"Yeah, that's the last time I saw you."

"I was actually coming in for work that day," I huffed.

"What do you mean? I thought you'd already turned in your resignation."

"Yeah, but I didn't mean to." I told Andre everything that had happened and how I'd gone on a shopping spree and was now in an even bigger financial mess, although the items had been returned.

"Wow," he commented. "I'm sorry that that happened," he said sympathetically.

"Yeah, but you have to be glad to some degree. You got a great promotion out of it." I chuckled.

"True, true. But still, I'm sorry for what happened on your side of the fence."

"Thanks."

"So what are you doing now?"

"Teaching classes at the gym and thinking about selling my house."

"What? Why? December, don't sell your house."

"Andre, I can't afford it!" Hearing my frustration, he was silent for a moment. "Don't beat me up about it, okay? It's a hard enough decision to make without being argued with." Suddenly, I was fighting back tears.

"Okay. Listen. My sister's a real estate agent. Let me give you her number." He paused, sensing that I was now crying, signified by soft sniffs. "Don't cry, Deece. Things will work out."

"I know." I sniffed again. "Just call back and leave the number on my voice mail, okay? I'll call you back later," I said shakily.

After hanging up with Andre, I sat on my bed, trying to rationalize where I was, where I was going, and what I was doing. I felt like a complete failure. Pulling myself together, I dialed Corey's number to fulfill the strong urge I had to hear his voice, thinking that it would give me some level of comfort. It had been weeks since our kiss; we really hadn't talked since then.

His phone rang three times before he answered.

"Hello, Corey?"

"Yes?" He sounded rushed, as if I was bothering him.

"It's December." Right there, I had nothing else to say.

"Yes, how are you? What can I do for you?" he said all in one breath.

"I . . . I was just calling to see how you were." This wasn't a good idea. There were a few seconds of silence before he spoke again.

"December, I'm very disappointed by the way you left the company. Somewhere in my mind, I assumed, which I shouldn't have, but I assumed that there was better rapport between both of us, where you could have shared your intentions with me." I bit down on my lip as I contemplated spilling the beans about my leaving. "And then for you to ignore my calls and—"

"Corinthian, I thought you said you were ready. We need to get going, baby," a woman's voice said in the background.

"Hold on just a second, December," said Corey.

Baby? Don't jump to conclusions. Don't make assumptions, I coached myself, but my coaching was ineffective. Normally, that wouldn't have been enough to make me cry, but I found myself doing all I could to hold back more tears. Regardless of my efforts, again they began to trickle down my face.

Corey said into the phone, "December, I'll need to talk to you another time."

"Okay," I eeked out.

"Thanks for calling." And at that, he was gone.

No job, no cash, no man, no house. In one big whoosh, my life was falling apart.

I spent the entire morning cleaning every corner of my home, making sure that it would show well. Had I had some extra cash, I would have called the maid company again, but this time I had to do it myself. With the help of an eighties CD collection, I was done in no time.

Just as I put away my mop and bucket from cleaning the kitchen floor, the realtor arrived.

"Good afternoon. I'm Anita Shivers, Andre's sister." She extended her hand for a shake as I let her in.

"It's nice to meet you," I responded, although I wished it were not under these circumstances. Near tears, but holding on, I walked Anita through each room of my home, pointing out its special features and upgrades. When we were done, she sat down to ask a few questions about what I owed on the property, how long I'd been in it, and that sort of thing.

"I can tell that you are very attached to your home," she began. "Why do you want to sell it?"

A number of responses went through my head, but I decided to just be honest. "I can no longer afford to keep up the payments on it." I shrugged it off like it was no big deal, but in all actuality, I was hurt and embarrassed to have said that.

"I see. Well, I had an opportunity to prepare a comparative market analysis so you can get an idea of what your home could sell for."

She handed me a package that showed homes in my area that had recently sold, what they had sold for, and how my home compared to them. When I looked at the figure that she thought my house could sell for, I was very surprised. I could make almost three times what I currently owed on it! All of a sudden, as much as I loved my house, I felt a few of those emotional and sentimental attachment strings pop. I'd have enough money to pay off all of my bills and my truck, take a trip to Paris, do some shopping. . . . *Wait, wait, wait. Get a hold of yourself, Deece. No trips and no shopping.*

Two hours later, my house was officially for sale, and within three days, I had four offers on the table, and all four buyers were willing to pay my asking price, which was a few thousand more than what the realtor had suggested. After a careful review of each offer, who the lenders were, and the loan approval letters (they all pretty much looked the same), I went with the buyer who had the earliest closing date. The earlier the closing, the sooner I'd be debt free. Anita slid the contract papers to me, pointing out every place that my signature or initials were needed. On the last sheet, I signed on the dotted line, and now, with three short weeks before I had to be out of there, I needed to find somewhere to live.

As soon as Anita left with the ratified contract, I drove around town, with a copy of an apartment guide, in search of a new residence. Of course, the best apartments were just as high as what I paid in mortgage and nowhere near as nice. I had to keep reminding myself that I would be out of debt; that was my motivation.

By accident, I located a small subdivision of privately

owned townhomes. That was exactly what I was looking for. I drove down street after street of the no outlet area, hoping that I could find at least one FOR RENT sign. Considering the beautiful brick fronts, single-car garages (perfect for pretending that I wasn't home), alcoved entrances, and well-manicured lawns, I could see myself being very happy in this neighborhood. As I pulled around the final bend, I found my pot of gold—a unit for rent. I didn't waste time jotting down the number; I parked, marched right up to the front door, and rang the bell, crossing my fingers that the owner was at home. A woman who looked old enough to be my mother and as stately as Lena Horne opened the door. Her hair was pulled back elegantly in a French roll.

"Yes," she answered politely, displaying a row of beautiful teeth.

"Hi. I was just passing through the neighborhood and noticed the sign in the yard, and I am actually selling my home and in search of a rental property. I know I don't have an appointment or anything, but I was wondering if I could view your home while I was here." In a split second, I became acutely aware of how raggedy I must have looked in a pair of baggy grey sweats, a pink baby T that read "hot girl" in rhinestones across the front, and a pink and grey ball cap on my head.

"Actually, I'm not the home owner. This is my daughter's house. I was just here taking care of a few things for her while she's out of town, but I guess you can come on in," she invited. She stood aside and held the storm door open for me while I walked through.

"Thank you so much," I graciously responded. The area where I now stood was a small foyer, with a half bath, a door leading to the garage, and a few steps leading up to the living-room and dining-room area, which was lavishly covered in the most plush carpeting I'd ever put my feet on. I must have sunk a full two inches just standing on it. A large fireplace separated the two spaces, and a double-sized French sliding glass door led out to a deck. Lena then led me up another short flight of stairs, to a level where there were two guest bedrooms, which shared a full bath in between. Another set of stairs led to a loft, which overlooked the living- and dining-room area and seemed to serve currently as office space. The more I looked, the more I fell in love and was ready to sign a lease. I'd even pay the whole year of rent up front (after I sold my house, of course). What I'd seen thus far had been absolutely beautiful, but I just wasn't ready for what was waiting for me on the very top level, which was solely the master bedroom. It wasn't a bedroom. It was a boudoir.

The room was decorated in all white with tan accents, which gave it a very clean, pure, and natural look. On one wall, situated on a six-inch platform, was a king-sized bed, centered between two windows, covered with a plush feather comforter, and surrounded by a hanging mesh canopy. I had to control my urge to run over to the bed and just fall backwards into it. The opposite wall was a full floor-to-ceiling window, adorned with white sheers, with a scarf draping across the top and down the sides, pooling onto the floor. There was a quaint breakfast-for-two setting at the window, overlooking a small lake.

For a minute Corey crept into my mind. I imagined him seated at the table, with his feet set apart, dressed only in a pair of cotton pajama pants, relaxed, and leaning back in one of the chairs. He patted his lap, beckoning me to him as I exited the bathroom (which had an awesome Jacuzzi tub), freshly sugar-scrubbed, buttered down, and glowing, clad only in a rich burgundy-colored bra and panties set, towel drying my hair.

"Come here for a minute," he said and gestured with his head.

"No, you're gonna make me late for work," I giggled.

"Girl, come here."

I sucked my teeth while I sauntered over to him. "If you make me late, you're taking me to dinner tonight."

Mmm," he moaned, running his hands up my back while I straddled him. "I can take you to dinner, but for right now I'ma take you to . . ."

"My daughter's owned this place for about five years." Lena broke into my fantasy and brought me back to reality. "She just had a new home built not too far from here."

"This is a gorgeous home. I am very interested in it. Do you know what she's renting it for?" I asked as we descended the steps back toward the foyer.

"I'm not quite sure, but I'll give you her information so you can give her a call. She'll be back here tomorrow night. Let me grab a notepad and jot her information down for you.

While Lena stopped on the loft level, I took the pleasure of peeking again at the guest rooms.

"Okay. This has her cell number on it, too, if you want to give her a call right away," said Lena. "I'm sure she'll be glad to talk to you about it."

"Thank you," I said, with a huge smile, reaching out for the paper. "Is there an application or something I need to take with me? I can also leave a deposit or the first month's rent or something," I offered, anxiously trying to seal the deal before I left.

"You would have to call and talk directly to my daughter for that. I don't know how exactly she's handling applications. Why don't I just take your name and number for now?"

While she spoke, I glanced down at the note she'd just handed me. As soon as I read the information, my smile disappeared and I lost all interest. Written on the paper was: *Janice Wheeler, 555-2746 home, 555-6822 cell.*

"What's your name, honey?" she asked, her pen poised on the pad.

"Uh . . . Lorraine Taylor."

"Okay, Lorraine," she said, writing. "I'll tell my daughter you stopped by."

"Thank you," I said, now with feigned enthusiasm.

Of all the homes in the whole wide world, how did I manage to end up at Janice's? My feet couldn't carry me fast enough to my car.

Twenty-Nine

There was no way I'd ever rent from Janice; I didn't care if the rent was two dollars a month, with all utilities included. I drove to three other rental properties, not really caring for any of them, before I went home and got my next shock of the day. Corey was standing at my front door, ringing the bell.

"Can I help you?" I said, with a slight smile, which I couldn't hold back. Casually dressed in a navy Burberry herringbone knit polo, khaki slacks, and a pair of tan leather loafers, he looked up, surprised to see me standing there. A slow smile crept across his face.

"I was just getting ready to leave you a note, since you don't return phone calls." Our eyes searched each other's, sending vibes and unspoken messages.

My eyes said, *"Great day in the morning, you look good!'"*

His eyes said, *"I've not been able to think of anything else but you, and right now I just want to wrap you in my arms and join my lips to yours."* At least that is what I think his eyes said. For all I know, they could have been saying, *"Why in the world are you dressed like that?"*

Then my eyes switched to, *"Wait a minute. Where is that hoochie-skeezer that was calling you baby? Does she know that you're over here?"*

"Let me get the door," my mouth said. He stepped aside, allowing me to move past him. "You aren't working today?" I asked, gesturing my head to refer to his clothing.

"Only a half day. I'd just left the office, and I don't know." He shrugged. "I just thought I'd swing by and see how you were."

"You really like doing the unannounced thing, huh? Come on in. Can I get you something to drink?" I tugged on my clothes as if that would make my T-shirt and sweats more presentable.

"Sure."

Silence hung in the air for a few seconds while he took a seat at the bar. I got two glasses and filled them with ice and sweet tea.

"So what are you doing now?" he asked. He wrapped his hand around mine as I offered him his glass. I tried not to blush but just couldn't help it.

"Um . . . nothing really. Just kind of taking some time for me," I lied, casually sliding my hand away, then walking back to the kitchen. In my mind, I fumbled for my next words. "Have you, uh . . . had lunch yet?" I opened the refrigerator as if I was going to cook something if he was hungry, knowing that the fridge was two eggs, a few slices of cheese, a jar of jelly, and a half-eaten bowl of ramen noodles away from being empty. Luckily, from where he sat, he couldn't see this.

"No, but now that I'm not your boss, I'd like to take you to lunch." My eyes bounced back and forth between the two eggs. I did not want to look at him while I said, in my most nonchalant, nonsarcastic voice, "Your girlfriend won't mind?"

"My girlfriend? What girlfriend?" There were definitely only two eggs. One, two . . . one again, two. Jelly, cheese, two eggs.

"The woman you're seeing."

"I'm not seeing anybody." He sounded confused. Then he added, "Yet."

I finally stopped hiding in the coolness of the fridge and closed its door as I peeked over at him. "Okay, well, the woman that you were with the day I called. You know . . . the one that said, 'Corey, baby, come on. You're supposed to be ready,'" I mocked in a falsetto voice, leaning back on the counter.

He gave a little chuckle as he crossed his arms and looked down at the floor while shaking his head. Then he rose slowly and walked around the bar and into the kitchen. I felt a small twinge of panic, hoping that he wasn't planning to help himself to some imaginary food or something. He stopped in front of me, faced me directly, then rested his hands on the countertop, one on each side of my hips, framing me with his arms. He leaned forward until his nose nearly touched mine.

"My mom doesn't sound like that." He paused, looking into my eyes. "Is that the girlfriend you're referring to?"

I couldn't even say anything, especially since he'd leaned in even closer and softly absorbed my lips into his. All of my insides began to turn into goo.

He broke the kiss and continued. "I couldn't talk to you when you called, because we were on our way to place flowers on Octavia's grave." With raised brows, his eyes now said, "Anything else?"

Ashamed, I folded my lips inside my mouth. "I made an assumption," I admitted. "I'm sorry."

He nodded slowly, then kissed me again. "Can we go to lunch now?"

I smiled. This man was gonna make me fall in love with him. He moved back to his seat at the bar.

Not wanting to seem too anxious, but all the while jumping up and down inside, I gave a second slight rebuttal. "I can't go like this." I raised my arms, showing off my "clean the house" outfit.

"I can wait for you to change," he offered.

"I don't know. I did have a couple of things to do today."

"Like what? Taking time for yourself means doing what you want to do at your own pace, right? Aw, come on, December. It won't kill you to stray off course for an hour to have lunch with me." I looked up at the ceiling, pretending to be in pensive thought.

"Okay," I agreed. "Just give me a few minutes."

He stood and tugged at his waistline, straightening his clothes. "I'll be back in, say, twenty minutes? Is that enough time?"

"Make it thirty." When I walked him to the door, he leaned over and kissed me on the cheek, bringing an instant and unwilled grin to my face.

"I'll see you in a few," he said.

It took me seventeen minutes to ransack my closet in search of something to wear. After trying on about eight different pairs of pants that made my butt look too big, too flat, or too wide, or were too short, too big in the waist, or were missing a button, I went with a pair of "faded in all the right places jeans" and chose a sleeveless white knit top with a ruched front.

Snatching the ball cap off my head, I was horrified. I had forgotten that I'd started taking out my microbraids just the night before and now had a huge circular patch of nappy hair right on the top of my head! I spent the next six minutes trying to camouflaging the patch with the remaining braids. Every time I thought I was done, I'd notice a nap patch trying to peek through. With seven minutes on the clock, I rummaged through my scarf drawer and found a piece of white knit material, wrapped it around my head in an elongated bun, asymmetrically angled behind my left ear, and secured it with a scrunchie adorned with a large turquoise and white flower. I added a pair of white hoops on my ears and slid my feet (probably for the last time) into my pair of dog leash sandals, which I had decided to get, anyway, despite Janice having a pair. With two minutes left, I applied a bit of eyeliner, a light coat of mascara to lengthen my lashes, and a clear gloss to my lips. Perfect! By the time I was dressed, my bedroom looked like my closet and dresser had both gotten sick and thrown up all over the place.

Corey looked stunned when I opened the door minutes later.

"You look fantastic," he complimented as he handed me a fresh bouquet of mixed flowers.

Naturally, I blushed. "Thank you, Corey. Let me put these in some water." Finding the same vase that the last flowers I'd received from Corey came in, I set the flowers on the dining-room table, then extracted one and, with a rubber band, attached it to my head wrap, replacing the scrunchie.

"Ready?" he asked. I nodded, grabbing my purse. "What do you have a taste for?"

"Mmmm, I'm pretty flexible, as long as it's not baloney."

"You don't eat baloney?" He crinkled his brows as if a person not liking lunch meat was unheard of. "Girl, I can fry you up a baloney sandwich that will make you think you're eating steak! You've probably only experienced the regular old two pieces of bread and mayonnaise, with a slice of cheese and a piece of baloney in between. That's not how you eat baloney."

"For real?" I asked, unconvinced.

"See you gotta take your time with baloney. First, you gotta get the kind with the string still on it, and you pull the string off." He drew his hand through the air in an imaginary demonstration. "Then you chew on that for about two minutes to get your taste buds ready, right?"

"Uh-huh."

"Now it's best to use beef baloney. All that other stuff is junk." Just then his cell phone rang. "Excuse me."

While he took his call, which seemed to be business related, I pulled out my cell and sent Kisha a text message. *Out with Corey!*

A minute or so later, her response came back. *Can't talk now—will call later.*

Coincidentally, Corey and I snapped our phones closed at the same time. "I forgot that I needed to swing by Hampton to pick up some files," Corey said. "Do you mind riding over with me?"

"I don't mind if you don't mind," I answered, knowing that Andre would no doubt see us together and make assumptions that I wouldn't be quite ready to confirm. Corey whisked his truck onto the interstate ramp, cranked up the music, and opened the sunroof.

In the thirty minutes it took to arrive at the Hampton office, I couldn't remember the last time I felt so carefree, even though I only had a little piece of a job and, in a few short weeks, would have nowhere to live. I just felt so good in Corey's presence that I tucked those concerns away and thought a million good thoughts. Such as that the woman I'd heard in the background had been Corey's mom, not a girlfriend, and that I could be his girlfriend. And how good his lips felt when they touched mine, and if he kissed me one thousand times in a row, I'd still want at least one more and . . ."

"What are you thinking about?" he asked, turning the stereo down while he parked.

"Nothing in particular," I lied, glad that he couldn't read my mind.

"You were thinking something, judging from the way you're grinning over there." I wasn't aware that I'd been smiling.

"It was nothing." I shrugged. I decided against speaking to Andre, for no other reason than if he saw the two of us together, he'd call me with questions that I just didn't want to answer right now. "I'll wait here," I said, then went back to my happy daydreams.

He returned inside two minutes with a handful of manila folders, which he placed on the backseat. "I know the perfect place we can have lunch. Unless you want something fancy?" he asked.

"No, wherever you choose is fine."

Corey drove to a small, seemingly family-owned and family-operated restaurant, Grandstand's Grill. "They have the best grilled chicken salad in the world," he commented.

"Better than a baloney sandwich that tastes like steak?" I teased.

"Yep."

"I'll take it then."

After ordering us both Chicken Greek Salads, which was the grill's specialty, Corey asked, "So what's going on with you?" He tapped the laminated menu on the table a few times before sliding it between the ketchup and mustard bottles and the napkin holder.

"Nothing and everything." I tried to give a light laugh, but it wasn't very believable.

"Nothing and everything," he repeated. "You flew out

of Wright-Way like a bat out of hell. I know you were looking for another job, but I did think you would at least grant us proper notice."

Should I or shouldn't I? I contemplated in my thoughts. There was really no reason to share with Corey the truth about my resigning. What was done was done.

"Umm . . . it was just the right thing to do. Maybe in the wrong way. I will admit that."

"So the promotion wasn't carrot enough for you, huh?"

"Actually, the branch manager position was a really good carrot, but I just wanted the opportunity to pursue some other things."

"Like what?"

Like what? Hmmm . . . like what. Good question.

"Like owning my own gym. You know, something small and personable." It was the only thing I could think of off the top of my head.

"Really?" He furrowed his brow as he nodded. "I didn't know you were a fitness buff."

"Yeah. I'm a certified personal trainer," I commented, nodding my head matter-of-factly.

"So you have a bit of an entrepreneur bug?" Our server brought two delectable-looking salads topped with seasoned chicken, along with two cups of tea.

"A little bit," I minimized, knowing that I'd never given owning a gym the slightest bit of thought. "This looks really good!"

"I'm impressed, December. Anytime a person is able to take a detour from the corporate rat race and venture out on their own is commendable. I'm proud of you for taking that step." He smiled. "When you just jumped up and quit like that, I really wondered about your stability and decision making." He stabbed into his salad with his fork. "And then I heard that you were teaching aerobics classes." He looked puzzled, then shrugged. "I was just thinking, how do you quit a real job to teach aerobics?"

Ouch.

"Well, let me bring some balance to your thinking," I offered. "Like I said, I'm a personal trainer. I received my certification long before I left Wright-Way." Actually, it wasn't long before, but *long* is a relative term, right? "And I am teaching classes because it's the perfect way for me to build up my client list, so that when I open my gym, I'll have some faithful patrons. So there's some truth to what you heard, but it's all part of a plan." It sounded so good, I almost believed it myself.

He nodded his head, then smiled and said, "A woman with a plan. That's what I'm talking about. You're more incredible than I've known about."

Now if only that plan were real.

Later that week, I had dinner with Shelley, catching her up on the details of the whirlwind my life had been over the past several weeks, the real deal behind me leaving Wright-Way, my decision to sell my house . . . and Corey.

"I knew you two were gettin' it on!" She emphasized *knew.*

"You didn't know anything, because we're not gettin' it on, as you so eloquently put it," I said.

"So you two are officially a couple?"

"I guess you could say that. I mean, he didn't write me a note that said, 'I like you. Do you like me? Circle yes or no. I want to go with you, but only if you want to go with me.' " We both laughed, remembering grade-school love notes.

"And why was it that only the ugly boys wrote us those notes?" Shelley asked, poking her baked potato.

"I don't know what you're talking about. I got that note from cute boys! Maybe you were ugly yourself in school," I suggested as I dipped a buffalo wing into some bleu cheese dressing.

"Whatever. I was a little funny-looking back then, with my new adult teeth bucking in the front and beady balls on my neck. I make up for it now, though. There's a table behind you full of brothers that are checking me out right now." I glanced quickly over my shoulder.

"Girl, they are watching the game." My head nodded toward a TV that was several feet behind Shelley's head.

"I bet one of them will stop over here before we leave," she said confidently. "But back to you. So you have been seeing Mr. Davis for how long? And don't lie!"

"Shelley, I don't have a specific date on the calendar that says, 'I'm now seeing Corey.'" I made quotations in the air with my fingers.

"But you've kissed," she argued.

"And what does that mean? That doesn't mean we're seeing each other."

"Has he been to the bank?" The bank was our coded reference for sex.

"Can he open up an account first? What do you think this is, a twenty-four-hour quick check cashing joint? As a matter of fact, I need to find out if my own bank account is still active. It's been so long since I've had a deposit, it might be closed!" Shelley quickly covered her mouth to keep from spitting food across the table while she laughed.

"I'm just asking since you're over there glowing," she said through a mouthful of chicken-fried steak. "Girl, if you're glowing like that over a few kisses, when he hits the bank, you are really going to be all to pieces." I could only shake my head. "So where are you going to live?"

"I have no clue. I am looking for a nice place to rent, but I have to find somewhere fast." I crunched into a celery stick. "And you will never believe whose house—" I was cut off by a huge, six-foot-three, looming and bobbing "Bruh-man"-looking brother who approached our table.

"Excuse me, ladies. I was just, uh, sitting back there with my boys, watching the game, but I had to come let-chall know, y'all is some fine sistahs." He smiled particularly hard at Shelley, revealing a missing front tooth, looking like a worn-out, run-over pair of brogans.

"Thank you," I said graciously while Shelley balked silently.

"So, uh, what-chall doing later on, 'cause we 'bout to go play spades at my boy's house, you know." He slapped a fist into his palm to emphasize his words. "An' we wanted to invite-chall ladies over to join us, an' all dat."

"Shenitha, do you want to go?" I asked Shelley, knowing she would have killed me if I'd blurted out her real name.

"Shenitha. Dat's a pretty name for a pretty lady," Bruh-man said.

Shelley finally cleared her throat and spoke. "Thank you, but we have plans."

"Oh, ah-ight, den," he said as he punched into his hand again. "Well, can I at least give you my numbuh just in case y'all change y'all mind?"

"Sure," I said. "We might be free a little later on." It was all I could do to hold myself together. Shelley kicked me under the table, causing me to yelp out loud.

"Ah-ight, cool!" He jotted his number on a napkin and handed it to Shelley. "Shenitha, I ain't gon' forget dat. Hope to see y'all ladies later." As he headed back to his table, he turned around and said, "Bye, Shenitha."

"Well, you did say one of them would stop by," I said as I laughed uncontrollably.

Shelley picked up a spoon, trying to see her reflection. "Girl, I must be still ugly!"

Thirty

I had spent the next two weeks trying desperately to locate an apartment, which I found out was kind of hard to do without a good-paying job and tenure at that job. At almost every apartment complex I'd gone to, the leasing consultant pretty much told me the same thing: a) my employment would have to be verified (I needed to be employed for at least six months), and b) my income would have to be verified. With my small gym salary and tenure, I didn't have the income to support getting an apartment, although I would have tons of cash in a few days. I couldn't believe how many apartment complexes were not willing to take a year's worth of rent money up front. So here it was, two days before my home would go to closing, and I had nowhere to live. Shelley offered me a room at her place, which I'd use as a last resort, but I wasn't quite there yet.

Corey even offered to let me move into his home, at least temporarily, until an apartment came through. That really meant a lot to me, and I appreciated his generosity, but at the same time, that solution didn't quite sit well with me, either. I didn't want to come into a new relationship using him as a crutch.

When I shared that thought with him, he seemed a bit offended and said, "I'm not being a crutch, December. I'm being a friend. I'm being more than a friend. Do you think I'd let just anyone move into my home?"

"It's not that, Corey. I just don't want to burden you or be in your way."

Nor did I want to sell myself cheap, offering the milk without the cow. I didn't know how true it was, but I'd read in one of my books that a man never marries a woman that he's living with, because he doesn't have to. He let out a sigh.

"If you need me, I'm here for you." He studied my eyes. "I'm here for you," he repeated as he nodded to reassure me about what he'd said. I just couldn't do it; moving in with Corey, even temporarily, would be too much like shacking up.

Coming in from a day full of office visits, I picked up the mail and started sorting through, following my usual routine of placing the bills in the back of the pile and reading the more interesting mail first. I slid my letter opener into what looked like a greeting card-envelope, which bore no return address. To my surprise, it was an invitation.

> *It is with joy that we,*
> *Geneva Lynn Johnson*
> *And*
> *Edward Jerome Thomas*
> *Invite you to share with us a celebration of love*
> *As we exchange marriage vows and begin our new life together.*

"Awww!" I said aloud. Eddie finally found himself someone to love. I was happy for both of them, and even happier that he'd no longer ask me out every chance he got. It always took a sister to assist with getting rid of that winter boot; I was going to have to send Geneva a thankyou card. I marked my planner for the date on the invite, filled out the RSVP card, then moved on to the next envelope. It was a letter from the Center for Plastic Surgery. Maybe they were having a sale.

> *The Center for Plastic Surgery*
> *Dear Ms. Elliott,*
>   *You recently visited our offices, but we have not yet had the pleasure of scheduling an appointment for you. Are there other questions you would like to ask in your decision-making process? We are committed to ensuring that you are able to make an intelligent and well-informed decision regarding our surgical procedures and will gladly answer any questions that you may have.*
>   *Please don't hesitate to give us a call or schedule an additional consultation appointment.*
> *Sincerely,*
> *The Staff at CPS*

With so many other things going on in my life, I had put my quest for implants on the back burner of my mind, but this letter brought it back to the forefront. So much so that I stopped reading the mail, went straight to my bedroom, and took off my blouse and bra. Turning slowly from side to side, I did a full assessment. There was something about my breasts that made them look more firm, more round, more plump. I counted back in my head to my last period. Every month, a week before my period started, my breasts would fatten up.

That wasn't the case this time as I'd just gone off my cycle a few days ago.

I then cupped each breast and lifted it slightly, trying to remember what I looked like ten years ago, or even just a few years back, prior to my weight loss. I was very satisfied with how my belly had flattened out and I'd loss several of the dimples and lumps in my thighs, and now that I worked out consistently and regularly, all of the lumps, humps, and rumps were gone, but the effect of the weight loss on my breasts was less than satisfying.

I moved on to the pencil test, taking two pencils from my nightstand and putting them in the crease underneath each breast to see if they would stay there or fall. Those pencils stuck like chewing gum up under a seat at the movie theater. Even with that, though, what I saw looked significantly different and better to me than what I remembered seeing months ago. I picked up the letter again, rereading it quickly, then glanced back up at the mirror. I'd need to give this more thought. I was obviously building up my pectoral muscles; maybe I didn't need implants, after all. I took off the rest of my suit and pulled on a pair of sweats and a T instead before heading back to my desk.

The next piece of mail that I opened was a letter from Cobblestone Luxury Apartment Living, telling me in writing that they were not willing to rent to me, as if the instant, face-to-face rejection hadn't been sufficient.

Ms. Elliott,

Thank you for your recent inquiry about Cobblestone Properties. Unfortunately, your income does not meet the requirements for apartment rental with us. We require that your total household income be at least three times the rent amount of the apartment you desire.

*We would love to offer you a home to come home to in
the future. Please keep us in mind if your income status
changes.*
Sincerely,
Brittany Farrior
Property Manager

This was depressing. I was about to be sitting outside
on the streets. Homeless, a vagabond, destitute, down-and-
out, living in a box (covered with one of my Egyptian-
cotton sateen sheets for privacy and lined inside with
my crinkled suede floor . . . well . . . box-bottom covering)
underneath a bridge, with a purse full of cash. When
did getting an apartment become so hard? College kids
got apartments all the time. How were they approved?
And what about people who got evicted from one place
but pretty soon were in another? How did they do it? I
was almost in tears, thinking about how my life had just
seemed to flip upside down in one day . . . and I was the
one directly responsible for the flip.

I balled the letter up, tossed it in a wastebasket, and
started searching the Net for extended-stay hotels. Most
of them offered free cable, soap, and tissue; included
utilities; and would clean up my room for me once a
week. Not a bad deal. Just as I picked up the cordless
phone to make a reservation, it rang in my hand.

"Hello."

"Yes, Ms. Elliott? This is Fawn from Water's Edge Apartments. How are you?"

"Fine, thank you. And yourself?" I responded coolly.

"Great, great," she sang in a white girl kind of way. "I
was just calling to let you know that everything went
through with your application, and all you need to do is
let me know how soon you want to move in."

Water's Edge was a very small community that I'd

pass on my way to the gym each day. The property didn't really appeal to me, but in my desperation, I'd stopped there to inquire about vacancies. The two-bedroom, one-and-a-half-bath town-house apartment was a little outdated, featuring a 1980 gas stove and a trash compactor in the kitchen, sad-looking grey carpets, and one single phone jack throughout the whole place. It did have a couple of features that I liked, however, like the loft-styled master bedroom, the ceiling fans, a sliding glass door leading out to a private patio off the dining area, and a corner fireplace in the living room.

I could tell by the look of the office that there might be a few loopholes in their processes, so I took a chance and filled out an application, showing a stack of old Wright-Way pay stubs as proof of employment and income verification. I had strategically ordered the stubs so that the most recent stub was at the bottom of the stack, hoping that after looking at several older ones first, the consultant would notice the pay frequency and amounts and skip looking at every single one. It worked! As soon as she said, "You meet the income requirement," I wasted no time writing a check for the application fee and another for the deposit. Overall, the apartments were below my standards, but right now, all that was beside the point.

"I'll take it!" I nearly shouted into the phone. After finalizing my move-in date, I ended the call, then got up and did my best cheerleader's jump ... the "jump up in a straddle and touch your toes" one. I got my feet only about six inches off the ground, didn't reach my toes by a long shot, and landed with a thud, but that was good enough for me.

Taking my seat once more, I opened an envelope from the consignment shop, which had an itemized list of the items they'd sold and a check for $1,457 tucked inside. That called for a triple backflip with a double twist, a handspring, and a forward lunge cartwheel thing a ma jig, complete with arms raised in an Olympian finishing pose! I'd be there first thing in the morning to drop off more items, upping my shoe count from ten pairs to twenty.

Suddenly inspired by these two successes, I transitioned to another initiative. On a blank sheet of paper, I began listing and defining my former job responsibilities. After thoughtful consideration, I became conscious of just how much business acumen I had. I reminded myself of the speech Janice had given me the day she'd offered me the branch manager's position.

When I review what it takes in order to accomplish a feat like that, I have to look at your ability to interview candidates effectively and fit them in assignments for which they are best suited, to maintain client relationships, and to be proactive in forecasting their staffing needs, as well as to balance various administrative duties, all of which you do extremely well.

I'd been birthing, cultivating, and maintaining business relationships; organizing and launching marketing campaigns; assessing job skill sets and developmental needs; tracking and submitting payroll; managing hours and efficiency; and creating and implementing effective growth plans . . . all for someone else. If I could do it so skillfully and successfully for someone else, surely, I could do it for myself.

On the back side of that same sheet of paper, I made another list of what I thought I would need to start my own business—not selling houses or offering to fix people's credit, but something I'd be proud to have my name on. In a few hours, I had a long list of action items that I'd immediately start working on. Everything from writing a business plan to developing my slogan: *Summer's coming . . . Get ready in December!*

* * *

I called Anita to ask her if she could show me a few commercial properties for sale or lease. Opening my e-mail, I reviewed my entire address book, counting names and remembering old friends and contacts, then downloaded every single address into a file to develop a list of potential client contacts. I then surfed Web sites for printing companies, browsing postcards, letterhead, forms, and other business branding supplies.

Maybe I did have a plan . . . and just had never realized it.

Thirty-One

The closing had gone as scheduled, and Corey, Shelley, and Andre all sacrificed their Saturday to help me move into my new place. The men toted the furniture and got the pieces situated in the proper rooms, while Shelley and I set up the stereo, cut music on, unpacked boxes, placed wall hangings, put away dishes, made beds, dressed the bathrooms, and hung clothes. By the time the sun went down, the apartment, although a little substandard, had come together nicely, and I reasoned that the place wasn't so bad, after all. It was better than living on the streets, hands down.

I'd ordered pizza and drinks for the four of us, which arrived just as we collapsed, exhausted, onto the living-room furniture and floor. When the delivery person rang, we all looked at each other.

"Get the door, Andre." That was Shelley.

"You get it," said Andre.

"I'll get it," I said, trying to heave myself up from the floor.

"I got it. I got it." That was my baby! Corey sprang to

his feet, answered the door, and came back with the boxes. By then, we'd all mustered the energy to sit upright and attack the pizzas as soon as he sat them down on the table.

"Turn the TV on," Andre said through a mouthful of food. "Don't you have some movies?"

"Somewhere around here." I located and shuffled through a nearby box with one hand and held my pizza with the other. "Let's see . . . I have *Stella, The Best Man, Malibu's Most Wanted, Brown Sugar*. . . ."

"I think I'm seeing a pattern here," Corey said, apparently noticing that all the movies featured Taye Diggs. "You have a thing for Diggs?"

"Well, you know." I shrugged. "Taye and I used to date a while back. Then he fell all in love with me and wanted to get married, but I was like, 'No, Taye. Think about your career.' He was like, 'I don't want my career more than I want you, Deece. You mean the world to me.' I said, 'I know, baby, but you have to go on to your destiny . . . Just send me your movies on DVD. That will be enough.' He said okay; then we just kissed and said good-bye."

Shelley grabbed a pillow from the couch and hurled it at me. "And then you woke up!" she said and laughed.

"What? I'm serious!" I said. "I couldn't let that man sacrifice his entire career for me."

That started a conversation on which celebrity we would date if we could. Of course, Halle and Beyoncé were at the top of the men's list.

"What's so special about Halle?" I asked and waved my hand. Andre and Corey just looked at each other.

"Halle got it going on!" Andre commented, slapping Corey a high five. "The woman is beautiful. No, she is beyond beautiful! She is some word that hasn't even been created yet that means beautiful to the tenth power."

"Okay, I can give her that, but she can look toe-up just like the rest of us. I look just as good as she does. Matter of fact, she used to call me every week for beauty tips," I replied.

"Yeah, right!" Andre said. We all laughed.

"All Beyoncé got is booty," Shelley exclaimed, standing to imitate the choreography from the *Crazy in Love* video. " 'Cause she can't sing worth a dime."

"What?" Andre said, disagreeing

"Y'all know that girl can't sing . . . Stand her up beside Whitney . . . um, before she got with Bobby. Put her up against Mariah . . . well, before she had a nervous breakdown or whatever was going on with her. Or how about Anita Baker? All three of them can sing her up under a table on their worst days," Shelley said.

"They can't shake them tail feathers, though," Andre added. Corey and Andre fell over laughing, then high-fived each other again. Shelley went on to comment that Denzel and Morris would be her choices.

"So you have to have two men? You can't pick just one, huh?" Corey teased.

"I like to keep my options open. What's wrong with that?" said Shelley. You and Andre are trying to share Halle and Beyoncé, so what's the difference?" She bit into her pizza, then continued. "Denzel called me just last week to let me know that he's all mine if he ever gets rid of Pauletta," she stated. "I'm seeing Morris right now, though, so it's Denzel's loss. He's not going to have me waiting forever."

"At least we were decent enough to pick single women. Both of you picked married men," Corey said and laughed.

"Wait a minute now," I defended. "I said Taye and I *used* to have a thing. I'm not seeing him anymore."

"Well, I'm still seeing my men. I don't mind them being married," Shelley stuck in.

"Girl, Denzel and Morris don't want you," replied Corey.

"And Halle and Beyoncé don't want you or Andre, so I guess we're even," said Shelley.

"I have my Hall-Oncé right here," Corey said, draping his arm around my shoulders, then leaning over to give me a kiss. "She's better than both of them put together." I blushed.

We settled on *Drumline,* but we all dozed off only a half an hour or so into the movie. Andre was sprawled out on the floor; Shelley snuggled down in the chaise, under a sheet she'd grabbed from the linen closet; and Corey and I occupied the couch. I sat on one end while he lay, with his head in my lap. The blaring music from the closing credits seemed to stir all of us at the same time.

Andre sat up, wrapped his arms around his knees for a few minutes, then climbed to his feet. "All right, Deece. I'm outta here," he said, clipping his cell phone to his belt. He slapped hands with Corey and said, "See you Monday, man." Shelley stood and stretched, folded the sheet, and left it on the back of the chaise, then gathered her things and walked toward the door with Andre. Corey and I followed.

"Thank you so very much," I said, truly grateful to have them as friends.

"I'll be back tomorrow to help you get the rest of your stuff put away," Shelley said as she hugged me. Andre just threw up a peace sign, got in his car, and sped off.

As soon as the door was closed and locked, Corey gently gathered me in his arms and began to place kisses on my neck. He enveloped my lips with his own, then began walking me backwards to the living room, and together, we eased onto the chaise. Our kisses became more intense and passionate as his hands first stroked my hair, then my face. As if on cue, the surround-sound speakers were silent momentarily, while the CD/DVD player rotated to an alternate disk, a collection of Babyface's love songs. It had been in the player, untouched, for months.

Corey's breathing was light and restrained, almost silent, rather than rushed and out of control. Moving slowly, he kissed beneath my chin, trailed down my neck, then began to unfasten the buttons on my shirt, exposing a red demi front-closure bra. With quick and skillful fingers, he undid the two tiny hooks that held the bra together and caressed and kissed me adoringly. He traced random circles on my flesh with his tongue, making it easy for quick gasps and soft moans to escape my lips. My hands found their way to his head, and my fingers massaged his scalp purely out of reflex.

While Babyface sang "Whip Appeal," I struggled to let go, and I struggled to hold on. Corey sensed both my desire and my hesitancy and said, "If you want me to stop, I will."

I didn't know how to respond. I wanted him, but I didn't want to move too fast. I wanted something real, something special, something worth bragging about, but my hips were beginning to rotate ever so slightly, asking for and anticipating more, wanting something now. When I took too long to respond, he carefully—while still releasing kisses—refastened my bra, eased back up toward my face, wrapped his arms around me, and kissed my forehead.

"I can wait," he said. "You're worth waiting for." I think I fell in love with him at that very moment. He rested his chin on my head while I nestled in his arms.

Before the CD ended, we were both asleep, but by the time the sun came up in the morning, I'd awakened him twice. Our clothes lay in a pile on the floor, and the sheet that Shelley had left on the chaise had been unfolded and semicovered both of us.

Corey had transitioned from a Stiletto to a Bedroom Shoe.

Thirty-Two

In the next few months, I met with so many people for so many reasons that my brain was exhausted and screaming out for mercy. I went from one office to another, filling out all kinds of applications and forms, from business licenses to tax identification numbers to insurance forms to inspection documents—just the whole gamut. Corey assisted with solidifying my business plan, helping me to look at its structure from all angles, played devil's advocate, and offered feasible solutions to potential barriers.

I'd used the proceeds from the sale of my home to pay off all of my bills, and I still had more than enough cash to put down a substantial down payment on a building. Finally, I was ready to sign a lease on a commercial property that I thought would be perfect for my gym. It was located in the center of a busy strip mall, and had at one time been a fitness facility, so it already had several of the structural features I needed, such as men's and ladies' locker rooms, offices, a huge group-session room, and plenty of space for free weights and equipment. The location even had a pool and sauna area, but it was in need of significant repair and would not be usable for quite a while. Still, it gave me a future vision and something to work toward.

Before I signed the lease, I asked Corey to come take a look at the property.

"We're going to have to go early," said Corey. "I have to drive to Richmond today, and I want you to ride with me."

Anita met us at eleven sharp, unlocked the door to the building, and let us waltz through on our own. Corey didn't say much but seemed to conduct a very careful inspection, stooping down to pull at the carpet, flushing all of the toilets, turning on faucets, looking at cracks, running his hands along the walls, picking at chipped paint, opening and closing lockers, and staring up at ceiling tiles, just to name a few things.

"This place needs a lot of work, Deece," he said, kicking at a small hole along the back wall. I was already prepared to roll up my sleeves and apply some elbow grease (and some cash) to get the place in functioning order.

"What do you mean when you say a lot?" I figured Corey could see things that I probably would give no thought to.

His forehead was creased as he raised his brows at me. "You should negotiate in your lease agreement that the realty company cover some of these repairs or significantly lower the lease amount." He dusted his hands against each other, then pulled out his phone. "Excuse me for a few minutes." He walked up to the front of the building, where we'd left Anita patiently waiting.

While he was gone, I walked the building again, envisioning new tile and carpeting, fresh-painted walls, cleaned mirrors, and updated fixtures and equipment.

I could make it happen. I knew I could. Even if I had to do it a small piece at a time.

I walked up to the entranceway, watching both Corey and Anita, who had stepped outside of the building. Corey had his arms folded across his chest and, with knitted brows, nodded his head. They both walked out to the middle of the parking lot, and he pointed upward, to the roof, at who knows what, then made several other hand gestures. This time Anita nodded, jotted some notes down in her portfolio, and nodded again. Together, they came back in.

"You ready, babe?" he asked. I looked back and forth between both of them, waiting for either of them to bring me in on the conversation they'd had. "We can talk in the car," Corey said.

"Okay," I said in more of a question tone than one of agreement.

"Anita, we'll let you know what we decide," Corey said as we prepared to leave. *We?*

He opened the passenger door of his truck for me, then let himself in, and we drove off. "Is that the place you want?" he began.

"Yeah," I responded, again pointing out all the reasons why I favored that location more than the others I'd seen.

"Okay. Well, let's make it happen." He pulled out his cell again and gave a voice command for it to dial someone named LJ. "Hey, man . . . Yeah, I'm on my way now. I'm just leaving though . . . yeah, . . . so who's working the grill? . . . Does she know what she's doing?" (Boisterous laughter.) "Well, don't eat it all up before we get there . . . Yeah, I did say we. I want you to meet someone."

He took his hand off the steering wheel to reach over and squeeze my thigh while winking at me. Then he spoke into his cell again. "Listen, man, I need to talk to you about something. I just looked at a place that I'm going to need your help with . . . commercial property . . . Right. We'll talk about it when I get there . . . All right, man. See you in a little bit." He snapped his phone shut, reached over to my thigh again, and rubbed back and forth. "Are you ready to meet the family?"

"What family?" I asked, panicked.

"My family. My parents, my brother, his wife, their kids."

"We're going to your parents' house?" I tried to keep a straight face, but my heart's pace had sped up significantly.

"No, to my brother's."

"Corey, why didn't you tell me I'd be meeting your mother today?" I yanked the visor down and started checking my hair and make-up.

"Because I wanted you to be yourself. The same self you were when I met you. Not the dressed-up façade you, but the real you." He glanced over at me digging through my purse to find lip gloss, eyeliner, something . . . anything! "And stop it," he commanded, pushing the visor back up. "You look great."

How does a man take a woman to meet his mother without giving her fair warning? Suppose I didn't want to wear khakis and a white oxford shirt to meet her. I might have wanted to wear a white linen sundress with my Eric Michael espadrilles. I might have wanted to get my hair rebraided, or bring her a "nice to meet you" gift or a bottle of wine. Oh, wait. He's a PK, so his parents probably don't drink. Anyway, I would have appreciated a little heads-up. I couldn't be too upset, though. He was taking me to meet his parents!

An hour and a half later, we turned into a cul-de-sac

in a subdivision of all brick homes and pulled up in front of an immaculate three-story home with a two-car garage, set on grass so lush, it looked like a carpet. I checked my reflection in the mirror once more and willed myself calm as Corey walked around the truck to let me out. All I had in my purse in the way of make-up was a tube of lip balm, which I quickly applied. Corey took hold of my hand, and together, we walked down the side of the house, toward the smoky smell of hickory and mesquite, which hung thick in the air, to the backyard. Two men stood with their backs to us, tending the grill, while an older woman and a younger woman sat up on a deck, sipping tea, and four little girls, almost identical to each other, sat at another table, engrossed in a game of Old Maid.

The older woman jumped to her feet and extended her arms when she saw Corey come around the side of the house.

"Corinthian!" she exclaimed.

"Hey, Mom," he responded, wrapping his arms tightly around her and rocking her from side to side. She was a rather petite almond-colored woman with bright eyes and jet-black hair. When Corey broke his embrace, he turned to introduce me. "Mom, this is December. I brought her with me so you and Dad could meet her." He winked at me. "December, this is my mom, Gail Davis."

"Hi, Mrs. Davis," I said, accepting the embrace she offered. "It's nice to meet you."

"Come on and have a seat with me and Tari. We were just chitchatting a little bit. Corey, your brother and daddy are out there trying not to burn up the food."

"LJ told me you were doing the cooking today," Corey teased.

"You know I only cook indoors," Mrs. Davis said. She swatted at Corey as he leapt out of her reach and off the deck.

I spoke to Tari, who I assumed was Corey's sister-in-law. "This is a beautiful home you have," I complimented, taking a seat at the table with the ladies.

"Thank you. LJ built it for us about a year ago. I just hope we don't outgrow it," Tari said, patting and admiring her belly.

"He built it himself?" I asked, amazed. Tari nodded to confirm. "He does it for a living. Do you want to see the inside?"

"I'd love to."

We stepped through a sliding glass door and into an eat-in kitchen, which was adjacent to a dining room. Circling around to the foyer, I was taken aback by the nine-foot ceilings, which nicely showcased a formal living room with a gas fireplace and hardwood flooring. The house had six bedrooms—including the master, with three and a half baths—and a completely finished basement. While Tari gave me a tour, she shared that she and LJ had been married for ten years, had two sets of twin girls, ages six and seven, and were expecting their first boy in a few more months.

"If LJ keeps getting me pregnant, he's going to have to build us a whole neighborhood of homes," she quipped, leading the way back outside just as the men were bringing platters of ribs, burgers, and hot dogs up on the deck.

"December, this is my brother, Lazarus John. We call him LJ. And my dad, Alan," Corey said. I shook hands with both of them.

"Nice to meet you," I said.

"Corey tells me you're about to open your own gym," LJ stated.

"I'm in the process of finalizing some major plans," I said. "I'm actually trying to make a decision on a building right now. Hopefully, I can have the gym up and running within the next six months or so." While I talked, Corey draped his arm around my shoulder, and in response, my arm circled his waist. He leaned in and kissed me on the cheek.

"She's the one, Dad. She's the one," Corey repeated as he bobbed his head. I blushed. His dad nodded as he chuckled and patted Corey on the shoulder.

"It's about time you brought somebody around. You ain't gettin' no younger. Y'all better come get some of this good food," Mr. Davis said.

We all ate, laughed, and talked, while the girls ran themselves ragged in the yard. Tari went in the house for a deck of cards after a dispute arose over who currently reigned as the king and queen of bid whist.

"Dad, you know, last time Tari and I beat you and Mom like you two stole something!" LJ said, laughing.

"Wait 'til she get back here with them cards. I'ma show you that I'm still the daddy and you still the child," Mr. Davis said, folding his arms across his chest. "Gail, you better tell that boy."

"I think we can show him better than we can tell him, honey," Mrs. Davis said and chuckled.

LJ tilted his head downward and raised his eyebrows up at his mom. "Mom, I love you and everything, but I'm not going to have mercy on you now. Just so you know."

"You play?" Mr. Davis asked me.

"No, sir. I've never learned how," I replied.

"Well, that's good for you, 'cause you ain't too new to take a whuppin' 'fore you leave." The whole table cracked up, including me.

"Go easy on her, Dad. I want her to be around for a

long time," Corey said, laughing and patting his dad on the back.

"I think I'm going to go play with the girls for a while," I said, rising from my chair.

"Good idea," Mr. Davis replied. "I'd hate for you to witness this terrible beatin' I'ma have to put on these boys tonight." As I walked off, I heard Mr. Davis say to Corey, "That's a good one there."

Thirty-Three

My fingers trembled as I cut the red ribbon with an oversized pair of scissors. No doubt, it had been a headache getting the building properly prepared and passing a barrage of city and building inspections, but finally, it had all come together, my very own establishment.

Corey had been phenomenal in negotiating a very reasonable purchase price (rather than a lease) for the building, after pointing out several structural flaws and concerns. He then hired LJ and his crew to come in and renovate the entire facility, at cost, which I partially paid for with the money I made from taking more things to the Sequel week after week. That money amounted to over fifteen thousand dollars. LJ had torn out and replaced the floors, demolished and restructured walls, enlarged the office spaces, and had done all else that needed to be done. He and his crew had even renovated the pool and sauna area, which I hadn't planned to have done until at least a year out. By the time they finished, the gym was state-of-the-art.

Shelley lent her interior design expertise in picking out the club's colors of blue, burgundy, and hunter green; helping me with carpet patterns; and designing a setup that would be most welcoming to guests.

I'd purchased thirty-two varied pieces of equipment, free weights, balance boards, step benches, body balls, and other miscellaneous pieces, offering something for everyone, from the individual who hardly ever exercised to the person who worked out for several hours every day.

Malaun, Jennifer, Keya, Wayne, and Troy—my new staff—stood by the door, perfectly matched in black pants, black and turquoise Double Dry sports tops and T-shirts, and matching Nikes. They greeted guests as they came in and handed out gift bags holding hats, water bottles, key rings, and wrist bands, all bearing the gym's logo, and a coupon for a free personal training session. Eddie and Geneva Thomas had done a wonderful job catering the event and had set up food and drink stations featuring light and nutritious appetizers in the foyer and throughout the large group-session room. I'd ordered a set of dance party mix CDs just for the occasion. Heavy bass sounds echoed through the room from the four speakers, strategically placed in each corner, adding to the charged atmosphere.

Shelley offered her services by manning the name badge table and encouraging guests to complete information cards for door-prize drawings, while Rodney and Andre gave tours of the facility. As I looked down at the foyer from the upstairs manager's office, I was overwhelmed by the number of people who'd taken the time to come out to the grand opening of December. Corey's parents came in, along with LJ and Tari. Monique was there, and nearly everyone from the Wright-Way office, although I'd not seen Janice yet. Even Terrance came. Friends I'd not seen in forever and then their friends filtered through the entranceway and slowly filled the room where the festivities were happening tonight.

I couldn't help but smile at how far I'd come, and how ironic it was that I would have never gotten here had it not been for Janice. I wondered if she'd come tonight. Probably so, just to be nosy or to find fault. I'd invited her, anyway, because I didn't discriminate when it came to potential clients. If she had money to spend, I had a place for her to spend it, and if she showed up, I'd have to thank her. Well . . . maybe not.

"You have really done it, girl," Kisha said, putting her arm around my shoulder. "And I am so proud of you!"

"Thanks, Kisha." We embraced tightly for several seconds. "I love you, man!"

"I love you, too. Now stop crying." She smudged away my happy tears with her thumb, then reached on my desk for a tissue. "I ain't wiping up no snot, so here." In both laughter and tears, I snatched the tissue from her and pulled myself together. "Come on. Let's get this party started!" Kisha cried.

Just as we came down the stairwell leading to the foyer, I saw this chunky, full-faced woman making her way over to one of the food stations. When she turned around, I was caught totally off guard. It was Janice! And she looked like she'd gained about forty pounds, with her carrot-eating, diet shake–drinking self. As she caught sight of me, her eyes popped wide open.

"Hi, Janice. Thank you for coming," I greeted cordially.

"Oh my God!" she exclaimed loudly, with an exaggerated smile, looking me up and down. "Look at you! You look fantastic!" She clasped her hands over her mouth. She could hardly believe that I was as toned and shapely as I was. I had dropped two dress sizes since leaving Wright-Way. By the same token, I could hardly believe that she'd turned into a wobbling Weeble. "What did you do!" she asked, still in shock. I shrugged.

"You know I own this place, right?" I asked rhetorically as I nodded. "I work out all the time, watch what I eat." I shrugged. "It's no big deal. Thanks again for coming out." I patted her hand and moved away. Strolling toward the group-session room, where most of my guests were waiting, I left Janice standing there, wide-eyed and green with envy. *Yeah, I know I got it going on, butterball,* I thought.

As I approached the doorway, the tempo of the music changed, and Earth, Wind & Fire's "In the Stone" began to play, making for a perfect entrance. As my staff, Andre, and Rodney took notice of me, they began applauding, which started the entire room clapping. In the front of the room, on the platform from where my class instructors would teach, there was a microphone waiting. I strolled over to it, picked it up, and brought it up to my mouth.

"Good evening!" I said. "I'm December Elliott, and I am so very honored that you all have come out to support the opening of my new gym, December." My audience applauded and whistled a second time. "I'm so overwhelmed by your presence. I don't quite know what to say."

"Deece! Deece! Deece!" Andre yelled, starting a group chant. I smiled and blew random kisses at no one in particular as my eyes scanned the crowd for Corey. My heart sank a little when I did not see him anywhere. As the chant ended, I refocused my thoughts and continued.

"Let me just start by thanking some very important people in my life, starting with both my mom and dad, who flew all the way here from Africa to be with me tonight." The crowd looked around to locate my parents, who stood in the middle of the room, nodding and smiling. I could tell by the looks on their faces that they were proud of me. "Mommy, Daddy, thank you so much for all your love and support." My mom and I blew kisses at each other; then I continued. "Then I want to thank my former boss, who's now my competition, for encouraging me to start my fitness career. Rodney Jacobs."

As Rodney waved his hand at the crowd, I saw Corey huff through the door. Immediately, we caught each other's eyes and shared a smile. Janice saw him, too, and wobbled herself right over to him and began pulling on his arm. He gave her an irritated look and practically snatched his arm away. She looked around, embarrassed, probably wondering if anyone had seen the exchange.

I went on. "I have to thank LJ Davis and his entire staff of talented workers, who completely transformed this place from this . . ." I grabbed an enlarged, poster-sized photo from behind me, showing how the building looked when I purchased it, and showed it to the crowd. "To this." I waved my hand all around the room, encouraging everyone to take a look around and compare what they saw to the photo.

"A million thanks to my staff, who greeted you all at the door and worked day and night for the past two months to get this place opened on time. They scrubbed, they filled out papers, they made phone calls, ran to the post office, sent e-mails, and put up with me at all hours of the day and night. Wave, team," I instructed. My staff of five smiled and waved from where they stood, grouped together.

I continued. "I have to thank my girls Kisha and Shelley, who listened to me cry during the hard parts of this coming together and helped me to celebrate the small successes along the way. Thank you to Andre, who's always been in my corner . . ." I thought for a minute if I wanted to spitefully thank Janice, then spoke again into the mike. "I have to thank my sweetheart, Corinthian Davis, for everything you've done to bring this to fruition. Everything."

And last but not least, I want to say a very special thank you to"—I paused for effect, and the room became calmed—"myself." I bit into my lower lip and felt some unexpected emotions rise up. "The part of myself that found the inner strength to recognize my own talents, overcome my challenges, keep me motivated and pressing forward, because it was, indeed, a struggle." I nudged away a tear and took a deep breath. "And for that, I want to say, 'December, I'm proud of you girl!' " The room exploded with applause once more while both my parents stepped forward to hug me. I just couldn't stop my flow of tears.

"You've done well," my father whispered in my ear as he embraced me. My dad was definitely a steel-toe boot man: hardworking, purpose-driven, and protective. "That's my girl!" As we pulled away from each other, he took the mike and began to speak.

"A toast!" he said. Guests who didn't already have a glass quickly grabbed one from the drink table. "To my daughter, my little girl, who has followed her heart and found her dream." He raised his glass and said, "Cheers!" As everyone lifted their glasses in my honor, even Janice, I felt like I had just won a million dollars.

My dad handed me the mike once more. "Please enjoy the food," I said, "and feel free to tour the facility if you haven't had a chance to do so already." Corey was making his way up to the platform area. "Again, I want to thank you for coming out to support me, and we will be available for membership sign-ups all evening," I added. It was then that Corey stepped up and gestured and I handed him the mike.

"Ladies and gentlemen," he began. "Let's give this wonderful woman one more hand." The sound of his hand hitting against the mike thumped through the speakers. "Now if I may," he said and then looked first at me, then turned to my dad. "Mr. Elliott, Mrs. Elliott, you have a wonderful daughter here, whom I have had the esteemed pleasure of working with . . . growing with . . . and falling in love with." He turned and looked at me, with the most soulful eyes I'd ever seen. "She is the most beautiful, incredible, tenacious woman I've ever met. And with your permission, I'd like to marry her."

The audience gasped, woo-hooed, and applauded as 2,573 butterflies took off flying in my stomach. My dad gave a slow single nod (although I knew he would thoroughly grill Corey later); then Corey dropped to one knee while he fished around in his pocket and pulled out a ring box whose robin's egg blue color distinctively said Tiffany & Co. He held the microphone and ring box in one hand and grabbed my hand with the other.

"December . . . I never believed in love at first sight until I saw my daughter's face," Corey said. "When I lost her, I didn't think I'd ever experience a first sight love again . . . and then I met you." My free hand rose to cover my mouth as I fought unsuccessfully against a fresh wave of tears. "From the first day I saw you, I knew you were the one. You are beautiful." His head moved slowly from side to side as he spoke, never taking his eyes away from mine. "I love you, I'm in love with you, and I'd be most honored if you would have me, Corinthian Paul Davis, as your husband."

He lifted my hand to his lips then, and with the assistance of Andre, who held the mike, he opened the ring box and slid a glorious rectangular Lucida diamond, set in platinum, on my finger. There was no question that it could be seen from clear across the room.

"December Elliott, will you marry me?" I wasted no time in delivering my response.

"Yes," I whispered as I nodded. He rose and embraced me tightly. And nothing else ever felt so good.

Thirty-Four

Nine months later, business at the gym was going incredibly well. Rodney had been awesome in assisting me with general business practices and staying on top of codes, compliances, and other legalities. Through effective advertising and other strategies, new members were joining every day. Group class participation was steadily increasing, and I'd been able to purchase more equipment. There were plans in place to enlarge the main group-session room and incorporate a child-care section, and a small drink, snack, and workout gear store.

I called Malaun from the airport to go over last-minute details that would have to be taken care of while I was away for more than thirty days. I had all confidence that things would run smoothly in my absence, as we'd had several meetings in preparation of my being gone for such a long time, and Malaun had my emergency contact numbers, although I didn't expect her to have to use them.

During the fourteen-hour flight, I drafted follow-up e-mails on my laptop, scheduled bill payments, created new marketing pieces, reviewed and revised the gym's group-session schedules, read *The Instant Millionaire*, and leaned on Corey's arm in between. Each time I did, he kissed me on my head and leaned his head down against mine. He, too, had his laptop out, making good use of the time.

We'd been flying over the Pacific for about two hours now and still had a couple of hours to go. Each time I glanced at my watch, I felt the flutter of those same butterflies that took off in my stomach nine months ago, anticipating landing in one of the most beautiful places in the world.

Despite my little-girl dreams of a huge fairy-tale wedding, I'd decided on a destination wedding on Oahu, Hawaii, with no one in attendance but the on-site officiator and our parents. As gifts to us, my parents paid for the wedding and the first portion of our stay, while Mr. and Mrs. Davis paid to have our stay extended by two weeks, lengthening our honeymoon from two weeks to a full month. There was a dinner scheduled for the six of us once we landed, which was right at 7:00 P.M. Hawaii time.

After getting our marriage license the next morning, Corey and I spent the next forty-eight or so hours apart. I don't know what he did with that time, but I spent it with my moms, current and new, at the spa, having our hair, fingernails, and toenails done, and enjoying body scrubs, massages, and facials.

I arrived at the pier on Waikiki Beach fifteen minutes before the ceremony was to begin and, from the darkened limo window, admired Corey, who was talking to our dads. He looked nothing short of incredible. A few short minutes later, he walked down the pier to a flowered arch, taking his proper place, while the dads strolled toward the limo to escort their wives to their places.

When my dad returned for me, I carefully lowered my veil over my face and, with elegance and grace, stepped from the limo onto a plush white carpet, which extended the length of the pier. The setting couldn't be more perfect: the sun was just setting, white birds still glided through the air, the water was a beautiful shade of bluish turquoise, and the pier's torches had been lit.

I was adorned in an incredible strapless, beaded floor-length gown that modestly showcased my figure, which, I could truly say, I was proud of, breasts and all. Dad lifted my bouquet of long-stemmed calla lilies from the seat of the limo.

"You look beautiful, baby," my dad said, taking my arm and running a gaze from the top of my head down to my feet. My French-pedicured toes peeked out from just beneath the hem of my gown. My dad took note of this. "December, where are your shoes? Do you need me to get them out of the limo?" I shook my head softly. Dad looked confused. "As much as you love shoes, you don't have any to put on today?"

"No, Dad"—I nodded my head toward Corey and smiled—"my Perfect Shoe is at the end of the pier, waiting for me."

Outro

The Shoe Dictionary—*(continued)*

The Timberland Boot
The Timberland is a rugged shoe, made for climbing, hiking, and roughing it in the wild. It's made to offer the best protection in rocky and uneven terrain. This best describes the Timberland Boot man; he's rough and wild. He likes to cuss, break stuff that he didn't pay for, and drink forties, and he pledges a strong allegiance to his "boys." He is all about offering protection, and he may own a weapon or two.

The Tennis Shoe
This shoe is a very comfortable shoe that offers support for your soles as you run around the gym, on an outside track, and around town, from errand stop to errand stop. Your Tennis Shoe man is just that. While he is supportive, he lacks backbone and will let you run all over him . . . He's not a take-charge and take-control kind of man at all. It's not nice to take advantage of people, but he makes it so easy!

The Loafer

This casual shoe is perfect for your casual, laid-back workdays. This is the shoe you choose when you really don't feel much like dressing up. In the same sense, the Loafer man really doesn't feel like doing much of anything. He's very casual and laid-back, complacent, seeming to be headed nowhere in particular. He lacks goals and initiative but enjoys life at the same time.

The Glass Slipper

Now, of course, there is no such thing as a wearable shoe made of glass (so we have the clear-plastic glass look-alike). However, if there were, you can imagine that this shoe would be extremely fragile to handle. Great attention would be given to how and where the shoe should and could be worn. The Glass Slipper man, likewise, is extremely fragile and requires constant words of affirmation of how wonderful of a man he is, or else you don't love him. Anything constructively critical you may say has the propensity to hurt his feelings and shatter his ego. You can barely crack a harmless joke about this man, because he'll take it seriously, and before you know it, a stupid argument is underway!

The Slide

Easy to slip into, easy to slip out of. That best describes the Slide man, who is generally so smooth, you can't seem to let go of him, although he slides in and out of your life whenever he gets good and ready. He shows up and says, "What's up, girl?" and before you know it, he's slid back in your bed, then out the door until next time . . . but only because you let him, which is totally your fault.

The Brogan

This shoe is made for working out in the field, which is exactly how the Brogan man presents himself . . . as if he has been in the field all day, in the hot, hot sun. Now, there is nothing wrong with a hardworking man, but can he take a bath first? How about scrub up under those fingernails? All of his under-shirts are dingy and yellowed, especially underneath the arms, and let's not even talk about his skid-row underwear. But the funny thing about the Brogan man is he is completely con-vinced that every woman wants him.

The Flat
This man is so dry and boring that he's almost not worthy of his dictionary space. Well, I take that back . . . He might be in-credibly smart and financially savvy. But he has no personal-ity, no style, no wit, and no sense of humor (yawn!). Special note: Beware of the flat-broke Flat, who may have style, wit, and all that other stuff, but in the memorable words of Gwen Guthrie. . . . "no romance without finance."

What kind of shoe is *your* man?